FRAGILE CREATURES

A THRILLER NOVEL

GARETH R.T. OWEN

ISBN: 978-1-7362712-0-9
eBook ISBN 978-1-7362712-1-6
Library of Congress Control Number: 2021900800

First paperback edition June 2021
Edited by Elizabeth Cartwright
Cover art by Flor Figueroa

Printed in the United States of America

www.GarethRTOwen.com

To all the J's, with thanks and love

Beware the dark pool at the bottom of our hearts. In its icy, black depths dwell strange and twisted creatures it is best not to disturb.

—Sue Grafton

GARETH R.T. OWEN

FRAGILE CREATURES

A THRILLER NOVEL

PROLOGUE

1994

The bulky Chevy Tahoe barreled along South Alameda Street, a cube of energy tearing through the dead of night. The twinkle of street lamps danced along the black paintwork, disappearing into the tiny voids of the bullet holes. And the lights from two cop cars pulsed red and blue in the rearview, the nimble Fords gaining fast.

Luca Messetti gripped the steering wheel with gloved hands and yanked it to the right, sending the SUV skidding through the tight turn onto Slauson Avenue, the thick tires screeching and whining.

A yelp of agony came from the passenger seat where Casey was slumped down, both hands applying pressure to the bullet wound in his belly. His black tactical overalls were unzipped down to his crotch, and the shirt beneath was stained a bright, wet red.

"Be careful," said Jimmy from the back seat. "If we crash, we're done."

"Fuck that," said Luca, his Bronx accent thick. "We gotta shake them."

A loud *pop* rang through the car, and Luca ducked instinctively. He glanced in the wing mirror and saw one of the cops' arms extended out of his window, his pistol aimed, ready to fire again.

"He's going for the tires!" yelled Jimmy.

"Well, hit him back!"

Cool night air swirled around the Tahoe as Jimmy lowered his window. He leaned out of the SUV, aimed his MP5 submachine gun at the front cop car and began spraying bullets, the rapid booms echoing around the vehicle like firecrackers in a tin can.

The cop car's windshield morphed into a web of cracks and golf-ball-sized chunks of metal tore from the hood. In a panic, the cop veered right and smashed into the back of a parked van, both vehicles crumpling under the force of the crash.

Jimmy focused his attention onto the remaining cop, quick-firing in his direction. The cop swerved out of the line of fire, then sped up toward the back right of the Tahoe, out of Jimmy's sight.

Up ahead, on the corner of Long Beach Avenue, the railroad crossing signal started blinking, and the crossing arm began to lower. They were a full half-block away from the crossing, but Luca gripped the wheel and punched the gas.

"We're not going to make it," Casey groaned.

But Luca kept his foot planted on the gas pedal as the orange cab of the freight train came hurtling into view from the left. Another bang rang through the SUV as the cop took out one of the brake lights. He was getting closer to the tire, and if he hit it, the crew would be done.

Jimmy shifted to the middle of the seat. He was about to take out the rear window so he could get a shot on the cop, when he noticed the train.

"Shit!" he screamed.

The Chevy engine roared as they neared the crossing, the barrier arm completely down now, the train only twenty feet away, it's horn booming. They hit the arm, shattering it into splinters of white, and the Tahoe thudded across the tracks as the train whipped behind them, missing the rear fender by mere inches.

Jimmy whooped, yelled, "Goddamn!" and slapped the back of Luca's headrest. But Casey only managed another yelp, this one closer to a guttural cry.

"Hang in there," said Jimmy. "You're going to make it."

"I'm losing a lot of blood, man," said Casey, his voice strained, desperate. "You gotta get me to a hospital."

"You know we can't do that," said Jimmy.

"Just leave me outside. You ain't gotta take me in."

"In this car?" barked Luca. "What are you, stupid?"

Luca sped through a red light and whipped the Tahoe left onto South Avalon, then turned back and said, "Check the bags. One of the stacks has to be tagged."

Jimmy pulled a GPS bug detector from his cargo pants and scrambled into the trunk space. There was a ripping sound as he unzipped the first of the extra-large duffle bags, exposing a wall of hundred-dollar bills. After twenty seconds or so, the ripping sound came again as Jimmy moved on to the second bag.

Luca's gaze flicked back and forth from the road to the rearview. "You see anything?"

"Not yet," said Jimmy.

"Well, hurry the fuck up!"

After a few moments, Jimmy called out, "Found it!" His hand sprouted from the shadows holding a black transmitter the size of a deck of cards.

"Good," said Luca. "Toss it."

Jimmy did, and Luca watched in the side-view mirror as the little plastic box exploded on impact with the blacktop.

"We're golden. Get us back to the lot."

"Wait," said Casey, the word barely more than a groan. "I won't make it if I don't get to a hospital."

Jimmy looked as though he was groping for the right words to say to ease the kid's fears, but before any came out of his mouth, Luca said, "You knew the risks. Now, it's time to be a man and accept them."

The car fell silent and Casey's eyes fell to the blood oozing from his wound, at his very life spilling through his fingers.

They made it back to East 62nd Street in less than four minutes. The Tahoe sped under the endless row of power lines and pulled into the parking lot, gravel crunching beneath its tires. The lot was empty, save for the three, clean personal vehicles the crew left in wait: a blue BMW, a dark green Toyota, and a silver Ford Explorer.

A cool, stiff breeze greeted Luca as he hopped out and ran around to the back of the SUV, the smell of solvents and burned rubber lingering in the air from the surrounding factories. When he popped the trunk, Jimmy tossed him one of the duffle bags, and he caught it with a grunt. Then Jimmy hopped out with the second bag, and both men loaded them into the back seat of their respective vehicles. Luca's was the Explorer; he was less flashy than Jimmy with his BMW, and less practical than Casey, who had the Toyota.

Bags loaded, Jimmy yelled back at the Tahoe. "Let's go, Casey. We gotta move."

But there was no response or movement of any kind. The bullet-ridden SUV suddenly took on the eerie appearance of a crime scene photo.

"Keep going," said Luca. "I'll get him."

Jimmy nodded and began stripping off his tactical gear as

Luca rushed around to the passenger side of the Tahoe. When he flung open the door, he found Casey with one hand on his wound and the other holding his Nokia cell phone, his bloodied thumb hovering shakily over the buttons.

"The fuck are you doing?" said Luca.

"I gotta get help," said Casey through a mouthful of blood. "I'm not gonna make it."

Luca snatched the phone and tossed it into the footwell. "You stupid son of a bitch. You're gonna get us caught."

"I won't say a word, I swear it. I don't wanna die, man."

Casey was barely twenty-one, and unlike Luca, he'd never taken a bullet. As he trembled in the passenger seat, Luca could see the pain and fear of death swirling around in his head like a tornado, his panicked brain thinking about only one thing—survival. The kid probably even believed he wouldn't rat out his crew when faced with interrogation, but Luca had seen too many people go down that way to take any risks. He glanced over to the BMW, where Jimmy was still stripping off, then fixed his gaze back on Casey, his stare cold and calculating.

Casey sucked in a ragged, tortured breath. "Please, man. Help me."

Luca smiled as he slipped off his gloves and placed them in his pocket. Then he was on Casey, grabbing the back of his head and smothering his mouth and nose with a thick, calloused palm. Casey thrashed and flailed like a drowning swimmer, but he was weak and couldn't put up much of a fight.

Luca had no problem taking a life. And although he never killed just for pleasure, when he had to kill for business, he saw nothing wrong with taking pleasure in it. The surge of power almost aroused him, a shot of testosterone spiked with adrenaline as he stomped out a man's very existence. *The closest you could ever feel to being a god.*

Just as he felt Casey giving up, Luca stared into his eyes to watch the boy's soul leave his body. When he finally let go, Casey's head fell back, his eyes still open, lifeless and vacant.

"Jimmy, get over here!"

After a few moments, Jimmy's tall frame appeared at Luca's side. His eyes locked onto Casey's body, his face a mix of anger and regret.

"Nothing we could have done," said Luca. "Fucking cops."

Jimmy slipped the rolled-up ski mask from his forehead, then ran his free hand through his mess of damp blonde hair. "God damn it. What are we gonna do?"

"Nothing. We've wasted too much time already. We need to move now."

The faint whine of police sirens had begun to grow in the distance, and it was clear they were working on borrowed time. Jimmy gave a reluctant nod, then slowly closed Casey's eyes with a swipe of his hand.

Luca headed back over to his Ford, stripped down to his shorts and shirt, and tossed his gear and MP5 into the trunk. When he slammed it shut, he turned back to find Jimmy standing next to the Tahoe with a can of gasoline hanging at his side, his expression all hesitation and uncertainty.

"What are you waiting for?" said Luca. "Douse it and light it. Make sure you torch the Toyota too."

Jimmy looked down at the gas can in his hand as if he wasn't sure how it'd gotten there. The sirens were louder now, and Luca thought he could hear the distant whirring of helicopter blades.

"Jimmy! He's dead. Now do it."

Jimmy looked at Luca, and suddenly all the uncertainty was replaced by absolute conviction. He nodded. "I got it. Get out of here, I'll see you in twelve hours."

Luca nodded, then rounded the Ford and hopped into the driver's seat as Jimmy began dousing the Tahoe with the gas.

. . .

Luca was three miles from the lot, cruising just under the speed limit with the windows down and one hand on the wheel, when a sweet wave of relief washed over him like a cool shower on a hot day. It was the biggest job he and Jimmy had ever done, and it had been a success. *With one less person to split the take with,* he thought with a smirk. He would meet up with Jimmy in the morning, then it was off to Panama City or Medellin to live the rest of his life like a king.

The glimmering mirage of his paradisiacal future breezed across his mind, and he couldn't help but lean back to unzip the duffle bag on the back seat. He gazed upon the sea of tiny Benjamin Franklins, all of them staring up at him with judging eyes. But as he flicked his gaze back and forth from the bag to the road, he noticed something—something very wrong. He reached back and pushed some of the top piles of cash out of the way, revealing black-and-white print.

He whipped the car to the side of the road and skidded to a stop, his heart pounding in his chest. Flicking on the interior light, he turned to the bag and began rummaging through it. What he found made acid race from his stomach to his throat: the bag was filled with newspaper.

Then something else caught Luca's eye. He reached in and pulled out the GPS transmitter, its red power light pulsing like a heartbeat. He stared at the transmitter for a moment, dumbfounded, then turned back and punched the dashboard with three heavy blows.

"Shit, shit, shit. Jimmy, you snake son of a bitch!"

With no time to think about how the double-cross had unfolded, he tossed the transmitter out of the window, spun the Ford in a tight U-turn, and began speeding in the direction he'd come from, hoping he could shake whoever was tracking him.

But less than half a mile down the road, the wail of sirens rang out. Two police cars appeared from nowhere, blocking Luca's path. He slammed on the breaks and skidded to a stop twenty feet short of the cops, tossed the Ford into reverse and stomped on the gas—only for two more cop cars to pull in from a side road, blocking him in from behind.

The doors of all four cars flew open. A swarm of officers with guns drawn converged on the Ford. One of them screamed, "Hands, hands, I wanna see hands!"

Luca wrestled with the thought of reaching for the pistol in his glove box, but it was too late. They were on him, squawking radios and beaming flashlights, all guns pointed at his face.

All he could do was raise his hands, grit his teeth, and hang his head.

1

SCARLETT

TWENTY-FIVE YEARS LATER

The store was bright and smelled of sweet coconut and cherry, not the leather dungeon Scarlett had imagined. Instead of a creepy guy with a lingering stare manning the register, the clerk was a smiley woman in her twenties, with a pixie cut. *Better together* by Jack Johnson gently sauntered out of unseen speakers, and the only other customers in the store were a young couple who kept exchanging soft chuckles.

But Scarlett still felt strange scanning the aisles in her nurse scrubs, as conspicuous as an eight-year-old in a cocktail bar. She passed gadgets and gizmos, some with batteries included, some batteries required, not knowing exactly what she was looking for. She'd hoped she would know when she saw it; a *voilà* moment.

But after ten minutes in the store, she just felt confused. Most of the products posed more questions than answers; *Is this too much? Will he just laugh at this? What even is this?* She picked up a small whip with a tasseled handle, but after testing it on the palm of her hand—the crack so loud it echoed around the store—she quickly placed it back on the shelf and moved on.

But just as she was beginning to give up hope, her short lunch break almost at an end, she came across the handcuff section. They were perfect: not too intimidating to be weird, and not too girly or silly to be laughed at. With four color options, she played it safe and grabbed the gray ones, then rushed over to the counter.

"I have the pink ones of these at home, they're awesome," the clerk said as she rang up the purchase.

Scarlett blushed, trying to force the very intimate image out of her head, and for some reason said, "Thanks."

After an interminable silence with undertones of allure, the clerk handed her the little red store bag and receipt, then winked and said, "Have fun."

Scarlett left the air-conditioned store and stepped into the early-summer sun, the heat ripples rising from the asphalt, and the distant honks from traffic-weary drivers stuck in overheating cars.

With her head down, clutching the little bag close to her chest, she hurried down the sidewalk to her Honda CR-V and hopped in, the dashboard stating that the heat had crept into triple digits.

Scarlett's days were made up of driving from neighborhood to neighborhood and house to house: Reseda to Northridge, Thousand Oaks to Simi Valley, Glendale to Woodland Hills, rows upon rows of generic, single-story, pastel-colored homes—rectangular wood boxes that *safely* enclosed the lives that dwelled within. Each street was scattered with three-foot chain-link fences, limp American flags, and sun-worn deck chairs perched on porches under dangling wind chimes. Trucks and old-model sedans sat parked next to high curbs and weed-riddled sidewalks.

But there was something that made Scarlett's stops unique from the other houses on the block—inside, there was always someone dying.

Scarlett pulled up outside the Abbott household and re-entered the afternoon heat; the Honda's fan kicked into overdrive as she wandered around and popped the trunk. Her car was a hospital supply closet on wheels, the back half-filled with disposable mattress pads, bandages, antiseptic sprays, diapers, *et cetera*. She often fantasized about pulling up to some catastrophe, popping the trunk, and handing out supplies to the injured, like a heartwarming scene in an action movie—but she'd had no such luck so far.

She plucked her black shoulder bag out of the mess, headed up the driveway, past the orange "beware of the dog" sign, and rang the duct-taped doorbell. A few moments later, a raspy, tired voice called out from the other side of the door: "Just a sec!"

Mark Abbott opened the door wearing what he usually wore; a faded polo shirt that clung to his protruding belly, baggy stonewashed jeans, and thick-rimmed milk bottle glasses. He flashed a confused look and said, "Oh, it's you," as if he was expecting someone else and Scarlett wasn't scheduled to be there at this exact time.

"Hey Mark," she said, mustering a smile. "How are you?"

Mark grunted a half response and looked down at his bare feet. "You better come in outta the heat."

Mark was the type of man who favored interactions with as few words as possible, and little to no eye contact. Scarlett had come across plenty of men like that in her life, and she always had the same effect on them. Her smooth, caramel skin, small, freckled nose, pink lips, and bright eyes always roused the keen, confident men and unsettled the nervous, shy ones. Mark was definitely the latter.

She stepped inside and entered the past; the house had remained completely unchanged since it went on the market back in the 80s. Except now, it was faded and worn and stained, like a grainy Polaroid of how it used to look. Stifling, stale air hung in the house, suspended and still like a drop of blood in a glass of water. Inch-long white hairs clung to every surface, clustering together in piles at the base of the walls, despite the fact the family dog had passed over six months prior.

Mark led her towards the back bedroom—toward Letty, his mother, the reason for Scarlett's visit.

"How's she doing?" asked Scarlett.

"Same, I guess," said Mark. "Still dying."

As they reached the doorway to the bedroom, Mark stepped aside and said, "I'll be in the backyard, case you need me," then slinked off toward the kitchen.

Letty was sitting upright in bed, facing a closed window, the boxy TV in the corner lifeless, the stench of rubbing alcohol and urine as thick as soup. Scarlett had to hold back a gag as she rounded the raised, hospital-style bed and cracked the window.

Letty suffered from advanced-stage Parkinson's and had lost the ability to move or talk, but her big brown eyes still lit up at the sight of her nurse, a feeling Scarlett enjoyed despite everything else.

"Good afternoon, Letty," Scarlett said, pulling a pair of rubber gloves from her bag. "You ready to get to it?"

Getting to it meant cleaning and redressing the pressure sores Letty got from being bed-bound.

That was the job: go from patient to patient—advanced-stage Parkinson's to brain cancer, CHF to COPD—and clean wounds, check vitals, talk, calm, mitigate, and sometimes just listen. Scarlett used to think of it as meaningful work, bringing comfort to people in their final months, weeks, days... but that was back before she had some years on the job under her belt. Back before countless patients like Letty, all of them clouded in the same morbid finality. After a while, she began wondering how long she could keep doing it. How long could she keep watching these people fade and die with no *real* purpose but to simply bear witness?

Like most of the patients on Scarlett's roster, Letty was in a poor state—her face coated in a layer of grime and sweat, her hair a mess of matted clumps spilling around her head like a dropped plate of spaghetti. And, worst of all, when Scarlett slipped on the gloves—the rubber catching on her engagement ring—she found Letty's diaper hadn't been changed. She held back a long, frustrated sigh for Letty's sake and got to work.

When she was done, she wandered through the kitchen, past the grease-covered cabinets and car-sized microwave, and popped open the back door. Mark was in the weed forest of a back yard where he said he'd be, hunched on an old wooden stool, attempting to put together an IKEA coffee table. He was studying the instructions as though they contained the answers to life's eternal questions, and small bits of wood and metal littered the floor around him like a miniature barn had exploded. Scarlett guessed he was in his late forties, and all she knew was he worked nights. He may have been a warehouse worker, delivery man, security guard... serial killer? They were all equally plausible.

"Hey Mark, can I have a word?"

"Shoot," he said flatly, without looking away from his project.

"This is the third time I've arrived here to find your mom in a soiled diaper," she said, trying to coax Mark's eyes up to hers.

"Okay," he replied.

"She needs to be changed regularly to make sure she's kept dry. It's very important."

"Uh-huh."

"You understand, right?"

"Yep."

Scarlett felt her patience wearing thin, so she took a long breath before her next words: "Well then, please start taking some responsibility. She is your mother, and she needs you."

Mark finally met her gaze, the muscles in his face tense, a hollow sadness in his eyes. "I'm trying, okay? This is hard for me."

Scarlett wanted to come back with a stern response, to scold Mark and remind him how hard it must have been for Letty to raise him. But she feared that Mark would see through her righteous act.

The fact was, deep down, she understood his actions. What child wants to accept their mother's imminent death, let alone change their diaper? She knew better than most how demoralizing and heartbreaking it was for families to watch a loved one fade away before their eyes. And even worse to be Letty, the one fading, trying to appear brave in front of your family despite the pain and fear.

Scarlett often felt a strange pleasure at how her mother went—fast and painless, or so the doctors assured her. A clot in the brain unbeknownst to her or anyone else, right up until the second it killed her in the departure lounge of Burbank Airport. The woman who raised her. The black French immigrant who scrubbed toilets, folded laundry, and wiped kids' snotty noses for wealthy LA families. One minute she was that woman, waiting for a coffee or looking up at a screen to find her gate, and the next... nothing.

"I know this is hard," she said. "Maybe she'd be better off in an assisted living facility? There are some affordable options these days."

"No," said Mark, his tone firm. "No homes. No way. She's not ending up in one of those places, you understand?"

Caught a little off guard, Scarlett tried to keep her voice calm. "Look, I just—"

"No, you look. It's your job to come here and help my mom, right? So, why don't you just *do* your job and leave me the hell alone!"

A flash of heat rose up Scarlett's back as anger and frustration swelled in her gut. She was angry at Mark, angry at herself, but mostly angry at the job—the job that was supposed to... do what? *Make her happy?* It sounded so wrong now, like reading an old diary entry from her years as an unruly teen.

She wanted to fire back with a scathing response, a witty rebuke to leave Mark remorseful, but she knew it would fall on deaf ears. Really, she just wanted so much to help, to do something, but as always, she found herself useless—escorting disaster, trying not to make matters worse.

Taking a deep breath and burying her frustration, she nodded bitterly. "Of course," she said, and headed back through the house, and out to her car.

She sat in the Honda in silent reflection for a moment, before her phone buzzed from her purse. She fished it out, and it told her she had a text message from a number that wasn't saved to her contacts. But it didn't need to be; that 310 number had been seared into Scarlett's memory forever.

The text was from *him*. It was from Anton.

She slowly unlocked her phone, a strange, anxious feeling buzzing through her body. The text simply said, *Hey. I'm back in L.A.*

2

LUCA

Luca's cellmate, Hooper, set down his magazine on his cot. With his long southern drawl, he said, "I don't like that look in your eye, man. Not one bit."

Luca had been in the same spot for almost two hours: sitting on the cold floor of their cell, watching beams of sunlight cut through the reinforced glass, his nose long since immune to the chemical tinge of cleaning products that filled the air. He was thinking back on his life, the heist, the arrest. And he was thinking about what he always thought about: revenge.

Hooper sat up and turned so he was side-saddle on his bed. He looked like a biker with his wide chest, forearm tattoos, and thinning white ponytail. "You hear me talking to you, man?"

"What?" said Luca, snapping out of his trance.

"I said I don't like that look, brother. If it were me, I'd be bouncing off the fucking walls, and you're just sitting there staring into nothin'."

"I'm just thinking about what I'm gonna do."

"What's there to think about? You call up some friends

from the old days, hit a titty bar, or what have you. It doesn't need the type of thinking you're doin'."

"It's not that simple for me. You know that."

He had told Hooper all about the money, the robbery, the set-up. He'd also told him what he planned to do to Jimmy as soon as he tracked him down. He trusted Hooper—a rare honor bestowed on very few people. That were still alive, at least.

"It *could* be that simple," said Hooper. "You've done your time."

Luca didn't reply. He didn't need to; after spending years locked in a confined space together, they'd learned how to read each other.

Hooper took a long, slow breath. "I ever tell you the one with the guy and the tree down in Texas?"

"I don't wanna hear it," said Luca, raising his palm.

"Come on, come on. One for the road?"

Hooper liked to tell stories and old tales to get his point across. Although not big on stories himself, Luca humored his cellmate because... well, shit, there wasn't much else to do. Also, Hooper had a way of telling them. He delivered them with such enthusiasm and carefully placed emphasis that even some of the stories Luca had already heard seemed to carry a new, more profound meaning when Hooper told them. And Hooper was smart. A little crazy, but definitely smart. On more than one occasion, his advice had even saved Luca from being sent to solitary or taking a shank in the kidney at yard time.

"Fuck it," said Luca. "One for the road."

Hooper grinned and eagerly rubbed his hands together. "So, a couple of hundred years ago, a Texan called Henry decided to break it off with his girl. This poor girl was so heart-broken that she went and killed herself. Now, the girl's brother, not too happy with the premature demise of his sister, decided to hunt Henry down. After finding and shooting Henry in the head, the brother turned the gun on himself, blowing his own brains out. But the thing was, our old boy Henry wasn't dead; the bullet had only grazed his face and then lodged into a tree behind him."

Using the tips of his index and middle fingers to represent the bullet, Hooper mimicked the trajectory of the bullet, running his fingers along his cheek, then sailing past his head.

"Lucky guy, right?" he went on. "So, twenty years later, Henry decided he wanted to get rid of the tree. He knew it would be a pain in the ass to cut down, so he decided to blow it up with a few sticks of dynamite."

Hooper leaned forward and lowered his voice, campfire style. "So, he set the dynamite around the tree, rolled out the fuse, and let 'er rip. But the explosion didn't only take out the tree; it propelled the bullet, which had been nestled in that same spot for twenty years, straight into his head. Killing. Him. Dead."

Luca sat there for a moment, letting the *moral* of the story—if one could call it that—sink in. The first of Hooper's points was simple: if Henry had left the tree alone, he could have died an old man in his bed. But by deciding to rid himself of the past, he ended up shooting himself in the face.

Luca had survived a long career as a criminal and a quarter-century in prison. He *could* walk away from it all and salvage some form of a life with his remaining years. But if he went for Jimmy, there was every chance he could end up back in prison. Or even the boneyard.

The second point was more subtle: if Henry had decided to remove the tree when he was a younger, fitter man, he could have been rid of it in an afternoon with nothing but an axe. Luca was no spring chicken anymore—he had bullet fragments buried deep in his left knee which ached every time he put weight on it, and he hadn't fired a gun in over two decades.

He looked Hooper in the eye. "What if Henry ha—"

But his voice was drowned out by the yell of a guard outside. "Open cell one-twenty-four!"

Another guard, this one further away, responded: "Opening cell one-two-four."

A heavy metallic *clunk* rang around the cell, followed by a slow squeal as the cell door rolled open. A guard by the name of Johnson stepped into the opening, his linebacker frame nearly filling the space. The man was as tall as he was wide, with a voice box stolen from a bullhorn.

He stepped into the cell, puffed out his chest, and said, "Looks like your time has finally come, Luca."

After twenty-five years and three months in prison, the great state of California had decided it was safe to let Luca back on the streets—on parole, at least.

"Looks like it has," Luca said. "You gonna miss me, big guy?"

"Like I miss having the clap," said Johnson. "Now get moving, I ain't got all day. And no goodbye grab-assing with your boyfriend, either. I don't wanna see that shit."

"Fuck you," said Luca, putting his hands on his knees and slowly rising to his feet.

Johnson gave the cell a once over, eyeballing the posters and sketches taped to the wall like he was in the world's worst art museum. "If you wanna take any of this shit, you gotta carry it out now. We ain't in the business of shipping nothing to you, so don't bother asking."

"Trash it," said Luca.

Johnson unclipped the handcuffs from his belt, held them out, and cleared his throat.

"You're cuffing me to walk out?" Luca asked.

Johnson chuckled. "You ain't free yet."

As the cuffs were going on, Luca glanced over to Hooper on

the bottom bunk. They shared a look; no words were said, but the half-smile and a single nod carried a silent message: good luck.

Walking down the long hallway with Johnson on his hip, Luca glanced around the place he'd called home for so long and felt nothing but pure contempt. He thought back to the sentencing, the judge a seething tower of biblical fury as she ran down Luca's long list of priors like a preacher denouncing Satan at a sermon. It took four guards to stop him from ripping her heart out when she looked him dead in the eyes and said, "Twenty years."

Add to that four counts of violence toward other inmates, two counts of disturbing the peace, and one escape attempt that saw him snagged on the razor-wire fence encircling the prison loading bay, and instead of serving only eighty percent of his sentence, he had ended up with five additional years tacked on.

A redheaded guard with "Miller" on her nametag was working the processing counter. She gave Luca a curt nod, then slid across the $434 income he'd earned working in the laundry room, minus state and federal taxes. Then she handed over his personal effects: a brown leather wallet with an expired driver's license and no cash, a box of matches from the Vanilla Club, and...

"Where's my watch?" asked Luca, anger riding his voice.

"This is all that was there," said Miller.

"Where's my fucking Rolex?"

Luca had hard black eyes, a sharp mouth, and a dented mound of flesh for a nose, which gave him the fierce countenance of a cornered Pit Bull, but Miller seemed far from intimidated. Her gaze remained flat and emotionless, and this pissed Luca off.

He was about to yell, to demand his property, but Johnson stepped over and put a hand on his shoulder.

"You wanna get out of here, or not?"

Luca turned and looked up at the bigger man. "I want my fucking watch back."

"Well," Johnson raised his eyebrows. "You could file a report, but that will take some time. Then if we find it, someone here will reach out to you. But I gotta tell you, a lot of stuff gets lost in processing, and most of the time, it tends not to show up. So I wouldn't get ya hopes up, if you know what I mean. Now, you want me to get the forms for the report, or you wanna get outta here?"

Those thieving bastards. Luca breathed hard, burying his rage somewhere deep down inside himself. The Rolex was worth four, maybe five grand, and he needed that money. He would have killed for less on the outside, but inside these prison walls, the guards had all the power, and they loved to wield it.

Luca turned back to Miller and scowled. "Let's get this over with."

Johnson pushed open the main entry/exit doors, and they stepped out into the sunlight, the hot afternoon air hitting Luca in the face like a blow-dryer. The feeling of freedom was nothing short of immense. He'd spent twenty-five birthdays, twenty-five Fourth of Julys, and twenty-five New Year's Eves locked in a cage, wasting away like a piece of garbage in a landfill, surrounded by hundreds of other pieces of garbage, all basking in everyone's accumulated stink. Finally, he could feel that stink lifting off him like steam from a winter jogger.

Johnson waved up to a guard in a watchtower to the left of the gate. The guard nodded, then disappeared out of sight. A buzzer rang out twice, and the gate slowly rolled open—one of the best sounds Luca's ears had ever heard.

"Swing a left after you get through the gate—should be a cab waiting for ya," said Johnson. "Good luck."

He said the last part like a child being forced to say thank you by their parents. But then he turned to face Luca and held out his bear paw of a hand. Luca reached out and shook, and a tiny piece of folded paper transferred from Johnson's palm into his. It was so seamless that even if someone was watching through a camera from the control room, they never would have noticed.

Luca tucked the paper into his pocket and walked out a free man—older, more broken, un-rehabilitated, but free. He stopped just outside the gates for a moment with his eyes closed and nose up, filling his lungs with deep breaths. Here, the air smelled sweeter somehow, as if the gates were a force field, blocking out anything good from ever reaching the prison walls.

He walked around the corner and found the taxicab in the passenger loading bay, just as Johnson had said. But there was no one else; no smiling faces to greet him, no family members with homemade banners and balloons—no one to claim him at all.

He knew no one would be there, of course. He was never the type to make many *friends*. Even so, he was still struck by an unfamiliar sense of loneliness, just strong enough to cut through the thrill of getting out.

As he neared the cab, the driver, a Puerto Rican man in his fifties, rolled down the window.

"Need a ride?" he said, his accent still thick from his motherland.

"No shit," said Luca, before opening the rear door and climbing in.

The driver turned back with a toothy grin. "Where to, brother?"

Luca thought about how other inmates might answer that question: To the closest bar? A fast-food restaurant they'd been craving for years? A strip club? *Home*? The cabbie's smile faded as the question lingered in the air like a bad smell.

Finally, Luca replied, "Downtown."

"Damn, man," said the cabbie. "Traffic's gonna be crazy getting over at this time of day."

"Better get moving, then."

He sighed. "You got an address?"

Luca did have an address. That was what set him apart from most of the other washed-up ex-cons walking out of those gates—he had a plan. And that plan had a first step.

"The Capital Motel," said Luca. "South Central and East 23rd."

The cabbie nodded, bobble-head style. "I know the place. Used to work that area a few years back before it got really bad."

He didn't say anything else, but his expression telegraphed what he was thinking—*you just got out, and that's the first place you're going? You poor bastard.*

3

SCARLETT

The knife pattered on the cutting board with the rhythmic precision of a sewing machine as Scarlett diced thyme. Beef seared in a pan beside her, the whole house swimming in the aroma of sautéing asparagus and melted butter.

She'd been gliding around the kitchen like a figure skater for almost an hour, her nurse scrubs replaced by yoga pants and one of her fiancé Josh's baggy UCLA shirts. She'd thought about waiting until Josh got home before starting cooking, just in case he wasn't home by 7pm—even though he'd promised he would be—but her mind was racing with thoughts of the text from Anton, all those old feelings coming to the surface. She'd hoped that by throwing herself into dinner she would be able to steer her mind away from him, but it was only half working.

They'd dated on and off for three years before he moved to New York, and Scarlett got her life together and went to nursing school. It was the most turbulent, insanely passionate, and violently sad relationship she'd ever had. The best and worst time of her life.

Her cell phone buzzed from the center island. Scarlett

glanced over nervously but was relieved to find it was a call from Yvonne. She grabbed the phone, answered, and pinned it to her ear with her shoulder as she kept working on the dinner.

"Hey."

"Hey, girl," Yvonne said. "I know you're busy tonight, but I just wanted to make sure we're still on for tomorrow?"

"Of course," said Scarlett, scraping the thyme in with the vegetables. "8pm at Mill's."

"Good. If I don't get a night away from these kids, I might crack."

They had one of their double dates planned: a quarterly tradition which usually consisted of Scarlett and Yvonne indulging in gossip while Josh and Yvonne's husband, Danny, droned on about office politics.

"I heard they changed up the menu," said Yvonne. "Candice was there last week—she said the new beef stroganoff is incredible."

"Not for me. I can't do those heavy carbs."

"Boo. You gotta live a little."

"I'm living."

"Bullshit," said Yvonne. "Speaking of living, did you get a *special gift* for Josh like we talked about?"

Scarlett thought about the little red bag from the store. "Yeah, I picked something up. It was so embarrassing."

"Well... what the hell did you buy?" Yvonne said excitedly.

"Nothing too crazy."

"So... are you going to make me guess, or?"

"Okay, okay... I got handcuffs," Scarlett admitted.

"A little bit PG-13, but a good start. You gonna use them tonight?"

Scarlett turned the heat off the beef and thought about it. "Yeah, I don't know yet."

"Why the fuck not? I mean, that's what you bought them for, right?"

"What if he's not into it?"

"Then at least you tried, instead of just complaining to me all the goddamn time."

That was what Scarlett liked about Yvonne: her directness, her fearlessness to express how she truly felt without worrying about offending anyone. They'd first met at Josh's office Christmas party three years prior. It was Scarlett's first time meeting Josh's colleagues, and she was nervous about mingling with the "cutthroat, backstabbing brown-noses" that Josh had told her so much about.

"You'll be fine, baby," Josh had said. "Just be yourself."

But two hours into the party, Josh vanished after a trip to the bathroom and left Scarlett to fend for herself. She spent twenty minutes at the bar as creepy older men approached her with finger food plates, sporting red wine smiles and giving handshakes that were either way too tight or way too soft, which made her equally uncomfortable. And she could feel the men's wives giving her elevator stares up and down her dress, which now looked far more low cut than when she'd tried it on in the store.

She was about to leave and head home when Yvonne and Danny approached her. The first thing Yvonne said was, "Don't you just hate these things? They're so fucking boring," loud enough for the whole room to hear.

Her next question instantly endeared her to Scarlett: "You wanna do a shot?"

After *several* shots, Josh reappeared with an apologetic story about getting dragged into the CEO's office for glasses of Brandy. But Scarlett didn't care. She and Yvonne left the guys at the bar discussing Q1 projections for the firm and danced to

Jingle Bell Rock and All I Want For Christmas Is You, their heels and purses on the floor between them.

"Anyway, I gotta go," said Yvonne through the phone. "The little one is trying to chew the eye off a stuffed kangaroo. I swear Danny dropped her as a baby and didn't tell me. I'll see you tomorrow, okay? Love you."

"Love you. Bye."

Scarlett hung up the phone feeling lighter and more upbeat than when she'd answered it, all thoughts of Anton and his text replaced by anticipation for the night with Josh.

Tonight was supposed to be a small celebration—three months since their engagement—and she'd cooked up Josh's favorite dish: ribeye steak with sautéed vegetables and homemade peppercorn sauce. The meal had shaped up to be one of her best efforts yet; the steak medium rare, and the vegetables seasoned to perfection.

But 7pm rolled by without Josh making an appearance. Then 7:30pm, then 8pm, then 8:30pm, all with no word. She tried calling him but only got his voicemail, and if she didn't know him so well, her annoyance might have morphed into worry. By 8:45pm, Scarlett was on the couch watching TV, the food in plastic Tupperware, and the night nearly over.

For the first time since moving in, the new, spacious house seemed empty, lonely even. The house was open plan, with the staircase running a U-turn up to the second floor. It sat in the middle of a neighborhood that was a nicer, newer version of the neighborhoods where Scarlett's patients lived. They were still cookie-cutter designs, but two stories instead of one; had paved herringbone driveways instead of patchy lawns; alarm-coded front doors instead of creaky screen doors with dog claw tears.

At 8:52pm, Scarlett heard the garage door open, then close. Josh came through the front door with his tie loose around his neck and a—*what a day*—look on his face.

"I am so sorry, baby," he said and pulled a bottle of wine and a half dozen pink roses from behind his back. "Is there still time to celebrate?"

He was all business in a blue suit and brown leather dress shoes, despite his company's casual dress code. He was what Scarlett liked to refer to as *all-American handsome*; his almond-colored hair brushed to a side parting, his face sharp and angular with liquid hazel eyes atop high pronounced cheekbones.

"What happened?" she asked. "I've been trying to call you."

"I know, I know," said Josh. He set the wine and flowers on the kitchen island and headed toward her. "First, I was stuck at the office because of that damn Chicago deal. Then I hit a wreck on the freeway and was in standstill traffic for over an hour." He flicked his head back and grimaced—the universal *why me* gesture. "To top it all off, the shitty car phone charger I got at the gas station decided tonight was the night to quit on me."

Scarlett tried to mask her annoyance and disappointment. She knew if she tried to push the subject, she would just come off as unreasonable. After all, his reasons were legitimate. And she knew what a stressful time it was for him. This wasn't the first time the—*make it or break it, verge of making company history, god damn*—Chicago deal had kept him late at the office. She also tried reminding herself that Josh coming home late because he was a workaholic was far better than him strolling in at 2am reeking of booze and perfume, the way Anton used to.

Josh slipped onto the couch beside her and enveloped her in a hug. "I know you worked hard on dinner, I'm really sorry I'm late. And I'm going to make it up to you, I promise."

And he would, probably in the form of a new purse, jewelry, or maybe a dress he thought would look great on her.

"Are you still hungry?" Scarlett asked with a sigh.

"Famished."

"Well, I hope you like cold steak."

"I love it," said Josh. "As a matter of fact, the guy at the store said this wine is the perfect pairing for cold steak."

Scarlett smiled slightly, despite herself. She started to get up to get Josh's food, but he stopped her.

"I got this baby, you relax." He headed for the kitchen, grabbed the bottle from the island, then turned back and said, "Oh, and I've got a surprise for you, you're going to love it."

"What kind of surprise?"

"You'll see."

Using Josh's excellent track record of previous gifts as a reference, she tried to think of what it could be. Then she remembered her own surprise, the one in the little red bag, and suddenly felt a little nervous.

The steak was still tasty despite it being cold, and the wine did turn out to be a good pairing; go figure. With empty plates in the sink and the second bottle of wine open, Josh set his laptop on the coffee table and said, "I can't wait to see your face when you see this."

He faced the screen away from Scarlett as he found what he was looking for, then swiveled the laptop so she could see. On-screen was the image of an enormous gothic-style building set back on a vast courtyard.

"What is this?" she asked.

Josh beamed a smile from ear to ear. "This... is our wedding venue."

Scarlett's brain stuttered for a second. "What?"

"One of the partners at the firm; his wife's a wedding planner, and she got us a special price."

Scarlett took in the picture for a moment. It resembled a gigantic French chateau built to look like a castle. Whitestone walls with black roof spires and twinned towers either side of a suspended balcony. The courtyard was a labyrinth of lush lawns and gravel pathways encircling a wide water fountain.

Josh leaned across and flicked to the next image—a grand ballroom with gold decor and intricately carved details, capped with over a dozen chandeliers.

At that moment, Scarlett saw the grand wedding in her mind, the guests, the food. Then she saw their lives together as husband and wife, a rapid reel of future snapshots. She thought about Josh and her as an old couple: a senile partnership of the gray and slow.

Not too long ago, she'd been renting a shoebox apartment, living paycheck-to-paycheck, playing an insane game of *break up, make up* with Anton. Now she had this handsome, successful guy trying to plan their dream wedding at the most incredible venue. Some people would say she hit the jackpot; she was the luckiest girl in the world. But she struggled to look past Josh's inconsiderate ways and how she sometimes felt neglected. And then there was the sex.

No, Scarlett told herself, *don't do this again, don't go down that rabbit hole.*

It was true Josh was far from perfect, but he did have lots of redeeming qualities, the type she needed in her life. He was generous and driven and loyal. He was a gentleman, and he would make a good husband. And more importantly, he gave to her what Anton never could: a future.

Scarlett snapped back to reality and became aware that Josh was watching her expression, so she flashed a smile. "It's so beautiful. But don't you think it might be a little much? I mean, I only have a few people coming from my side."

"Not at all. It's perfect. This is your day, and we only get to do it once, so why not do it big?" He paused, watching her, still beaming. "So, do you love it or what?"

"Of course," she lied. "Like you said, it's perfect."

Josh's grin grew somehow wider. "Oh, baby, I can't wait to marry you."

He wrapped her in a tight hug, his body warm and firm, the sweet musky scent of his skin filling her nostrils, his heartbeat so heavy it seemed to beat inside her too. Then he leaned back, swept a curl of hair behind her ear, and kissed her, his breath hot with wine, his eyes drunk with love.

Five minutes later, they were in the bedroom kissing and caressing. Josh peeled off his shirt while Scarlett unhooked her bra. He laid her on her back, and she wrapped her legs around his, locking her ankles behind his knees, absorbing his warmth and energy. He began kissing his way from her neck to her navel, his thin but tender lips leaving soft wet tracks down her naked chest. She hesitated for just a second, her nerves battling the intense moment, but she decided to go for it. As Josh worked his way back up her body, she reached under the bed and pulled out the little red bag. He lifted his head, confusion seeping into the pure lust in his expression.

"What's that?" he asked.

"I got you a surprise too. Open it."

Josh gave an inquisitive smile, plunged his hand into the bag, and pulled out the pair of gray handcuffs. He eyed them with uncertainty. "Kinky."

"I thought we could use them tonight."

With Josh being reserved in the bedroom, Scarlett had mentally prepared herself to convince him with soft encouragement—*it's just a bit of fun, let's just try it.* But to her surprise, he took her wrists with conviction and locked them to the bedpost above her head.

She looked up at him with wanting eyes, her bare chest rising and falling with heavy breaths. The energy between them was palpable, a sudden explosion of hormonal fireworks. She was sure this would be the night.

But she was wrong.

The sex began slow and gentle as it always did—that was Josh's way. Even when they first started dating, he was always too delicate, too soft, too polite. Never really taking control of her the way she wanted, the way she craved. The handcuffs were her not-so-subtle way of telling him what she really wanted without crossing the line and questioning his sacred masculinity. But it hadn't worked, he was still thrusting away with the boring exactitude of an accounting spreadsheet.

On a whim, Scarlett decided to give him one more push, to double down on the night's efforts, all or nothing. She leaned into his ear and whispered: "Choke me."

He pulled back with a look of bemusement. "What did you say?"

"I want you to choke me," she repeated.

Josh's face went blank. There was no sign of embarrassment or confusion, just a blank stare.

"It's okay," said Scarlett. "It's just for fun. You won't hurt me."

"No," he said, his voice baritone.

"What's wrong?"

"Nothing. I just don't want to, okay?"

Knowing she'd pushed him too far, Scarlett backtracked. "Okay, it's fine. Just keep going, I was almost there." A lie.

Josh hesitantly assumed the position and went back to his mechanical thrusting. But after thirty seconds, his mind was lost and his penis slack. He hung his head and rolled onto his back, the look of a man defeated by himself.

"What's the matter?" she asked.

"I don't know. Maybe I'm just tired."

"It's okay, baby. You wanna rest for a minute, then try again?"

Josh ran his hand through his hair and sighed. "Can we just do it in the morning?"

Scarlett did a poor job of hiding her disappointment, then said, "Sure. Of course. Can you get the key?"

He released her from the handcuffs without making eye contact, then headed for the en-suite bathroom while she lay there, looking up at the ceiling, holding back a long, unsatisfied sigh.

She just didn't understand why he couldn't indulge her desire to get a little rough. She knew most men would jump at the chance for that kind of intimacy with their partner, but Josh wouldn't even talk about it. Was it so wrong for her to want to be pushed against a wall and dominated?

With the heat of desire still strong inside her, she closed her eyes and slipped into a state of erotic dreaminess as lustful snapshots flashed across her mind. Craving the sweet release, she checked the en-suite door was closed, then slid her hand beneath the covers and began touching herself.

The intensity swelled, and her mind wandered to memories of nights when reckless abandon ruled over sensibility and fear. Back to when passion consumed her. Then she realized, for the twentieth time since receiving the text outside Letty's house, she was thinking about Anton.

4

LUCA

The cabbie was right about the traffic. The journey from the California State Prison to the Capital Motel took almost three hours.

Luca observed the chaos of the city as it passed by. The new-model cars hummed along almost silently. Old family businesses had been replaced by boutique coffee shops and salad bars. Kids in skinny jeans and white t-shirts with the sleeves rolled up rode along on plastic electric skateboards, making Luca feel like he'd entered both the past and the future simultaneously. And then there were the office workers, laborers, students, kids, and their parents—*everyone* staring down at their mobile phones like zombies.

The city had moved on and left him behind.

The sun was setting blood-red by the time they reached the neighborhood where the motel was located. It was part of the city that had been conveniently forgotten during gentrification. It had been bad even before Luca went away, but now it was worse. On one corner, they passed an abandoned, battle-weary pit bull chained to a fire hydrant, it's guttural bark competing with the distant howls of a car alarm. On the next, a group of youths stood next to a burned-out Chevy El Camino, each of them following the cab with their dead eyes.

The Capital Motel itself was a crummy two-story building with dark-gray bricks and faded red doors. It was a seedy haven for drifters, dealers, hookers and their pimps. It used to be Luca's go-to spot whenever he had a lot of heat on him and he needed to lie low. It also happened to be the place where he kept his emergency stash, hidden within the walls of one of the rooms. And now he had to find a way to get it back... *if* it was still there.

The cabbie passed a flickering red vacancy sign as he parked in front of the reception office. He looked over his shoulder at Luca with a knowing expression. "Good luck, brother."

Luca nodded. He paid the man—the ride only slightly less expensive than a Learjet—and hopped out.

The motel manager was a troll of a man with the droopy face of a basset hound and a red, pitted nose like a strawberry. He was reclined in his tattered office chair, both feet up on the desk, shoveling greasy Chinese food into his mouth from a Styrofoam carton. His eyes were locked on a re-run of the 2016 NFL season game between the Raiders and the Cowboys, which played through a laptop that looked older than him.

Luca approached the desk and said, "I need a room."

On the laptop, one of the Cowboys players burst through two tackles before getting hit out of bounds. The manager kicked his feet on the desk and yelled, "What the fuck was that? You gotta put him down early! That's bullshit defense." He said it with the conviction of a man who thought the game was live and that the players could hear him.

Luca rapped his knuckles on the desk. "I said I need a room."

The manager finally turned his head, as if only just noticing Luca standing there. He looked Luca up and down from eyeballs to boot-heel, like he was a psychic trying to get a read on the other man's energy. "You ain't got no bags."

"Well, ain't you a fucking genius," said Luca. "Nothing gets past you, huh?"

"You a cop?" the manager asked, straight-faced.

Luca couldn't help but smirk at that. The question wasn't an unreasonable one. Any undercover cop could post up in one of the rooms for a few days and they would see and hear enough to create a year's worth of open cases. And, of course, that would be bad for business.

"I ain't no cop—just looking for a place to stay."

The manager gave a quick jerk of his eyebrow. "So what happened, you just get back from a *long* stay somewhere?"

Luca shot a threatening look, and the manager threw up his hand in response to his own question. "Hey, it's fine. I don't need to know anything about your business. But just remember," he jerked a thumb toward the rows of motel rooms across the parking lot, "those rooms are my business. You got it?"

Luca despised it when people tried to stamp their authority on him, but he was too tired to argue and he needed to get his stash. He swallowed his annoyance and said, "Fine. Just give me a room."

The manager scooped more chow mein into his mouth, then spoke through his food, sending small chunks firing down onto his sweat-stained bowling shirt. "Twenty-nine bucks a night, plus ten deposit for the towels."

Luca tried to think of a clever, roundabout way of asking his question, found none, and said, "Is room eighteen available?"

The manager looked as though he'd been asked for the speed of gravity. "Come again?"

Luca flashed a smile. "That's my lucky number."

"That room's taken," the manager said, suspicion in his tone. "I'll put you in twelve." He swiveled around to the key rack, his chair creaking and moaning under his weight. As he skimmed through his mess of keys for number twelve, Luca leaned across the desk and quickly swiped a couple of large paperclips from a small stationery tray. The manager turned back and placed the key on the desk, then used two fingers to slide it across the counter, like he was at a blackjack table placing a bet. But as Luca reached out, the man pulled it away.

"Cash up front."

Pulling out the rest of his petty cash, Luca laid down two twenty-dollar notes and said, "I'll take my change in coins."

The manager gave another quizzical look, then began counting out the change, as if he'd lost interest in their conversation.

Luca glanced around and took in the shoebox of a space. The walls were stained and bubbling from water leaks, and the mud-brown carpet was worn down to the under-fiber. "I'm surprised this place ain't been torn down by now," he said.

The manager looked up, a greasy grin spreading across his droopy face. "Not in this city. There will *always* be a need for a place like this."

The motel had twenty rooms in total; ten rooms on the ground level, and ten more stacked on top. Rooms twelve and eighteen were both on the upper stack, either end of the walk-way. As Luca crossed the parking lot toward the central stair-case, he straightened out one of the paperclips and began bending the end with his teeth.

A scrawny girl with a black eye and puncture wounds in her left arm appeared in the doorway of number seven, sucking hard on a cigarette. She called out to Luca in a child's voice. "You looking to party, handsome?"

He guessed she was in her twenties, but years of meth abuse had given her the appearance of someone older. He used to see a lot of that in prison. Some guys would come in on a first offense, all muscular and aggressive, then get released and six months later come back as a twisted, gaunt addict. The transformations were shocking, the meth sucking the life out of them, like a type of cancer you could pick up on the street corner.

He walked past the girl with no response and headed up the central staircase. She called out after him, "Asshole."

At the top of the stairs, he turned right, past an ancient vending machine with a handwritten *out-of-order* sign, while he used his front two teeth to mold the second paper clip into a small squiggle. Then he made his way down the walkway, past *fifteen, sixteen, seventeen,* and stopped at the magic number: *eighteen.*

With his thumb covering the peephole, he placed his ear against the door as if checking the room for a pulse—he didn't hear one. But there was no real way of knowing if anyone was in the room. He had no choice but to rap his knuckles on the door, without any idea what he was going to say. Half a minute passed with no answer, so he knocked again. After another half minute, he got to work.

Luca slotted the first clip—bent at ninety degrees to create a tension wrench—into the keyhole and twisted it. Then he slotted the other clip, the makeshift rake, above the wrench and felt around for the lock pins. He kept his head on a swivel as he went to work on the lock. He felt rusty, like a teenager fumbling around in a girl's pants for the first time. But eventually he heard a loud click announcing his success, and the door cracked open half an inch.

Before going inside, he braced himself to find a truck driver pointing a double-barrel shotgun at him, the guy's finger on the trigger with a—*you fucked with the wrong room*—look on his face. After all, this wasn't the type of motel where it was considered wise to go busting into people's rooms.

But he jolted the door open in one sharp motion—and found the room empty.

He quickly slipped inside and closed the door behind him, the thick stink of stale smoke and old sex hitting him like a punch. The tiny room looked as though a giant had ripped the roof off and dumped a garbage skip inside. There were clothes and odd shoes strewn across the floor and a mound of empty soda cans, chip packets, and fast-food wrappers beside the bed. On the nightstand was a thin glass pipe and several pieces of burned tin foil, all the remnants of a *good* night. The room's occupants were likely hiding out after a score, smoking and eating whatever cash they made until they ran out; rinse, repeat.

Luca crossed the room to the far corner and, keeping his eyes out for any loose needles, kneeled down by the air vent at the base of the wall. He pulled a dime from his pocket and went to work, loosening the four screws supporting the vent. The old rusted screws were worn, but he managed to get the top two off by applying extra pressure. As he moved on to the bottom screws, he heard footsteps and chatter coming from the walkway. He froze.

Jumping to his feet, he slipped over to the door as the chatter morphed into wild, drunken laughter right outside. Through the peephole, he saw the source of the sound—an older man in a cowboy hat with a young hooker, her hair dyed gas-flame blue. Two blurry figures, swaying, laughing, touching, like a hazy memory from a drunken night before. They stopped outside the door, and the metallic rattle of a key trying to penetrate a keyhole sent Luca into autopilot, his brain turning his body sideways, his hands balling into fists.

I ain't going back to prison, he thought. And he meant it. He would take them both out before allowing them the chance to call the cops. And if all he had was his bare hands, then so be it.

But through the rush of adrenaline, Luca heard a voice. The hooker's voice, asking, "What are you doing, stupid?"

"What's it look like?" the old man replied.

"That's the wrong room."

"The hell it is."

"You said nineteen, stupid."

"You better stop calling me stupid."

"Yeah? And what you gonna do?" said the hooker in a sing-song voice.

"I guess you're gonna find out."

Still poised for a bloody confrontation, Luca remained a statue, listening to the shuffle of feet. Then he placed his eye to the peephole once more and found them in his peripheral, at the next room—nineteen. The door opened, and they walked in.

Luca chuckled—his version of a sigh of relief.

Out of danger, at least temporarily, he went back to work on the screws. Before he could get to the fourth screw, the high-pitched squeak of bodies bouncing on old mattress springs penetrated through the wall from the next room. The *couple* had wasted no time getting to their *business*. In a way, it made Luca a little jealous—it'd been a hell of a long time since he'd had that kind of fun, whether it was real or purchased. But all that would have to wait. He had business to take care of before he was allowed to think about pleasure.

He finally finished with the fourth screw, popped off the vent casing, and reached inside.

As he felt the damp wrinkles of the brown paper bag he'd

placed there so many years ago, any remnants of jealousy instantly evaporated.

Moving as quietly and quickly as possible, he got the hell out of there and rushed down the corridor to room twelve. It was a slightly cleaner, slightly smaller twin of eighteen—the same dull, dusty box, with ingrained stink. The bedsprings also squeaked under Luca's weight as he sat on the edge and opened the paper bag, releasing the musty smell of old books.

He tipped the bag upside down and let the contents fall onto the bed beside him. The rats hadn't gotten to it. It was all there: $3470 in cash and a 9mm Beretta 92 semi-automatic pistol. He stared at the money and thought about checking into a better hotel, one with a king-sized bed, clean sheets, and fluffy pillows. One that didn't remind him of his prison cell.

But he needed the money for whatever lay ahead.

Plus, he was exhausted. The day's excitement had zapped all his energy. Not even the promise of room service and cable TV could get him to go back out and face the world.

Before getting sent away, Luca had always been fired up, full of fierce energy, forever looking for action. But a very long stretch in prison changes a man—though not in the way the system intends. Life inside was a perpetual state of wariness, and simple pleasures like eating, sleeping, and using the bathroom became nothing more than moments of vulnerability. Any youthful spark he once possessed had been stripped from him, his will ground down to fine dust. This old, tired shell was all that remained.

But before allowing himself the pleasure of sleep, Luca pulled out the piece of paper Johnson had handed him, unfolded it, and looked at the ten-digit number sketch in tiny handwriting. He picked up the landline phone from the bedside table, punched in the numbers, and waited.

The other line picked up on the fourth ring.

"Detective Brooks, homicide," a man's voice said.

"Detective?" said Luca. "I thought you'd be a lieutenant by now."

"Who is this?" the other man said, a hint of concern in his voice.

"What's the matter? You don't recognize your old friends?"

There was silence on the other line for a moment, then, "Ah, fuck."

5

SCARLETT

Scarlett woke up with a much worse hangover than four glasses of wine warranted, a sour taste coating her mouth, and a throbbing pain behind her left eye. Her phone read 7:33am, which meant she'd forgotten to set her alarm and was running late.

The space in the bed beside her was empty. She figured Josh had already left, no doubt still pissed at her.

She didn't feel guilty for what happened, but she still felt bad for Josh. It was supposed to have been a fun night to celebrate three months of engagement, and it had ended with him feeling... what? Inept? He must have snuck silently out of bed and got dressed in the en suite, the way he sometimes did when he had an early meeting and didn't want to wake her.

But then she heard the squeak of feet falling on the staircase and the mumbling of Josh's deep voice. She couldn't make out what he said, but she felt a jolt of happiness and suddenly yearned for his embrace. The bedroom door opened, and Josh came in wearing a pin-striped gray suit. Scarlett opened her mouth to speak, but he pointed to his Bluetooth earpiece and mouthed the words—*I'm on a call.*

Scarlett mouthed—*Sorry*, then watched with dismay as he walked over to the wardrobe, pulled out his weekend suitcase, and set it on the bed near her feet. He flashed her an apologetic smile, then spoke into the earpiece. "I know what the client said. We have to underbid this. It's ours to lose."

He opened the case and began shoveling in rolled boxer shorts and socks from his underwear drawer at random. "I understand, tell Mae to do everything she can until we get there, okay? I'll see you at the airport."

He hung up the call, and Scarlett said, "The airport?"

"I'm sorry, Scar. That was Jenkins. They need me in Chicago."

"Now? But... How long will you be gone?"

"Couple of days, max." He crossed to the closet and pulled four suits from the rack.

"But we have plans," said Scarlett. "Dinner with Yvonne and Danny. It's been planned for a month."

"I know, I know. Trust me, the last thing I wanna do is get on a plane right now. But Jenkins didn't give me much choice."

"You always have a choice."

Josh didn't respond. He just kept his head down, carefully folding the suits and placing them in the case.

Scarlett wanted to push, to ask him if there was anyone else that could go instead of him, but she knew what he would say. There was a reason he'd made it from an entry-level associate to a senior manager, and he was on the fast track to becoming a partner, all in the time Danny had remained in the same position.

"Look, I know we had plans," he said finally, "but I promise we can do the double date when I'm back."

"Well, what about last night? We need to talk about what happened."

"There's nothing to talk about," Josh said, zipping up the

case, but his tone was far from sure.

"I think there is," Scarlett said defiantly.

Josh picked up the case, took two steps toward the door, then stopped and turned back. "Look, I gotta go, but if you still want to talk when I get back, then we can, okay?"

She wanted to say no, to make him stay and talk it out, to clear the air. But she didn't. Instead, she said simply, "Okay," and watched him leave.

By the time she made herself presentable and doused the burning alcohol taste in her mouth, Scarlett had gone from a little late to just late. She made a quick pit stop at the medical center to pick up some supplies, then spent the morning tending to a single man in Winnetka with advanced liver disease. Then she assisted a doctor at a sweet old couple's house in Canoga Park, the wife only sometimes remembering the man she married fifty-three years ago.

During her lunch break, she parked under the scattered shade of a poorly groomed tree in a strip mall parking lot, leaned against her Honda, and lit a cigarette. She hadn't smoked in years, not since the time of her life she liked to refer to as her *period of rebellion*. Even then, she didn't really smoke. Only when she was with her *friends*, only to fit in. But in the past weeks, she'd begun to feel anxious and stressed—the wedding, the job, the new patient—all of it compounding, and for some reason slapping her with a yearning to smoke. And now there was the text from Anton and the failed night with Josh.

She watched as the Valley's population traipsed in and out of the array of fast-food options; Little Caesar's, Jack in the Box, Taco Bell. Her mouth watered at the aromas, or was it the cigarette? It was the first one out of the pack of Camels she'd hastily purchased from a Chevron gas station, feeling a reckless elation as she handed over the money like a kid with a fake ID.

But after only a few drags, her throat was sore and her head floaty.

She tossed the still smoking cancer stick to the floor and ground it out with her Nike. Then she hid the pack deep in the glove compartment where Josh wouldn't chance upon it. He wouldn't be mad if he found the Camels, just confused, inquisitive. She'd never told him about her period of rebellion, or what went on then, and there was no need for him to find out.

She climbed into the driver seat and pulled her phone from her purse to find she had a new message from Anton's 310 number, the text bubble demanding to be noticed. She tentatively opened the message and read it: *If you're free tonight, stop by Bar 91. Would love to catch-up.*

How typical. All those years with no contact, and now he texts her out of nowhere, asking to grab drinks. It annoyed her that he had the audacity to act so casually after the way he treated her, after the way he left things. Was he that oblivious to how weird that was, or did he just not care?

She tossed her phone back into her purse, took out her Tupperware container, and shoveled a plastic fork full of homemade salad into her mouth. The taste of tobacco and the accumulative aromas of the surrounding restaurants overpowered her dry lunch, and she almost heaved.

The day had started badly, but it was only going to get worse. Because *he* was her next patient; the old man with COPD, Mr. Francis. He was the only one of Scarlett's patients that made her uneasy, his overly inquisitive nature poking holes in her life like nails through drywall. She'd even found out the creepy old man had requested Scarlett by name. Apparently, he'd been given a referral from someone at church, or so he said.

Either way, during every visit, he always gave her the feeling he was building up to something, and it definitely wasn't anything good.

The old man's house sat on one of the tight roads that snaked up the back of Sherman Oaks, toward Dixie Canyon Park. It was a section of LA that looked borrowed from another, more rustic part of the state. The steep hillside was covered in tall grass and prickly bushes, both the color of satin brass. A small dust cloud whipped around the Honda as Scarlett pulled into the dirt driveway.

As she approached the front door, she took in the bungalow's imperfections—the cracked roof tiles, the rusted window screens, the peeling paint… she had a strange feeling it was somehow staring back, alive and aware, as though it had been waiting for her.

To the right of the door, a smattering of daffodils protruded from a rock bed, the yellow flowers leaning crookedly, as though drunk on the sun's rays. She grabbed one of the rocks—a smooth, palm-sized stone with a slightly lighter hue than its neighbors—opened it, and pulled out the key.

Scarlett opened the door to the gentle flow of distant classical music: angelic choir voices over a masterful pianist. It would have been beautiful if it wasn't so eerie.

The inside of the house had thick wood wainscoting, low ceilings, and smelled of pine and smoke. It felt hectic in its emptiness, like it had recently been abandoned, the occupants scrambling to take whatever they could carry on their way out. The whole house carried a strange vibe, like something bad had happened there and the very walls were tainted by it.

Scarlett called out down the empty hallway in front of her. "Mr. Francis? It's Nurse Scarlett."

With no reply, she slipped off her Nikes and followed the music toward the living room, her mismatched socks falling softly on the mint carpet.

"Hello? Mr. Francis?"

Still, no reply.

As she slipped through an open doorway into the living room, she spotted the old man in the center of the space, sat in his wheelchair at a red card table, the only piece of furniture in sight. He was reading from a thick leather-bound Bible, his face a mask of concentration.

A long tube ran from his sharp nose to an oxygen machine in the corner, the machine taking over the role of his weak lungs. And next to the device was a stack of aluminum oxygen tanks, like artillery shells ready to be loaded.

Scarlett yelled over the swell of instruments, "Mr. Francis!"

The old man lifted his head, panic flashing across his face which quickly evaporated into a soft smile.

"Scarlett," he said in a slow voice, heavy with a borrowed breath. "I didn't hear you come in."

"I called out to you."

"Sorry," he said, reaching into his lap for the stereo remote.

He turned the music down, the hum of his oxygen machine taking its place. "Mozart's Lacrimosa," he said with a smile. "Such a powerful piece."

He was wire-thin, with marble eyes and rubbery skin like melting plastic. His hair was a ruffle of white and gold, like the surf of a wave crashing against the sand. The chronic obstructive pulmonary disease had transformed him into a withered shell of a man; a living, breathing ghost.

"How are you feeling, Mr. Francis?"

He shrugged. "Like I smoked a pack of cigarettes every day since I was eighteen. I guess that's how that works, huh?"

Scarlett thought of the cigarette she'd just attempted to

smoke and felt instantly sick. She set her bag down and removed her stethoscope and blood pressure machine.

"Just need to check your vitals, okay?"

He nodded and wheeled back two feet from the table. She placed the stethoscope to his chest, listening for his weak heartbeat, and he looked up at her with a child's eyes. After a few moments, she pulled the device away.

"Any more sharp pains in your chest?"

"Occasionally, yeah."

Scarlett gestured to the medical alert necklace around the old man's neck. "Make sure to use that thing if the pain worsens or persists for an extended period."

Instead of saying yes or nodding, he just smiled; a token gesture of goodwill. As she took his blood pressure, the machine buzzing and purring around his frail arm, Scarlett's eyes fell on the Bible in the old man's lap. It was an antique King James Bible with brown leather and faded gold script.

"Just a bit of light reading, huh?" she asked, trying to keep the topic light, trying to keep it off her.

"You read it? It's a good one."

She jotted down his results in her notepad—132/85. "It's not for me."

"Of course it is. It's for everyone."

Scarlett smiled defiantly, "I prefer non-fiction."

Her mother had taken her to church as a child, and she'd enjoyed it—the pageantry, the singing. But as the years rolled on, her faith frayed. There wasn't a defining moment when she suddenly stopped believing, but a series of moments of senseless hurt and unanswered questions. Even if her faith had lasted into later life, the pain and suffering she'd witnessed through her patients would have likely quashed any sincere hope of a merciful creator being out there in the ether.

And of course, there was also her mother, the most generous, kind, and religious woman Scarlett knew, who was plucked from the Earth without warning.

Mr. Francis gave an inquisitive frown. "So I suppose you don't use *your* necklace when you need help?" He pointed at her chest.

Scarlett looked down to find her gold crucifix necklace had come free of her collar and was resting on her scrubs; a flag of contradiction. Annoyance crept through Scarlett's body, her internal defense mechanisms sparking to life. That is what Mr. Francis did, he found and pointed out discrepancies, subtly calling her out. She hated when people did that, it made her feel like a child.

She quickly tucked the necklace under her shirt. "It was my mother's," she said, then tossed her instruments into her bag and snapped it shut like a bratty kid.

The necklace was one of the few pieces of jewelry her mother had left her. She had never been the type to put much value on material things—something that had rubbed off on Scarlett. To some degree, at least.

"I'm sorry," he said. "I didn't mean..."

"Forget it," she said coldly.

A conspicuous silence fell on the room, both of them too entangled with their own thoughts to talk. Then finally, the old man cleared his throat. "How long do I have you here?"

"Same as every visit: an hour."

"Right. Of course," he said. "Can you do something for me? There should be a parcel by the door. Can you grab it and bring it over?"

Scarlett peered into his gray-blue eyes, and suddenly the pettiness of her irritation embarrassed her. She let her face soften. "Sure, Mr. Francis. No problem."

The old man grinned. "Thanks. And by the way, Mr. Francis was my grandfather. Please, call me Jimmy."

6

DETECTIVE BROOKS

Detective Henry Brooks had been parked across the street from Schmidt's Tavern for the best part of thirty minutes, eyeing the passers-by, checking the rooftops.

The street was bustling with frantic energy, as was usually the case in this part of town: The skinny addict couple jittering along in a half walk-half run, bickering over where or when they're going to get their next fix; The four punks cruising by in their shit-box hatchback with the music volume cranked up to the max; And the middle-aged woman on the bus stop bench, the years of monotonous drudgery stuck on her face like a mask.

Brooks liked to say that if you sit on any street for long enough, you always see the same thing. Different people from different backgrounds, detached from the comforts of wherever they call home. None of them lost, but all of them searching.

After a few more minutes of watching, teetering between boredom and paranoid fantasy, Brooks swung open the driver's door of his Cadillac and pulled himself out of the car with the grace of a KO'd boxer whose legs wouldn't let him fall. The veteran warhorse was pushing sixty-five and dealing with more busted parts than a scrapyard, making even the most routine tasks painful ordeals. But being broke and stubborn didn't mix too well with an LAPD medical plan.

He waited for a gap in the cars, then made his way across the street, still scanning his surroundings for a potential ambush. From the outside, Schmidt's Tavern looked like a generic store that had been closed for business since the Clinton administration, a tired, rusted facade with blacked-out windows and chipped wood siding. If it weren't for the *Jameson's* sign out front, you might not even recognize it as a bar at all.

As Brooks got to the door, he reached into his thin jacket and flicked the safety catch off his Remington R1 pistol and muttered to himself, "I'm too old for this shit."

He pushed opened the front door of Schmidt's and daylight poured in around him like he was a back-lit comic book character—*Captain Crooked*, he mused absently.

He let the door close behind him and scoped out the space, which was far bigger than it looked from the outside. It was a long, windowless rectangle of wood and worn brass, with black, rubber floor tiles that clung to decades of stink from spilled drinks, vomit, and cigarettes.

Four regulars sat on battered velvet stools at the long piece of scarred oak that was the bar. They were more like furniture than customers; the type of guys who thought of drinking elsewhere as worse than cheating on their spouse, each of them facing off against a Budweiser bottle and a whiskey chaser. They squinted at Brooks with less interest than a pig shows the moon, then went back to sipping their beer.

In the back, playing pool at an ancient purple billiards table, was a young couple with matching skinny jeans, beanie hats, and sticker-style arm tattoos. They both stared at Brooks for a moment, each of them sporting the look of someone hiding from something, then simultaneously decided he wasn't a threat and went back to their game.

It looked like a normal day at Schmidt's, except for the stocky guy seated in one of the flaky leather booths to the left. He had his back to the door, but even from behind, Brooks knew it was Luca. After so many years as a cop, he'd learned to spot the little details and pick up on body language. It was Luca's stillness that gave him away. He didn't even so much as flinch when Brooks walked in.

Brooks approached the bar and nodded to the bartender, a man by the name of Jack Molten. He was a weary-faced guy with a thick mustache and eyes that looked like they'd seen three world wars and four great depressions. In a voice that matched his face, he said, "Afternoon Detective. What'll it be?"

"Pilsner," said Brooks.

As Jack poured the drink, Brooks leaned over the bar and asked quietly, "That him? In the booth?"

"Believe so," said Jack. "He's been here over an hour. Only ordered one drink."

Jack was a good man. When a local gang had tried to tax some of his profits a while back, he'd turned to Brooks for help. Brooks discovered the gang was just some small-time punks trying to make a name for themselves, so he took the leader—a twenty-one-year-old kid called Addison—and locked him in the trunk of a car for three days in July, with nothing but a single bottle of water. Addison barely survived the ordeal, but he and his friends never set foot in Schmidt's again.

Jack was so grateful, he promised to be there anytime Brooks needed him. He also began keeping a 20-gauge Mossberg shotgun behind a dummy panel under the bar.

Jack slid a frosty beer mug across the bar to Brooks, who sipped it, and said, "Be ready, okay?"

It was only twenty feet or so from the bar to the booth, but to Brooks, the walk felt like a grueling hike, his black Oxford shoes slapping on the tiles like a high-pitched snare drum. The whole time, Luca didn't move a muscle, not even when Brooks rounded the booth and the men came face to face for the first time in a quarter of a century.

Luca was sat back with a half-empty beer in front of him and a blank stare on his face—the look of a man with a honed sense of patience.

He was only around five-foot-seven, but he was stocky and powerful and carried himself with the menacing air of an unhinged man. He hadn't changed much at all, except for the fact that his once black hair was now smoke-gray and thinning on top. And there were four new scars on his face to add to the others—landmarks on the road map of his violent, turbulent life.

Brooks sat his beer on the table and slid into the seat opposite. "You're early."

"So are you," said Luca.

Brooks shrugged. "It's been a long time."

"Time flies when you're having fun. You got fat."

"Yeah, well, fuck you too."

The men stared at each other in silence for a moment, two silverbacks, both dominant in their own world, neither giving anything away. But there was no doubt in Brooks's mind: Luca's borderline psychosis and unpredictable nature made him the true alpha.

Brooks had thought about what he would say in this very situation a hundred times. He'd even free-styled long speeches in his head, explaining how he couldn't have possibly had anything to do with Luca being set up, and how he didn't benefit from it at all. But with that hypothetical situation now before him, all that came to mind was, "I didn't know."

"That right?" Luca said morosely.

"Of course it is. All I did was give you a time and place for the hit. And that info was good."

Luca didn't respond, only glared at Brooks with soulless eyes.

A sudden loud crack rang out at the back of the bar, and Brooks jumped in his seat and reached into his jacket for his pistol, ready for all hell to break loose—but it didn't. It was just the couple on the pool table starting a new game with a heavy break.

Luca didn't even twitch, he just chuckled—a hoarse cackle of a laugh. "You think I called you so I could whack you?"

"Crossed my mind."

Luca gestured to the front of the bar. "How many of them guys yours?"

"You start something, I guess you'll find out."

Luca's lips pursed into a grotesque attempt at a smile. He wrapped his mitt of a hand around his glass, drained the rest of his hour-old beer, then said, "Why didn't you find Jimmy?"

"You think I didn't try? The son of a bitch turned into a ghost."

"How convenient."

"God damn it, I lost money on that too," Brooks barked. "I should be retired, and look at me."

Luca did look at Brooks for a moment, his black eyes giving nothing away. Then his lips curled into that same half-smile. "Well, lucky for you, you got a chance to redeem yourself."

Brooks didn't even want to know the answer, but he had to ask: "What are you talking about?"

"A source inside told me he's back in town."

"Bullshit."

"Does it look like I'm joking to you?" said Luca, pointing to his own rigid face.

"You're telling me your source has seen him?"

"No. But I trust the info." Luca jabbed the table with his index finger. "Jimmy *is* in LA, and I want *you* to find him."

Brooks raised his palms and shook his head in earnest. "No way, you can forget it. I don't want any part of this."

He started to stand, but Luca grabbed his arm with hands as thick and rough as charred steaks and yanked him back into his seat.

Jack looked over, but Brooks gave him a subtle wave with his free hand—*not yet Jackie boy*. Then he turned his attention back to Luca. "I ain't getting mixed up in your shit. Not again."

But Luca pulled him closer and said, "Listen to me, you cockroach. You might've forgotten the old days, but I haven't. When you're inside, all you got is time and memories, and I remember *everything*. *Every. Fucking. Thing.* Now, you do this right, and maybe, *just maybe*, I'll call it even. But if you don't, you're gonna wake up breathing dirt. You got that?"

Brooks yanked his arm free. "You better watch who you threaten. I'm a cop, you dumb prick."

Luca seemed to relish the confrontation, his eyes wide and drunk on hatred and revenge. "And you think that makes you untouchable?"

It wasn't Brooks's first time facing off against a wild-eyed killer with nothing to lose. It was almost common practice in his line of work. But he knew Luca. He wasn't just some punk with a big mouth, trying to earn his stripes. Brooks had seen first-hand what Luca was capable of when he let his rage take over. And it scared him. It would scare any sane man.

"Maybe I should just take you out right now," said Brooks; a weak attempt at a bluff.

"Shoot an unarmed man in front of a room full of witnesses? Even you ain't that stupid. No—it ain't that simple for you and me. We got history. We got *unfinished business.*

And whether you like it or not, now is the time we finish it. You *are* going to find Jimmy, and you're gonna do it fast. That's the only way you leave this party."

And just like that, Brooks was along for the ride. If he didn't want to live the rest of his crappy life constantly looking over his shoulder—at least more than he already did—then he didn't have a choice.

He took a slow, deep breath and hung his head slightly. "I'll see what I can do."

Luca stood up and placed his hand on Brooks's shoulder.

"Don't see. Do."

Luca left Brooks in the booth, frozen, small, and impotent. He was right where he didn't want to be: back in bed with a murderous psychopath. It was just like the old days.

And he hated the old days.

7

SCARLETT

Scarlett came back into the living room of Jimmy's house carrying the package in front of her like a food tray. She set it on the red card table in front of the old man.

"Can you open it?" he asked. His voice was slow and weak.

She tore it open, fished through the mass of packing balloons, and pulled out a blue cardboard box with the image of a cheap wooden chess set on it.

"It's not exactly the best set on the market," said Jimmy, "but they had next day delivery."

Scarlett flashed him a confused look, her brow furrowed.

"You mentioned you liked to play," he said.

It had come up briefly in one of their previous conversations, and Scarlett had quickly changed the subject to something medical. That's the way she always was with Mr. Francis, dishing out information about herself with a measuring spoon, careful not to give too much.

"I haven't played for a long time," she said.

Jimmy pulled the set from the box and placed it on the table. "Well, I thought we could play now."

Scarlett shook her head lightly. "I don't remember how."

"Well, I'll teach you as we go. You're a sharp woman, it's easy enough to pick up."

"Okay, fine. But I can't promise we'll finish the game."

Jimmy grinned, all teeth. "Good enough."

As he set up the board, he gave Scarlett a breakdown of the rules and what each individual piece could and couldn't do.

"I'm never going to remember all this," she said.

"It's okay, you don't have to, I can coach you as we go. Just remember each piece has its own capabilities and restrictions, and, therefore, vulnerabilities. Each move should be either a calculated action or a reaction." He nodded at the board. "Go ahead, you can take the first move."

Scarlett flashed the look of a bored child, then lazily moved one of her pawns. Jimmy leaned across and made his move, but before his hand was back to his side, Scarlett moved another pawn—a hasty move with no real purpose other than to move the game along. For the next ten minutes, the game went the same way, with Scarlett making unplanned rash moves. She quickly found herself in checkmate.

"Let's start again," said Jimmy.

"Why? We played, and you won—game over."

"Because you rushed and didn't take it seriously."

"I thought it was supposed to be a *game*?"

Jimmy began resetting the board, placing the pieces in their respective starting places. "Please. I want you to try again, but this time I want you to take your time before you move. This is a game of strategy, remember? Calculated actions or reactions. In a way, the game is similar to life."

Scarlett cocked an eyebrow, the sunlight glinting off her green irises. "Life?"

"Sure," said Jimmy. "Just like this game, life is all about choices. Each choice is bound by the dual realities of causality and sacrifice. These choices decide what paths we go down and what possibilities arise, and just like in this game, those possibilities are nearly infinite. That's what I love about it. No two games are alike, just like people and the lives they lead.

"Take you, for example: the choices you made to become a nurse. You must have weighed things up, the pros and cons, the gains and sacrifices, potential advancements and limitations."

"Of course," said Scarlett, "and I see the metaphor. But these are just pieces of wood on a board."

"True. But if you learn to assess the board and make calculated decisions while trying to think three moves ahead, you can apply that skill to decisions in the real world."

Scarlett thought about that for a moment. It was an interesting point. She considered herself as a planner, but more out of worry than strategy. It was smart to take a breath and look at the bigger picture sometimes, and maybe it was a good idea to get some practice at that. She picked up a piece, considered the board, and made her first move. Jimmy smiled. "That's better."

They exchanged a few moves, the game shaping up to be far more competitive than the last. "Tell me, why *did* you become a nurse?"

"It's a good job. You get paid for helping people." Her answer came out quicker than she'd intended, like a rehearsed response to a question she got asked all the time. In some ways, it was. Although the question usually came from herself.

Jimmy picked up on the fact. "Come on, what exactly drove you to pick that particular career. Was it a childhood experience at a hospital? Someone you knew in a similar role?"

"Nothing like that."

"Then, what?"

Scarlett slowly held up one of her knights, turned it in her fingers as she considered her answer. She took one of Jimmy's pawns. "I wanted to be happy."

Jimmy moved his bishop. "I don't follow."

She placed her hands in her lap and stared at them for a moment. As much as she didn't like the way the old man fished for personal information, at that moment, she saw him as a lonely old man just trying to make conversation, trying to take any pleasure he could in the little time he had left.

She took a long breath and felt the tension ease inside her. "I've never been what you call a happy person. I mean, I can be happy, things make me happy. But I've never really found natural contentment—mostly the opposite, in fact."

"I'm sorry to hear that, I truly am. But I'm not seeing the connection between that and you becoming a nurse."

Scarlett sighed, and they exchanged a few moves. "When you feel that way for long enough, you start seeking out things to fill the void. Most of the time, that involves partying, drinking, and what have you—but that never lasts. So you're forced to find something else, something more permanent. For me, it's acts of kindness towards others that make me happy—or at least, it was. Nursing was the perfect outlet for that."

"So, you made a choice to go down a very specific career path in the theoretical hope it would bring you happiness? That was very brave. Most people just chase money or security. Tell me, how has it worked out for you?"

She wanted to tell him it hadn't, that nursing was like everything else in her life. It had made her happy to begin with, but that happiness quickly faded. It was the vicious cycle she lived in, never appreciating what she had and always wanting what she didn't have.

Instead, she said, "I don't know yet." Then she folded her arms, suddenly feeling defensive and wanting to shift the focus away from her. "What about the choices you made, did they work out for you?"

Jimmy chuckled. "I regret almost all of them. *Almost.*" He

leaned back in his chair. "See, my life wasn't what you'd call conventional. You know, I wasn't always a religious man. Faith came and went throughout my life, depending on its convenience. Most of the time, I considered myself a product of my environment, a man with no choice but to get what he needed in any way possible. I mean, how can anyone grow up in a world this shitty and not turn to crime or violence when times get tough, right? But I know now that I was just naïve and selfish." He leaned over, moved his queen, and said, "Tell me, Scarlett—do you think one great gesture can make up for a life of sin?"

A little unnerved by the question, Scarlett simply said, "I don't know."

"That's right, you prefer *non-fiction*, isn't that how you put it?"

She shrugged. "We all know right from wrong."

"Maybe so. Maybe God gives us free will and the wisdom to know good from bad, and it's on us to steer a righteous path. But sometimes things have to be done. Things that make you have to ask for forgiveness."

A thick wet rumble of a cough worked its way from Jimmy's lungs to his throat, and he only just caught it in a handkerchief. As he pulled the handkerchief away, Scarlett noticed fresh red blood spots. Jimmy caught her looking, glanced at the handkerchief, then tucked it away.

"You know, when you get sick..." he said. "I mean really sick. To the point where you can feel death inside you like a creeping shadow. That's when you understand what we really are; sacks of blood, bone, and muscle in a constant state of survival—conscious or otherwise. Your lungs and heart and brain working relentlessly to keep you alive from the moment you're born. When we're young, we live with an unearned sense of invincibility; an imaginary cloak of armor. We like to think we're strong and resilient, champions of our own world. But sooner or later comes the realization that we are all such fragile creatures, on this earth for the blink of an eye, then gone forever. Once you understand that, you can truly let go."

Scarlett narrowed her eyes, gave a tight-lipped smile and a slight shrug, "Why are you telling me this?" And before Jimmy could respond, she went on. "Ever since our first session, you've been probing me about my life and asking questions about redemption. I mean, I see a lot of patients who seek answers, but with you, it's different. It feels like you're... like you're building up to something."

Jimmy smiled. "You really are sharp, Scarlett. Very sharp, indeed. And you're quite right, of course. I guess I've just been a little nervous."

I knew it, she thought.

She held her palms out to him. "Then please stop playing these games and just tell me what you need."

Jimmy nervously touched the skin below his Adam's apple and fixed his gaze on the chessboard, as though he hoped the pieces would help him articulate what he wanted to say. Then he looked up at her, his eyes searching. "I... I want you to help me die."

"What?" asked Scarlett, although she'd heard him just fine. "What are you talking about?"

"Well, I'm ready to go, and I was hoping you could help me. You know, like euthanasia."

Scarlett let out a short nervous laugh. "You can't be serious."

"Actually, I am. I know it sounds a little extreme, but really, it's not. It's already legal in Canada and some states here. They even say it's going to be legal in California by the end of the year. I just need your help."

He said it as though he was asking her to pick up some groceries or to give him a ride to the bank.

"No way," she said. "I can't. That's crazy!"

He reached out to touch her, but she pulled her hand away, her lips twisting into a frown of disgust. "I won't do it. I *can't*."

"It's okay to be afraid," said Jimmy. "I know I am."

"I'm not afraid."

"You're not?"

Scarlett ignored the question, stood up, and grabbed her bag from the floor.

"Wait," said Jimmy. "Please, can we talk about this?"

"What do you want to talk about, huh? How you want me to risk destroying my life for you? You know how selfish that is? Not to mention *insane*."

"Maybe I am selfish. But can you blame me for wanting this? I don't want to sit here waiting for death to come to me. Not like this."

"Then why don't you do it yourself?" Scarlett blurted, the words tumbling out in anger.

Jimmy glanced over at his King James Bible, his brow furrowed. "I can't. I wish I could, but I'm on a different path now. A path that requires me to ask for help." He looked into her eyes, and his features softened into a hopeful half-smile. "*You* are the only one that can give me control over my destiny."

"No," said Scarlett. "I really can't."

Then she turned and walked out.

8

LUCA

Luca had the cab driver drop him across the street from what he hoped was still Sandra's place and hit the guy with a tip just large enough that he wouldn't be remembered. The sky was a clear liquid blue, and the temperature was still in the low eighties, but the street was empty, despite it being after school hours. No kids were outside enjoying the summer sun, running and yelling, tossing pigskin, or playing stickball. *I guess what everyone says about video games and computers is true*, thought Luca.

He stood there for a moment and took in Sandra's place; a nondescript two-story house that was once white, but now a faded pearl with flaky brown trim. But it wasn't the house he was interested in—it was the driveway, the empty driveway.

If he was going to succeed in his plan, Luca needed a set of wheels. And he'd left his Toyota Tacoma on that very driveway twenty-five years prior.

Sandra was the closest thing he'd had to a steady girl before he was set up. But she went dark on him after the sentencing.

You have a collect call from a Los Angeles state correctional facility, do you accept the charges?—Nope.

All that didn't matter now, though, and he hadn't come to reminisce. He'd come for the Toyota. He'd come for what was his.

As he crossed the street, an ice-cream truck came around the corner, its high-pitched jingle announcing its arrival. As if in a cartoon, front doors all along the street popped open and excited kids funneled out, making a beeline for the truck, frantic for their sugar rush.

Luca marched up Sandra's driveway to the front door and tried to peer in through the living room window. There were no silhouettes or blurred movements of any kind, so he rang the doorbell and knocked hard for good measure.

As he waited, he glanced back and watched as a mess of kids stood at the ice-cream truck window, waving dollar bills at the driver, calling out their orders like they were betting on a dogfight.

Luca thought back to the summer when he'd convinced two friends to hold up their local ice cream truck driver—Big Charlie—with ski masks and box cutters. It was the end of a long shift on the hottest day in July, and the score was over twenty-bucks. To a couple of twelve-year-old kids way back then, that was like a million. Luca could still feel that cash in his hand—and the rush it gave him.

But Big Charlie had recognized his voice and called the cops. Luca's father broke four of Luca's ribs with a chair leg—from a chair that'd been broken over his back. But Luca wasn't beaten because he'd robbed Big Charlie; he was beaten because he got caught.

When Sandra's front door finally opened, Luca found himself face to face with a skinny teenage boy with crewcut ginger hair and freckles so pronounced he looked like he'd lost a fight with a red marker pen. He looked about fifteen or so and was wearing a hand-me-down Dodgers shirt and jeans that were ripped, but not in the name of fashion.

"Hi. Can I help you?" the kid said.

"That depends," said Luca. "Sandra here?"

The kid paused, confused, and it suddenly dawned on Luca just how pointless this trip had been. It had been so long, Sandra could be living anywhere by now—Phoenix, or Dallas, or Hell. But instead of saying no outright, the kid said, "Well, that depends. Who are you?"

Luca leaned down so their eyes were level, "I'm Santa Claus, you little shit. Now is she here or not?"

A woman's voice came from somewhere behind the kid, hoarse and broken, like the word had to fight its way out of her throat. "Luca?"

The kid shifted, and there she was, standing there with a dumbfounded look on her face. Her once long, blonde hair had been cut into short, black spikes, and she was around twenty-pounds heavier—but it was her. She wasn't as hot as the skinny blonde Luca remembered, but the new look suited her. The look of someone secure in who they were. She looked like... a mom.

Sandra stepped forward into the sunlight and put her left hand on the boy's shoulder as if claiming him, her maternal instincts as recognizable on her face as war paint.

"What are you doing here?" she said, a tinge of fear in her voice.

"That's how you greet an old friend?" said Luca. "What's the matter, you ain't happy to see me?"

The kid looked at his mother, "Everything okay, Mom?"

Her eyes didn't leave Luca's face when she said, "It's fine, Max. He's just a guy I knew a long time ago."

Luca glanced around behind him, and although no one was

paying any particular attention to them, he had the urge to take the conversation out of the public eye. "Ya know. It's a little hot out here, mind if I come inside to talk?"

"I don't think so," she said.

Luca pursed his lips into a humorless smile and jerked his eyebrows. "Oh, is now not a good time? Perhaps I should come back later tonight?"

A glimmer of dread flashed across Sandra's face, and she hesitated for a moment before she responded, "Fine. But you've got five minutes."

"Oh, that's plenty."

Sandra and Max shared a look for a moment, and without speaking a word, she said to him: *It's okay, give me five minutes, and I'll get rid of him.* And he replied: *This guy better not give you any trouble.*

Luca wondered where the dad was and why he wasn't the one giving Sandra that look. A not so small part of him wished the guy would step out from somewhere so he could have a bit of fun. He wanted to tell the guy in great detail just how well he knew his woman.

That's how Luca's mind worked. His subconscious longed for confrontation and the explosive action that followed, like a dog bred to fight.

Just like Sandra, the inside of the house was the same, but different. The same layout, but different furniture. The same structure, but a different feel. With a skateboard and piles of shoes in the hallway, it felt more like a home, a real home, which, for a reason he didn't fully understand, pissed Luca off.

They stepped into the living room—an open space with a long couch and a staircase leading up to the second floor—and Luca got his answer about the father. There was a photograph hanging on the wall of a man with a bushy red beard. Above the photo was a plaque with two angels carved into it, and the words "Lost but not forgotten." Luca let his eyes linger on the photo for a moment to let Sandra and the boy see that he noticed it. Then he turned and said, "Looks like a lot's changed since I went away."

Sandra glanced at her son, "Why don't you go listen to some of your records in your room?"

"But Mom..."

She threw up her hand. "Just go, Max. Please."

Max huffed an angry, bitter sigh, then shot Luca his best tough-guy look. Luca flashed his front teeth, then winked. "Off to your room now, kid. Us grown-ups gotta talk."

Sandra waited until Max was upstairs, with his bedroom door closed, before she bored her eyes into Luca with a scowl of pure hatred. "What the hell are you doing here? You can't just show up like this!"

"You don't answer someone's phone calls or letters, sooner or later they're gonna come knocking."

"Damn it, what do you want?"

"Why don't you sit down," said Luca. "You're getting a little excited."

Sandra didn't move. She just stared back, defiant and unblinking, like a cat being asked to rollover. Luca clenched his jaw and hissed through his teeth, "Sit down!"

She backed up carefully until the backs of her legs hit the couch, then lowered herself onto it. Then she placed her hands in her lap and stared at them for a moment as she considered her next move.

"I'm sorry I didn't reply to your letters, okay? But that was a long time ago. I was a different person back then. I was young and selfish."

"Really? But I seem to recall you being *very* generous, a real giver."

Sandra grimaced slightly at the comment, at the memory of

their intimate nights. Luca barely remembered the feeling of being with her, but as he tried to think back on the times they'd shared, he couldn't help but feel there was something special there. He pictured her on top of him, biting her lip, strands of damp blonde hair hanging across her face. He imagined her kissing his chest and stroking his arm, something powerful in the tender embrace. Then, he thought of himself alone in his cell, betrayed, abandoned, and forgotten, and suddenly, all he felt was rage.

"Fine, you wanna skip all the pleasantries, then let's get straight to business."

"Which is?" she said with slight relief.

"I want my truck."

"What truck?"

"My blue Toyota. The one I left out there on the driveway. I want it."

Sandra cocked her head to one side, "That's what this is about? Are you fucking kidding me? The truck you left here, what... twenty-five years ago?"

Luca grinned and spread his arms. "Now you're getting it. I need my ride back. I mean hey, don't get me wrong, I love being locked behind immigrant cab drivers reeking of pungent dishes from their homeland, but it's just not practical, if you know what I mean?"

"Well, I'm sorry to say, but that piece of crap has been gone for years."

Luca let his smile fade. "You gave my truck away?"

Sandra shifted in her seat and bit the inside of her lip, her confident persona shrinking. "Well, yeah, you were away for a long time."

"So let me get this straight, just so I'm clear. Not only did you ignore my phone calls and letters and leave me to rot alone like a piece of fucking garbage. You took my truck, something that belonged to *me*, and tossed it without my permission. Without even dropping me a line. Have I got that right?"

Sandra started rubbing her index finger with her thumb, slowly and deliberately, as if she hoped a genie would come out. It wasn't hard to guess what she'd wish for. "Well, I guess."

Luca decided to play with her, have a little fun at her expense and make her squirm "Ah, screw it," he said. "It is what it is, I suppose. It was just a shitty truck. And I get it, I got locked up and life goes on."

Sinking deeper into the couch, Sandra let out a long sigh, "Really?" Her relief was palpable, like a guy on two strikes getting an innocent verdict from a jury.

"Sure, it's not a problem. These things happen." He looked over at the photo of Redbeard again, at his unassuming look, the look of a man blissfully unaware of the consuming blackness that was coming for him. Sandra started saying something, trying to wrap up the conversation and get Luca out, but he wasn't listening. He kept staring at the photo, and then he said, "There was this kid in prison by the name of Warren. A skinny white kid about twenty-one or so, up for possession or some petty shit like that. He was soft, never done any real time; you could tell just by looking at him."

Luca glanced at Sandra, confusion spilling over her face like blood on a tile floor.

"Second day in the joint, three Hispanic kids beat him with socks filled with batteries and told him, in no uncertain terms, that he belonged to them now. So Warren went to one of the head guys in the Aryan Brotherhood and offered to pay them for protection. See, he figured if he paid them, then he wouldn't have to earn his stripes by shanking a rival gang member in the yard, or having his sister stuff balloons of Suboxone up her snatch and smuggle them into the visitation hall."

Sandra stared at him deadpan, her eyes like dinner plates,

and Luca was starting to see why Hooper told so many stories—they were fun.

"For the Brotherhood," he went on, "it's a win-win. They get paid for beatin' on some spics, and they get a young kid joining their ranks. So, they do what needs to be done, put an arm around Warren, and all is well in the world."

Luca moved closer to Sandra, his broad frame looming over her, like a bear on its hind legs.

"Except there's a problem—Warren can't get the money he promised, something to do with lawyer fees or some bullshit. Now the Brotherhood, they can't get embarrassed like that, not for nobody. So they decided to take payment another way and have seven of their members surround Warren at shower time and take turns showing him just how *physical* prison can be. They left him right there on the shower floor, beaten, weeping, and bleeding from every orifice—and I do mean *every one*."

Sandra's frightened eyes found the floor, so Luca pinched her chin and tilted her face up toward his. "So you see, you took something from me, and now you owe me. And if you don't have a vehicle to give me, well then, I guess I'll have to take another form of payment."

He looked her up and down with the cold evaluating stare of a butcher at a cattle market. "As you said, I've been away for a *long* time."

Sandra pulled her face from his grip and fixed her gaze on the photograph of Redbeard, as if asking him for help, or maybe asking him for forgiveness. She turned back to Luca, her eyes glazed with tears. "I got a motor you can take, but it's not a truck or a car."

"That right? So, what is it?"

. . .

Luca whipped off the thick, blue tarp and stared down at what lay beneath.

"Very nice," he said. "It run?"

"Of course," said Sandra. "Max has been taking care of it. He starts it all the time, trickle charges the battery, the works." She looked down at her feet, then back up at Luca with eyes that seemed to have dulled. "It was supposed to be his when he turned eighteen."

Luca chuckled. "Oh yeah? Well, you tell him to come and find me on his eighteenth birthday. I'll have it waiting with a bow on it."

They were standing in Sandra's garage, an immaculate workshop so abundantly stacked with tools and equipment, it might have passed for a mechanic's shop. Between them was a Yamaha V-Star, a beefy black gorilla of a bike with chunky tires and chrome pipes that twinkled under the fluorescent lights. It wasn't a Harley, but it was more than enough kit for what Luca needed. He'd always liked bikes; they were fast and easy to dump in a tight fix, plus the helmet gave you an inconspicuous way of hiding your face.

Sandra reached into her jeans pocket and pulled out a thick chunk of keys, then worked the black Yamaha key off the ring and held it out to him. Luca stroked her hand as he took it from her, and she recoiled slightly, forcing him to fight off the sudden urge to hit her as hard as he could.

A pair of his and hers Arai helmets hung from a wood beam above the bike. They were both black, but one was a little smaller and had a pink decal running around the side. Luca tapped on the ladies' helmet and grinned at Sandra. "You wanna take a ride?"

"No thanks," she said. She looked ready to say more, but must have thought better of it.

Luca slotted the key into the ignition, but before he could

turn it, the kid—Max— appeared in the doorway, his skinny chest heaving up and down with heavy breaths, his face screwed into a red ball of rage. The little shit had been listening in.

"What are you doing with my dad's bike?" he barked, desperation riding his voice.

"It's my bike now, kid."

"Bullshit it is. That's my dad's. And it's gonna be mine."

"Your dad's dead, kid. Ain't no point leaving his leftovers unused." Luca ran his hand along the seat and looked at Sandra. "Or should I say, unridden?"

Max started marching forward. "Fuck you, man."

"Reel him in, Sandra," said Luca.

Sandra put her hand across her son's chest, and Max stopped and looked down at it as if he'd never seen an arm before. Luca laughed, then turned the key in the bike and pressed the ignition. The bike rumbled to life, the big engine sending tremors through the concrete floor. Max pushed his mother's arm away and yelled in a broken voice, "That's all I got from him. You can't take it!"

"I can do whatever the fuck I want, kid. I'd be taking this bike even if it was your dad stood there instead of you. I could see from that photograph exactly who he was. When I looked into his eyes, I saw a little bitch—just like you, kid."

Max lunged at Luca, fingers spread like the claws of a feral cat. He moved with no hesitation despite the size difference between them, and Luca knew instantly this was a kid who was used to getting his ass kicked, a kid who'd felt the power of a heavy fist many times and no longer feared it. He kind of respected the little bastard for that, so he decided to go easy on him.

Before the outstretched hands reached him, Luca swatted them away with his left arm and grabbed Max's throat with his right. Sandra screamed and begged Luca to let go, so he jerked his arm and sent Max headfirst into the wall. The kid's legs buckled, and he hit the ground with a thud, a cut opening up on the hairline above his right eye. Sandra screamed again and dropped to her knees next to her son, half shaking and half comforting him.

"Max, no!" She looked up at Luca, her eyes wide and crazed. "What have you done?"

"Don't be so dramatic. He'll be fine."

"He's just a kid. You didn't have to hurt him, you son of a bitch."

"He chose to come at me, this is the consequence. The fact he's a kid is the only reason he won't be swimming in concrete tonight."

Max came to and let out a groan like a hog with a knife wound. Sandra stroked the side of his head, "Max, honey. You okay? Please say something."

Luca pressed the garage door opener, climbed on the bike, then turned back to Sandra. "Now... you sure you don't wanna go for that ride?"

9

SCARLETT

For the rest of the afternoon, Scarlett felt like she was watching her life through a pane of frosted glass, the volume and brightness turned way down. When she got home, she was three minutes into her shower before she realized the water was way too hot and her caramel skin was turning pink. She was a mess. But she supposed that was normal after someone asks you to kill them. Your brain gets beaten to mush by your own never-ending cycle of questions—*How could he ask me to do that? Is he for real? Is it even possible? Would I get caught?*

Scarlett stared at the side of Yvonne's face as she ordered a bottle of Pinot from their blonde waiter. When she'd called to cancel the double date, Yvonne suggested—or rather insisted—they keep the reservation and just have a girl's night instead. Scarlett thought of being alone in the house with her questions, then heard herself say *yes*.

Mills was packed. Every table was full, and the excited chatter of fifty concurrent conversations echoed around them.

"This is so nice," said Yvonne. "I'm so glad we did this."

She was a little overdressed for a weeknight—even for LA standards—in a midnight-blue sequin dress with crystal earrings, her mousy hair in a tight updo. There was a slight desperation about her look, like a recent divorcée on her first date in a couple of decades.

Scarlett forced a smile. "Me too."

The wine was soon served, and Yvonne began telling Scarlett about her oldest kid giving the middle kid a black eye; how she was called into daycare because the youngest had bitten one of the teachers; then something about a neighbor's broken window. Scarlett tried to give her full attention, to offer a few kind words of encouragement, but the old man's voice kept rattling around her head, forcing those horrible questions to resurface. Soon her internal dialogue overpowered her focus, and even the chatter of the room faded to a low hum.

"Scarlett," Yvonne snapped. "Are you even listening to me?"

"Sorry. I must have zoned out for a second."

"Yeah, no shit. Everything okay?"

"Of course, I'm fine," Scarlett lied. "Just a long day."

The waiter appeared and asked if they were ready to order, but Scarlett stared blankly at the menu for a moment, then looked up and asked for a few more minutes.

When he left, Yvonne leaned in and said, "So, how was last night?

"Last night?" said Scarlett absently.

"Yeah, last night. How did it go with Josh and your little surprise?"

Scarlett thought about lying to avoid a deeper conversation, but she was too tired to feign enthusiasm. Instead, she said simply, "It didn't," and took a long sip of her wine.

"Oh, Scar, is that what's bothering you? What happened?"

Scarlett waved her hand at the question as if swatting away a fly. "It's nothing; it doesn't matter."

"Of course it matters. Come on. You know you can talk to me."

Scarlett hadn't planned on talking about her problems, she had just wanted to get out of the house and avoid being alone. But Yvonne's warm almond eyes and soft, comforting smile disarmed her.

The next thing she knew, her mouth was open and words were pouring out. She started with the night of the handcuffs, then moved on to her wedding jitters, and the way she sometimes felt neglected when Josh chose work over her. It felt good to get it out and to focus on something other than the old man and his grotesque request for a while. She did think about telling Yvonne about Jimmy, but something stopped her—perhaps her ingrained respect for maintaining patient confidentiality. She wasn't quite sure.

At the end of her ramblings, she dabbed her eyes with a napkin and took a big gulp of wine while Yvonne waved the waitress away for the second time.

"I know he loves me, and I know he works so hard, but am I wrong to want more?"

Yvonne looked into her eyes and said, "You wanna know what I think? The honest truth."

"Of course," said Scarlett, unsure if she was truly ready for a dose of Yvonne's candor.

"You are one of the luckiest women I know."

"Really?"

"Of course. I mean, so what, he works a lot. It means he's ambitious. You want a couch potato with no aspirations?" Before Scarlett could give a reply, or even think of one, Yvonne said, "Trust me, you don't."

"But Danny's not like that."

"Girl, please. That man gave up on self-betterment years ago. Now he just drinks beer and yells at the TV while I chase after the goddamn kids." She gave a slight shake of her head, as if reliving the experiences as a flashback. "But Josh is a good man. Yeah, he's career-focused, but he's got a good heart, and he wants to do well for the *both* of you. And that's what a good marriage is based on. You need to have your independence, your own goals and aspirations, but work as a team to help each other reach those goals. And I know it sucks, but sometimes helping comes in the form of sacrifice."

Scarlett nodded, gave her best *I understand* look and said, "I guess you're right."

"And as for the sex thing," Yvonne went on. "Well, I hate to be the one to break it to you, but that's just life, sweetheart. When Danny and I first started dating, we fucked like rabbits on Viagra. But after we moved in together and got married, all that just flittered out. Hell, I'm lucky if I get a drunken fumble these days." She scanned around the restaurant and leaned in again as if about to tell a secret, but her voice got louder, "That's why I've got three different kinds of vibrator."

The couples and families on the surrounding tables looked over and gasped, and Scarlett laughed despite herself.

"Why do you need three?"

"Oh, honey. You got a lot to learn."

Scarlett and Yvonne stood on the sidewalk, more than a little tipsy from the second bottle of Pinot they'd shared, and stuffed full of beef stroganoff. The night was still warm, the air calm yet filled with anticipatory energy, a pre-weekend Thursday night buzz as people spilled in and out of the bars and restaurants along the street.

"Thanks for that," said Scarlett. "It really helped to talk."

"You kidding? It should be me thanking you—you got me out of the house."

Yvonne's Uber pulled up across the street, and the driver gave a weak but familiar smile.

"This is me. Look, anytime you wanna talk, you just call me, okay?"

Scarlett smiled and nodded, and they shared a quick hug. Then Yvonne turned and headed for the car, calling over her shoulder, "And tell Josh I said hi."

It *had* helped to talk, to take her mind off the afternoon with the old man. And deep down, Scarlett knew a lot of what Yvonne had said was right. Most of the time, girlfriends giving relationship advice were right. But it hadn't been what she wanted to hear. In some ways, it had even added to her confusion.

She pulled her phone from her purse to order her own Uber, but she automatically went to her messages instead. There it was, the message from Anton she'd received earlier in the day—*If you're free tonight, stop by Bar 91. Would love to catch-up.*

She snickered softly to herself at the idea flashing across her mind, but flattened the curve in her lips immediately. *No way, that's definitely a bad idea*, she thought. *Remember who he is.*

But her brain was lubricated with wine, and questions began to surface. Could one drink really hurt? They weren't kids anymore, she was almost a different person, and he must have changed too. And there was nothing wrong with two acquaintances catching up over a drink... was there?

10

DETECTIVE BROOKS

Brooks took a sip of his coffee, hovered both his index fingers over his computer keyboard, and slowly tapped the name 'James Nealson' into the search bar for the seventh time. It was dark out, and the precinct was mostly empty—the detective cubicles unmanned, the desk phones on their hooks. The obscure database spat out a list of matches, and Brooks scanned them, trying to find his man. With no luck, he sat back in his chair and let out a sigh.

He'd been at it for hours and was running out of ideas. Usually, if he needed to find a perp's address, he would run their name through a license check. If they'd kept their info up to date, *voilà*—and if that didn't work, he would check NCIC to see if there were any outstanding warrants, then call the issuing department and ask for info. But none of those things had worked with Jimmy, just like they hadn't worked back in 1994.

Brooks heard the click-clacking of high-heels on the linoleum and turned to find his occasional partner—a young hotshot detective by the name of Chen—carrying a thick binder toward him. He grabbed the mouse and quickly closed the search bar just as Chen slapped the binder onto his desk and said, "The Armstrong file. I read it front to back, but nothing new popped out at me. I thought you could give it a try, maybe you'll get some luck."

"Uh, sure," said Brooks.

Chen perched herself on the edge of his desk. "You okay? You look like you haven't seen your bed in a week."

Chen wasn't the typical two creams and three sugars kind of cop. She was petite and spritely, with the polished look and enthusiastic attitude of someone with well-established career goals, and maybe even political aspirations. She was a good detective and model cop, but Brooks didn't hold it against her.

"Just a little fried," said Brooks, rubbing his temples. "I think I might be getting a migraine or something."

"You want me to grab you some Aspirin? I think I got some at my desk."

"No, thanks. Those things don't work on me."

"Fair enough," said Chen. "You know, it's probably all this screen time. This is the longest I've ever seen you at your desk doing actual..." she leaned over and looked at Brooks's blank screen, "police work."

Brooks stammered, "I, uh... I was just sitting here thinking over my cases. You know, old school detective stuff."

"Whatever you say, old-timer." She tapped on the binder. "Well, let me know what you see in there."

"Will do."

Chen slipped off the desk, motioned to leave, then stopped and leaned down to Brooks as if to tell him a secret, even though there was no one else around. "Hey, by the way, if you want to close a window on your computer without making it obvious, try pressing 'Alt' and 'F4' instead of clicking off it."

Brooks blushed. "Sorry, old habit. You never know who's sneaking up on you."

Chen grinned. "I guess so."

As Chen moved away, Brooks ran his hand through his hair and let out a deep breath. He had to be careful. If someone noticed him searching for Jimmy, then Jimmy's body turned up somewhere, they might look into the past and connect some dots.

He looked around to make sure the coast was clear, then reopened the search results and double-checked the long list of people that weren't Jimmy. It was hopeless trying to find him through the limited department searches. Sure, there were other searches he could do, but that would require proving probable cause and getting a warrant. If he had a warrant, he could get all the records of anything Jimmy did on the grid—credit cards, bills, phone records—anything. But judges aren't too fond of issuing search warrants when the aim of the investigation isn't to find the person and arrest him, but to hand him over to a crazy ex-con to be tortured and murdered.

As frustrating as it was, deep down, Brooks knew his only chance of finding Jimmy quickly was to call in the big guns, and his big gun was a guy by the name of Eric Sanderson. But the problem with using Eric, was that, ironically, Brooks had to find him too. And finding him meant speaking to known associates. It meant going out onto the streets.

Brooks worked his way south, stopping to talk to the few people he thought might know of Eric's location. He managed to gather a few pieces of information and a couple of rumors, but they all amounted to nothing. He soon found himself where he knew he would end up: the Strip.

The Strip was a row of apartment buildings that had been derelict for a generation, decayed buildings sprouting up from the ground like rotting teeth. Brooks hiked up the stairs and knocked on the door to number 308, then flicked the safety catch off his Remington. After nearly a minute, a gaunt woman with a tattooed cheek cracked the door to the length of the chain and said, "Who the fuck are you?"

The heady smell of sweat and marijuana flowed out of the room like heat from an open oven. Brooks flashed the detective badge on his hip, and the woman moved back a few inches, then froze, panicked.

"You going to open the door, or do I need to knock it down?"

She hesitated for a moment, then closed the door, released the chain, and reopened it. Brooks pushed passed her and marched toward the living room, but the woman screamed, "Randel, it's the cops!"

Randel was one of Brooks's old snitches, but he also happened to be a heroin dealer, and there was no telling who would be in the apartment with him. Without time to falter, Brooks pulled his Remington and burst into the living room to find Randel at a fold-out table, frozen in the motion of counting out grimy stacks of bills. To the right of him, a skinny guy sat in an armchair rolling a joint. A pistol-grip shotgun rested on the edge of the table between the men.

The skinny guy quickly reached for the shotgun, but Brooks aimed his pistol at him.

"Don't even think about it, you piece of shit."

"What the fuck, man?" said Randel.

Brooks ignored him and kept his eyes locked on the skinny guy. "Move away from the gun."

The skinny guy looked at Randel, who nodded. Then he moved his hand away from the shotgun in a big looping motion, as if he suddenly feared the gun was radioactive. Brooks stepped forward, grabbed the shotgun, and let it hang by his side. He turned to find the woman standing behind him, her arms folded with a pissed-off look on her face.

"This is bullshit, he just burst in here," she said to no one in particular.

Brooks pointed to the space on the couch beside Randel. "Why don't you take a seat?"

She huffed an audible sigh like a frustrated kid, then wandered over to the couch and sat. Brooks glanced through to the backroom, which resembled a WWII medic tent: four paper-thin mattresses lined the floor, each one hosting a semi-conscious man or woman with a needle protruding from their arm. What little floor space that wasn't occupied by the mattresses was littered with old skin magazines, empty soda cans, and crushed cigarette packets. One of the dopers was a kid, no older than sixteen, but that fact no longer invoked surprise or sorrow in Brooks. He was numb to it.

"The fucks going on here, Brooks?" said Randel. He was chubby, with the warm, genial face of a TV chef. Only his darting eyes and raspy voice betrayed his scheming, hostile mind.

"I just want to talk," said Brooks.

"We don't talk to cops," snarled the skinny guy.

Randel glanced over at his friend. "Relax, Leo. He's not gonna fuck with us." Then he looked back to Brooks. "But I ain't got nothing to tell you, man. The narco cops already jammed me up earlier this week."

"That's not what this is about." Brooks gestured to the backroom. "You can keep plugging those zombies with your shit until their eyes roll back, as far as I'm concerned."

"So… what?"

"I need to find Eric."

Randel and the skinny guy—Leo—exchanged concerned looks, and the woman shifted in her seat.

"I ain't seen him," said Randel, suddenly defiant.

"Bullshit," said Brooks. "Tell me where he is, and I'll be out of here."

In an instant, Leo was up on his feet, his whole body tense like a compressed spring. "Fuck you, man, we don't gotta tell you shit."

Brooks pointed the Remington at Leo's nose. "Sit down, now."

"Hell no, we ain't no snitches."

"If I was trying to arrest him, you think I would have come here come alone, you idiot?"

"I don't care. And you ain't gonna shoot me. I don't have a gun. And I don't see no goddamn warrant."

"Maybe I won't shoot you. But I'll slap you with the butt of this gun until your head opens up like a melon."

Leo took a half step forward, his face screwed into a ball of fury. "You try it, old man."

"Relax," yelled Randel, his palms up to the room. "Everybody chill the fuck out. Sit down, Leo. He's cool."

Still shaking with rage, Leo shot Randel a sideways glance. "This is bullshit," he said, then sat back down.

Silence fell on the room for a moment. The woman pulled a cigarette from her bra and lit it with a trembling hand. She expelled the smoke, then shook her head while she studied the floor and muttered obscenities under her breath.

"Look," said Randel. "I ain't talked to him in a minute. But last time I saw him, he said he was working on something big."

"Where?" demanded Brooks.

"An old brick building over in Wilmington. On the backside of all them warehouses."

"Which one?"

"Shit, I don't know the address. What do you want me to do, man, draw you a fucking map?"

Brooks did. And while Randel scratched down directions on a scrap piece of paper, Brooks tucked his Remington away, flicked the release lever on the shotgun, and racked the pump until he'd ejected all the shells. Then he tossed the empty shotgun at Leo's feet and said, "See, was that so hard?"

11

SCARLETT

Just one drink, a quick catch-up, then I'm gone, Scarlett told herself as she pulled open the door to Bar 91. It was a cozy wine bar with soft piano music and dim, warm lighting. The place was mostly empty, save for a few couples and small groups seated at wooden tables, sipping from long-stemmed glasses, candles flickering between them. She glanced around nervously, but there was no sign of Anton. His absence filled her with an odd sense of indefinable relief.

One drink, she repeated to herself. And if she didn't see him, then so be it.

She headed over to the bar, slipped onto one of the stools, and set her purse down on the seat next to her. A bartender in a black-and-white uniform with a name-tag—"Diego"—stepped over and spread his palms on the bar. He was tall and broad, with tight, cropped black hair and a curly black beard. And when he spoke, his deep voice was thick with a Russian accent. "Good evening. Would you like to see the menu?"

"No, thanks. I'll just take a glass of the house Pinot, please."

He nodded. "Of course."

Although Scarlett was still past the point of tipsy, the short Uber ride from Mills to Bar 91 had sobered her up a little. And as she sipped the drink the bartender slid over to her, she began to reexamine what a catch-up with Anton would really be like. With most normal relationships, it meant sharing fond memories and old inside jokes and asking about old friends. But their past wasn't filled with those things. All they could reminisce on was the days spent locked in his apartment, their bodies intertwined and slick with sweat. The three-day binge parties, waking up with strangers in their living room. Or the times he would scream at her and berate her and threaten her. Or best of all, the times when he made good on those threats.

As she considered this, a nameless dread swelled inside her, and she felt a sudden need to get out of there before Anton arrived. *This was a mistake*, she thought. *This is Anton, he won't have changed. He's probably worse.*

She swiveled on her chair, plunged her hand into her purse and fished around for her wallet, ready to toss a twenty on the bar and beeline out of there without a word to the bartender.

"Scarlett?"

She turned back, and there he was, standing at the other end of the bar, his face a mix of shock and excitement. "You came."

A plethora of emotions exploded inside her, all competing for dominance. All she could do was smile nervously and say, "Hi, Anton."

He moved toward her in his usual confident, gliding stride, then wrapped her in a tight hug, his warmth somehow familiar and nostalgic and unsettling all at the same time.

When he pulled away, he said, "It's great to see you. How long has it been?"

"A long time," said Scarlett.

They held each other's gaze, and in that instant, their passionate, romantic, tragic history played like a movie in the space between their curious eyes.

He turned to the bartender. "Diego, grab us a bottle of whatever's in her glass."

Diego nodded. "Of course."

"I wasn't actually planning on staying long," said Scarlett, her nervous, childlike voice betraying her attempted perception of cool.

"Bullshit, you just got here," said Anton. "There's a nice private table in the corner where we can catch up."

Before Scarlet could protest, he took the uncorked bottle from Diego and headed for the table, calling out, "Come on, let's go," over his shoulder.

It was so Anton, the confident power move, leaving her at the bar in his wake, socially obligated to accept such a polite offer. Predictably, she followed and joined him at a small candlelit table out of the earshot of everyone else in the bar. Seated there in front of him, Scarlett was so nervous that her mouth turned desert dry. She had to interlock her sweaty hands under the table to stop them from fidgeting.

"So, tell me everything," he said. "How've you been? What are you up to?"

Scarlett faltered, unsure how to start. Unsure how to tell this intense man of which she shared the most intimate of connections about her new—*better?*—life without him.

But when she finally managed to start talking—telling him about going to nursing school, choosing to be a hospice nurse, and moving to the valley—he just listened intently, occasionally leaning over to top up her wine when it got low, his warm expression free of judgment and jealousy. It was like she was talking to a different person, an older, more reserved version of a man she used to know.

He looked very much the same though, clean-shaven with his black hair cut short, accentuating his sharp features. And as they sat there in the warm candlelight, Scarlett realized she'd forgotten just how handsome he was. A rugged, powerful face, his brown eyes smooth and liquid like melted chocolate. They were eyes that demanded you look into them, truly look.

When she finished speaking, Anton bowed his head slightly and said, "It's good to see you doing so well," with not a trace of sarcasm in his voice.

"Thank you."

They held each other's gaze again, then Scarlett broke the connection asking, "So, what about you? How was New York?"

"Colder," he said. "Winters were a bitch. But it was fun."

"And how long have you been back in LA?"

"Little over six weeks."

"What prompted the return?"

Anton toyed with the stem of his wine glass, watching the crimson liquid swirl around. "My father died. He had a heart attack. They... uh, I thought it was time to come home."

"Wow, I'm really sorry to hear that. My mother passed too. About three years ago."

"Damn, I'm sorry," he said, and they shared thin smiles for a moment.

"So you're working here now?"

Anton chuckled. "No. We own it."

"Who's we?" Scarlett asked, although she already knew the answer.

Anton flashed a wry smile. "You know, the organization."

He was third-generation Russian, and when he used the word *organization*, he wasn't referring to a business, association, or club. He was referring to a network of other Russian immigrants who came to America but still took orders sent from Moscow. They owned and operated everything from construction firms to laundromats and florists. And many more, less-legal sources of income. When they were together, Anton did his best to never divulge any of the details of what went on in front of Scarlett, but he once told her the best way to wash money is to buy a business where customers pay in small bills and it's difficult for the taxman to quantify sales. Like a coffee shop.

Or a wine bar, she thought.

"So, how do you like being a nurse?"

Scarlett faltered, searching for the right words. "It's... it's great."

"That bad, huh?"

"No. I don't hate it. It can be very rewarding."

"But you don't love it?"

"There is a big gap between love and hate with a lot in between."

Anton pointed at her engagement ring. "You love *him*?"

"Of course," said Scarlett pulling her hand away.

His question and her answer hung in the air for a moment, extinguishing the tiny spark growing between then, causing a long, frigid silence.

"Look, I should get going," she said. "It was really nice to see you."

Scarlett motioned to stand, but Anton reached across and placed his hand on her arm. "Wait. I'm sorry. I didn't mean to cross any lines. Finish your drink."

She flashed him an uncertain look, and he said, "Please."

Scarlett settled back into her seat. Anton studied the table for a moment, then looked up at her, his face a mask of pure unflinching clarity. "Truth is, I actually asked you to meet me so I could apologize. For how I treated you. For everything."

Scarlett opened her mouth to speak, but her thoughts were too vague and hesitant to be born into words.

"I was an asshole," he went on, "plain and simple. And I've always felt terrible about how I left things. When I think back I... I just wish it didn't happen that way, you know?"

Scarlett swallowed hard and managed, "Me too."

Anton traced tiny circles on the table with his index finger, then looked up at her again. "Of all the women who've come in and out of my life, you were always the most special. My little Scarlett rose." His pet name for her rolled off his tongue as if he'd been saying it every day for months, and instead of unsettling her, it was warm and comforting. "We did have some good times though, right? In between all that craziness."

"One or two," said Scarlett, and her mind went back to those moments, the nights of lust and passion. Due to his lack of adventure and vigor, sex with Josh was only ever okay. But with Anton, it was incredible. He was persistently creative in finding new ways to pleasure her, to make her crave him.

When Scarlett broke from the reverie, Anton was smiling a brilliant smile, and she realized she must have been blushing. All those years with no contact, most of them consumed by hatred towards him, and now, after a few *sorrys* and a flirty comment, he had her reminiscing about the feel of his touch. That was his gift; he could turn on the charm like a light switch and completely disarm you, make you forget everything else.

She nervously picked up her wine glass, then quickly set it back down. She was already too drunk, her words seeming to form themselves, her thoughts patterns loose and unfamiliar.

"Well, thank you for the apology, Anton. I'm glad we did this. But I really had better be going—It's late."

"Sure," he said. "Hey, let me give you a ride home."

Scarlett shaped her lips to say no, but he said, "Come on. Least I could do."

She hesitated, her fuzzy brain swimming from the wine, and she wasn't able to process the pros and cons quickly enough. It should have been easy to come up with the right answer, a simple response, but things with Anton were never simple.

12

ANTON

In those few seconds of hesitation, Anton knew he had her. That brief moment when they held each other's gaze, the first domino tipped, the wheels set in motion. *You're special, my little Scarlett rose*—he couldn't believe how easily women fell for that shit. Always longing to believe there's a *perfect* guy hiding below the surface, and they're the ones to bring them out. Did he have some regrets about the past? Maybe. But such is life. And you can only ever worry about the here and now.

That was something his father had taught him: *There's no use in dwelling on what was, what could have been, or what isn't. All you can do is play what's right in front of you.* He wasn't exactly a wordsmith, Anton's father, but he made some good points from time to time. *All you can do is play what's in front of you.* Well, there she was, right there in front of him, and he sure as shit wanted to play.

During the half-block saunter to his car, Anton snuck sideways glances at Scarlett as she walked head down in concentration, her narrowed eyes on her shoes, trying not to sway. She did an excellent job of hiding her buzz, so much so that most people wouldn't even notice. But Anton wasn't most people. He knew by the way she clutched her purse extra tightly under her arm, and her short, deliberate steps that she was wasted, the alcohol no doubt hitting her like a train when she stepped out into the fresh air.

Anton clicked the unlock button on his keys, and his midnight-blue convertible Mercedes GT-C came to life, lights flashing, side-view mirrors opening in salute.

Scarlett stopped and eyed the car. "This yours?"

"You like it?"

"It's beautiful."

Anton bowed slightly and fanned the air like a butler. "Hop in."

He put the roof down, and they rode along to the deep purr of the engine. Scarlett leaned her head back against the headrest and ran her hand through the warm air as the city drifted by. Anton could tell how much she was enjoying the ride—the whole night, in fact—and knew exactly where it was going to end. Scarlett caught him staring and said, "What?"

"It's just strange to see you in that seat. After all these years, I mean."

"It's strange seeing you too. You're so different."

"Different good or different bad?"

She smiled. "Just different."

Scarlett's eyelids looked heavy, and her features relaxed, but Anton could still see that familiar play of curiosity flash across her face. He'd learned from a young age that the trick with women was to capture their attention, then pique their curiosity. It was even more important than confidence or looks—although they're a close second and third. And Anton was always able to read women, their needs and wants, to find whatever's missing—especially when it came to Scarlett.

As soon as he had seen her ring, he figured she'd gone

looking for the opposite of him and found herself some boring shmuck. An asshole in a Banana Republic suit who probably worked in finance, or operations, or law. Someone who could provide for her and rub her feet, but never give her the excitement that deep down she craved. That's why it had only taken a few simple texts and some flowery words to get her curiosity going.

He decided to play his hunch and took a left on Outpost Drive. Scarlett looked around, confused, but before she asked why they weren't taking the freeway, he said, "Back roads. More fun."

But when he took another left onto Chelan Drive, she said, "Where are you going?"

The house Anton was renting was a glass jigsaw piece cut into the side of the Hollywood Hills. Perhaps not a mansion by Hollywood standards, but it was sleek, modern, and screamed new money. And he liked that.

They pulled into the long driveway and parked.

"What are we doing here, Anton?"

"I figured we should stop by for a night-cap. The view from the deck is unbelievable, you gotta see it."

"I don't think so. I need to be getting home—"

"But it's still so warm out. It's the perfect evening for it."

"We live in LA. Every evening's like this."

"This is the first time we've seen each other in what, at least five years? Come on, I'm not done catching up."

She sighed. "No, I..."

But Anton hopped out of the car and headed for the front door. He fished his keys from his pocket, then stopped and turned back to find Scarlett still sitting in the passenger seat, her face a play of curiosity and worry.

"Come on. Let me just show you the view, then I'll get you home. You've gotta see my place; you'll love it."

He could see her drunk-girl brain assessing the situation—*he only wants to show me the view, he seems genuine. He's giving me a ride home, after all.*

"Fine," she said finally. "But quickly, okay? Then I've got to go."

Anton grinned. "Of course."

The inside of the house was decorated with cosmopolitan sensibility and NASA-like functionality; every item picked precisely for its purpose and location. Long, gray couches sat on woven silk rugs under black aluminum lights with white silica diffusers, all surrounded by limited edition fixtures and minimalist artwork.

"Wow," said Scarlett. "You *have* changed. Who knew you could be so..." she groped for the right word, "*avant-garde*?"

"I actually prefer the term sophisticated panache."

Scarlett raised her thin eyebrows, and Anton grinned.

"Come on, I'll show you the deck."

He led her up the stairs, through the den, and out through the rear sliding doors onto the deck, the teak planking and glass railings glowing under the pale moonlight.

"What do ya think?"

Scarlett stepped up to the railing, looked down at the pool glimmering electric blue against the gray slate of the patio, then at the distant twinkling lights of the LA skyline—the pulse of a city powered by dreams.

"It's amazing..."

A gust of cool air rose up the hillside and swept across the deck, and Scarlett shivered slightly into herself.

"Let me grab you a jacket," said Anton. "I'll be right back."

Before she could stop him with a comment about her not staying, he slipped back into the house and returned a few minutes later with one of his suit jackets and two glasses of wine. She looked at the glasses with a smirk, and he shrugged.

"You don't have to finish it. But it's criminal not to enjoy the fine nectar of the gods while taking in a view like this."

"I've had plenty of wine tonight."

"Well, you can always sip it and spit it back out."

He held the glasses out to her, and she took them while he draped the jacket over her shoulders. Then he took one back and clinked the other.

They both stood there for a while, taking in the view, before Scarlett said, "So, are you going to tell me what you've really been doing for your family?" her words coming slowly now.

"What do you mean?"

"I mean, you can't afford a place like this just from being a co-owner of a bar?"

Anton gave her a mischievous smile. "If I told you I'm a part-time male model, would you believe me?"

"Nope."

"Well, you should believe me. I'm a trustworthy guy." He moved forward, closing the gap between them. "People trust me with their secrets all the time." He ran his fingertips up her arm, and her body reacted instantly, her weight shifting ever so slightly toward him.

"What kind of people?"

Anton set his wine glass down. "The type who have secrets."

He leaned in and kissed her; her lips tasted of red wine and cherry lip gloss. She tilted back, trying to pull away, but he wrapped his arm around her lower back and pulled her in close. He slipped his tongue between her lips and pressed his body up against hers. Her body and breath were warm from the wine, and although she tried to withdraw, it was a weak attempt.

Anton reached behind her, threw open the sliding doors, and backed her into the master bedroom.

"No, wait," Scarlett mumbled.

But Anton took her wine glass from her and kissed her again, his thirst growing more lustful and intense. He threw the door closed behind them and began grabbing and tearing at Scarlett's clothes like a wild animal, with pure unchecked desire.

Then he grasped her by the throat and pushed her against the wall. She grabbed his arm, her eyes wide, taken off guard. A look filled her face, and Anton couldn't tell if it was fear.

But then her hands dropped from his arms, her eyes softened, and her jaw relaxed—the expression of complete submission. He turned her around and pushed her on the bed. Then he was on her, ripping off her panties and tossing them to the floor. As he pushed himself inside her, she groaned. He leaned into her ear and said, "I missed you, my little *Scarlett rose.*"

13

DETECTIVE BROOKS

Just after the sun graced the California coast with its presence, Brooks fired up his Cadillac Deville, pulled onto the 110, and sat in bumper-to-bumper traffic for the better part of two hours, the whole time surrounded by a sea of fellow motorists who'd apparently just discovered how their horns worked.

Man, I love LA, he thought.

He followed Randel's map to a long, sidewalk-less road, marinated in the smells of labor: sawdust, welded steel, and melted plastic. Old rusted warehouses hid behind ten-foot steel gates lined with razor wire, each with a sunburned sign out front: *Ray's Lumber, Mayfair Towing, Philip's Auto.* The few that *were* still in business looked like they were on their way out.

From the outside, Eric's building looked like it could have been a tile distributor or small textiles factory: off-white concrete block walls, a few high windows, and a ramp leading to a roller-shutter door the width of a delivery truck.

The intercom chirped when Brooks pressed the button, inviting him to introduce himself. But he didn't say anything.

Instead, he glanced up at the camera perched above the door like a hawk and gave it his best smile.

After thirty seconds with no action, Brooks started to wonder if Eric had moved on to another building in another part of the city. Guys like him didn't stick around in one place for too long—that would be foolish. But just when Brooks thought about leaving, he heard shuffling boots, then the clank of a lock release. The door slowly creaked open, revealing the beefy frame of Ryan Daniels—Eric's "business partner," for lack of a better term. He was a tall, barrel-chested man with roles of muscle where his neck should be and an army-issue haircut.

"You ain't supposed to be here," he said.

"Yet here I am," said Brooks.

Daniels quickly looked around behind Brooks at his invisible entourage, then ushered him inside and slammed the door.

The inside of the warehouse was open plan, stripped and gutted of all its fixtures and finishes. The faded block walls propped up exposed roof trusses and steel pipes, with every window boarded up. The whole space glowed pale blue from the industrial fluorescents, and the tang of welded steel hung, trapped in the air with no route for escape.

To the right was the warehouse floor, where a Dodge Charger sat raised on a car lift, surrounded by tool chests, sheets of metal, and propane tanks. All four wheels and both front and rear windshields were missing, but what really caught Brooks's eye was that it wasn't just a standard, base-model Charger—this one came with all kinds of modifications. Like the ram bar, the lighting strip on the roof, and the lovely decal on the doors that read *Los Angeles Police Department.*

"You boosted a cop car?" Brooks asked.

Daniels scrunched his face like the question offended him. "I don't boost cars. Do I look sixteen to you?"

"Then where did you get it?"

A look of pride flashed across his big baby-face. "I built it. Well, I've almost built it."

Before Brooks could ask him why, a voice came from the other side of the warehouse—a loud voice, hoarse and aggravated. "What the fuck is he doing here?"

They looked up to find Eric standing at the top of a steel staircase that led up to the only room in the building, a twelve-by-twelve-foot cube made of panel walls and frosted glass. He was a wiry man with ropy muscles and a face like a skull; pale skin pulled tight over sharply defined features, his bald scalp as smooth and shiny as a billiard ball.

"Good morning, Eric," Brooks said.

Eric ignored him and looked at Daniels. "Be a pal and remind me what I told you this morning?"

Daniels shrugged. "Relax, it's only Brooks."

"I can see who it is," said Eric. "I'm not fucking blind. But I guess you're fucking deaf, 'cause that's not what I asked you. So tell me, what did I tell you..." he checked his watch, "a fucking hour ago?"

Daniels shrugged again. "You said no one in or out, not today."

"You do remember? So what the fuck is he doing stood down there with that smug-ass smile on his face?"

"I catch you ladies at a bad time?" Brooks asked.

"As a matter of fact, you did," said Eric, then he looked back at Daniels with a stare that demanded answers.

Daniel spread his hands, palms up. "What do you want from me, man? You want me to go back in time and not let him in."

"No, I want you to listen the next time I tell you to do something. We don't need this shit. Not today."

"I got it, boss."

Eric rubbed his eyes and sighed.

"Hey, you guys need a moment to kiss and make up? I can cover my eyes if it makes you feel more comfortable," said Brooks, beaming at his own fifth-grade insult. Eric glared at him, then back at Daniels, who shrugged yet again. That seemed to be his thing.

"For god's sake," said Eric, with the air of defeat and disappointment a parent shows a misbehaving kid. Then he hung his head and waved at Brooks. "Come up."

Despite the fact they bickered like kids in the back seat on a road trip, Eric and Daniels were pros. They were both ex-special forces with six tours between them. But Eric was dishonorably discharged when he was caught smuggling heroin into the states from Afghanistan. And Brooks—*accidentally*—busted him with a case of stolen Styler AUG assault rifles when he was following up on a homicide lead, only three months after he was released from Fort Lewis on the drug charge. Lucky for Brooks, he caught Eric off guard, and none of the weapons were loaded. And, luckily for Eric, Brooks liked to make deals.

Eric closed the door to the office, and they took seats on opposite sides of his fold-out desk. Almost everything in the room was flaking or peeling; the paint off the walls, the brown leather off the seats, the vinyl tile off the floor. It was like the underside of the hull on a neglected ship. But sat on the desk facing Eric was a laptop computer with a thick antenna and a forest of wires sprouting from the back, running down through a single hole in the floor. Brooks was as tech-savvy as an Amish elder, but even he knew that thing was powerful—probably able-to-hack-just-about-any-database powerful.

Eric lit a cigarette and spoke through the smoke, "I ain't even gonna ask how you knew I was here. Just tell me what you need and make it quick."

"I need you to find someone."

He sighed. "Don't they have ways of doing that in your office? I'm really busy, man."

"I can see that. But unfortunately, this particular job requires someone with your... special expertise."

Eric took a long drag of his cigarette, pulled the laptop closer, and hovered his fingers above the keys. "Give me a name."

"James Nealson, born in 1955."

"You know his social?"

"Nope. But I do know, without any reasonable doubt, that his favorite color is purple. And he might be in LA. That should narrow it down, right?"

"Jesus. How the hell did you make detective? I bet you failed the exam like fifteen times, huh?"

"There's an exam?" Brooks said in jest.

Eric shook his head and took another drag of his smoke.

"Man, I got a lot of people by the name James Nealson from that year, with a ton in California. Anything else you can tell me?"

"Our boy has a record. Burglary or theft in '80 and '89."

"Why didn't you say that in the first place?"

"I thought you liked a challenge."

"Asshole," muttered Eric.

Brooks glanced out of the door and down onto the warehouse floor. Daniels was on his knees near the rear of the Dodge, a welder's mask covering his face and sparks spilling over the floor below him like miniature fireworks. Brooks turned back, and in the few seconds he'd been looking away, Eric had stubbed out his cigarette and lit another. Eric had never been a model of stillness and calm, but this was the most anxious Brooks had ever seen him.

"What the hell are you two working on?" Brooks asked. "What's with the cop car?"

Without looking up from the screen, he said, "Trust me, old man. You do not wanna know."

"Well, on the contrary," said Brooks.

"Let's just say, some extenuating circumstances have forced us to get..." he looked up, "creative."

"Well, now I'm really intrigued. Come on, I'll pinky-swear I won't tell anybody."

"Just stop asking, man. I'm not playing. You don't want any part of this."

Before Brooks could press him further, Eric looked back to his screen and said, "I got him. In 1969 he was sentenced to three years in the Fred C. Nelles Youth Correctional Facility for aggravated burglary. Then we've got a short stretch in the early 80s, same charge. Then it looks like he went on trial in '89 but got off.

"That's our guy," said Brooks. "What can you tell me?"

"I've got information from back then; addresses, vehicle registrations... but in '94 he disappears. Got nothing after that. It's like he fell off the face of the Earth."

"Damn it. I'm having the same problem. We couldn't find shit back in '94, either."

"Wait, you were a detective back in '94? God damn, you're old."

Brooks flipped Eric the bird, and Eric looked back at his screen. "That's weird."

"What?"

"Well, before the juvie file, there's nothing, either. No birth certificate, no medical records, no parent information—nothing." Eric ran a hand through his invisible hair. "How can someone appear from nowhere, then disappear into nowhere... without my help?"

"A lot easier back in the day," Brooks said. "Everything was still on paper."

Suddenly Eric's eyes brightened, and he sat up in his chair, roused by the thrill of the hunt. "Maybe I could..." but he caught himself, his expression turning serious. "Hey, look. As much as I love playing detective with you, I wasn't fucking around earlier. We're dealing with some heavy shit down there. Now, I tried to help, but it looks like your guy's gone. So if you don't mind." He motioned to close the laptop, but Brooks reached out and held it open, all joviality draining from his face.

"I need your help, Eric. No fucking around now, this is real."

Eric considered this. "Who the hell is this guy?"

"Just someone from the past. But if you find him, you and me are square. No more favors."

A sting of shame rose up in Brooks. Fear and vulnerability were supposed to be hidden, especially in front of people like Eric. And there he was, practically begging. But there was no other choice, and by the look on Eric's face, he knew it.

"Okay, I got one thing I could try. But it's a long shot."

Brooks released the laptop. "What do you have in mind?"

Eric went back to tapping away at the keys. "I'm going to try and cross-reference any missing children from around the time he went to juvie and see if we find a match."

"Great, let's do it."

After several long minutes of tense silence, Eric clapped his hands together, and said, "Bingo. Got you, you sneaky motherfucker."

"What have you found?"

"James Francis, born in 1955 in Boston. I've got some medical records from Rose de Lima hospital in Las Vegas in

'64. Then both parents die in '68. He goes missing the same year our guy goes to juvie in California."

"Both parents?" Brooks said.

"Yep, and get this, the father's name was Neal Francis." Eric raised his eyebrows, "Neal Francis—James *Neal*-son."

"You think they could be the same guy?"

"Ya know, I take it back. Your detective skills are outstanding."

"Fuck you. Can you run a search on Francis?"

"Sure," said Eric, his cigarette clamped between his teeth.

"Well, I'll be damned. I got a hit. James Francis, born in '55, currently renting a house up on Dixie Canyon road through a company called Alonzo properties. Let me see if I can pull up the ad." After a few moments, Eric cocked his head back and raised his eyebrows again. "Wow, look at this place."

"That nice, huh?"

Eric swiveled the laptop around so Brooks could get a look at the screen. There was only one photo of the house under a brief three-line description. The photo was small and low resolution, as if it'd been taken on an old flip phone. And the house itself looked like an abandoned meth cookhouse.

"What the hell is he doing there?" Brooks asked.

"I don't know, but it says he's been there around three months."

"Something's not right here. This is all a bit *too* easy."

"Bullshit," said Eric, spinning the laptop back around. "If you'd gone to those dumb shmucks in your department, that would have taken days. I just make it look easy. Now, you want to hear the rest?"

"There's more?"

Eric flashed a wry smile. "Oh yeah."

14

SCARLETT

Scarlett's sleep was consumed by a vivid dream charged with deep emotion, her subconscious brain conjuring colorful scenes and projecting them onto the back of her eyelids. In the dream, she was a child—five or six—and her parents had taken her to the quaint bed-and-breakfast in the little coastal town of Morro Bay; it was the last memory she had of her father.

They were on the beach below the cliffs, and her father was holding her hand at the water's edge, sprinkles of saltwater kissing their faces as the waves crashed in front of them. She felt safe, her small hand lost in his strong grip. She looked back to find her mother watching on from a picnic blanket, her hair floating playfully in the breeze, her smile wide and full of love.

Scarlett woke slowly, her mind reluctant to break from the tranquility of the dream, reluctant to return to reality and face what she'd done. As her eyes crept open, a sharp pain exploded across her forehead, like an insect gnawing through her skull. It was her first time dealing with back-to-back, compounding hangovers in years, and she felt horrendous.

Anton was in the shower; the sound of water beating down

on his body seeped under the door of his en suite. She sat up; the room felt foreign and empty, yet pregnant with the conspicuous reality of last night's act.

Anton had been manipulative and forceful, but she hadn't put a stop to it. A tsunami of remorse and anxiety crashed into her, and she knew she had to get out before Anton came back into the room.

Moving as quietly as she could, she threw off the covers and spun her legs out of bed, her nakedness feeling shameful and wrong. As she got to her feet, the room tilted slightly. She had to swallow hard to avoid vomiting. She quickly threw her clothes back on and gathered the rest of her belongings, grimacing as she tucked her torn panties into her purse. She found the heel of her left shoe poking out from under Anton's jeans, but couldn't see the right one anywhere.

Dropping to her knees, she scanned under the bed and saw a sharp, black object cast in the shadows between two shoeboxes. She reached out and grabbed its cold and hard form.

When she pulled it out, her heart dropped in her chest: it was a handgun, a brand-new chrome pistol.

The shower stopped running in the en suite, and Scarlett's anxiety turned into something akin to panic. She knew who Anton was—what his family and friends did—and she knew he wouldn't hurt her, not like that. But holding the gun, the first gun she'd ever held, it was too real—too scary.

Tossing it back under the bed, she quickly headed for the door, fully prepared to abandon her shoe like some perverse adaptation of Cinderella. But as she turned the handle, she spotted it at the base of his chest of drawers. She picked it up, took one last glance over her shoulder at the bathroom door, then she was gone.

. . .

A hot shower did little to wash away the shame from the night before. And after drying off and putting on her scrubs, Scarlett picked up her phone to find two missed calls from Josh. Before she could even think about whether she was ready to call him back, the phone rang a third time, which sent a torrent of anxiety and worry coursing through her body. *Why three calls in a row? Did someone see me with Anton? Does Josh know I met up with him? Does he know everything?* The coward in her didn't want to answer, but she took a deep breath and nervously swiped the answer button.

"Hey baby," said Scarlett, injecting as much pep into her voice as she could muster.

"Where are you?" Josh's voice was flat, monotone, and void of emotion.

Scarlett stalled, trying to think of any reason she might have to lie. Finding none, she said, "At home, why?"

"Why didn't you answer my calls?"

"I was... I was in the shower," she said, again, finding no reason to lie. Silence fell on the line, so she broke it: "Everything okay, baby?"

Josh drew a long breath and sighed. "Not really."

Scarlett's heart rate quickened. *He knows.*

She started gnawing on a hangnail. "What is it?"

Another long sigh, followed by a silence so absolute it was deafening.

"Well," he said, and her body tensed up, "first off, my flight got delayed, so I arrived late to the first round of meetings..."

Relief spread over Scarlett, and she slumped onto the bed.

"Then, I find out Mae didn't send the term sheet to the valuation specialist. And if they don't get it done today, we're on hold 'til Monday. I mean, shit, is she trying to kill this deal?"

"I'm sorry, baby. That sucks."

Josh sighed again, and this time it seemed to ease the

tension living in his voice. "Yeah, well, I'm sorry, I don't mean to load all my problems onto you. I'm just exhausted."

"You don't have to apologize, it's fine."

"No, no, I was really just trying to catch you to say hi before I went back in. I'm probably going to be tied up for a while fixing this mess."

Scarlett sat up on the bed and tried to sound positive. "Well, grab yourself a coffee, and go in there and show them why Jenkins sent you. Do what you do best."

"Remind me what that is again."

Scarlett managed a chuckle, her nerves subsiding.

"You know," Josh said, "no matter how annoyed or down I am, the second I hear that adorable laugh of yours, I feel instantly better."

"Really?"

"Of course." He paused for a moment, then said, "Thank you, baby."

"For what?"

"I don't know. For always knowing the right things to say. For being you. For being mine."

A lump formed in Scarlett's throat, and she choked out the words, "I love you."

"I love you two, Scar. More than you know."

When Scarlett hung up, the tears came in cascades as she heaved wet breaths. Her mind flashed over the last thirty-six hours—the betrayal, the confusion, the guilt—and she lay back on her bed and sobbed into her hands. She was remorseful, exhausted, and overwhelmed.

And all with the knowledge that—after visiting a sweet old lady with esophageal cancer—she had another appointment with the old man.

15

LUCA

Before heading downtown for the first meeting with his parole officer, Luca picked up a small screwdriver from a corner store and headed over to the parking garage off South Grand Avenue. He found the row of motorcycle parking on the second floor and slotted the V-Star next to an old-model, black Kawasaki Ninja. And when he was sure the coast was clear, he kneeled down between the bikes and pretended to check his exhaust pipe while he unscrewed his license plate. Then he unscrewed the plate from the Ninja and swapped it with his.

With his PO's office on the same block as the sheriff's office, the courthouse, and city hall, Luca figured he needed to take some precautionary measures with the bike. He knew Sandra was too scared and smart to ever snitch to the cops about his little visit. She knew by giving him the bike, he'd be out of her life. But the kid, well, he might have done something stupid, like report the bike stolen. And getting arrested for theft or possession of stolen property would have really pissed on Luca's plans.

Plates swapped, he fired up the V-Star, slid out of the

garage, and headed toward downtown, the sun bouncing off LA's jagged skyline in the distance. He figured the new plates would buy him at least a week. If the kid did report the bike stolen, the cops were looking for a V-Star with the old plate number. If they happened to run the new plate, their computer would say it belongs to a 2007-ish black Kawasaki, and most cops wouldn't be able to tell the difference. And he didn't have to worry about whoever owned the Ninja—nobody checks their plates on a regular basis; most people couldn't even tell you what their plate number was if you asked them.

As Luca rode along, the bike purring below him, it dawned on him just how badly he'd failed to stick to his plan of being cautious and careful when he left prison. He'd only been on the streets for a few days, and he'd broken into a motel room, assaulted a teenager, stolen a motorcycle, and now stolen a license plate.

But hey, he had to admit, it felt good being back doing what he loved.

Luca's parole officer's name was Larry Pratt, a pencil neck with a soft handshake and weak-looking chin. He showed Luca into his office with an "Awesome to meet you, Luca," and a "Thanks for coming in," as if the meeting was optional. On first impressions, he looked like he wasn't going to be a problem. But Luca needed to dig deeper, find out what type of guy he was. Having a hard-ass PO would make life and plans for revenge a whole lot more complicated.

His office was a dreary, off-white cube filled with stainless-steel filing cabinets and cheap plastic furniture. It smelled of dust and old paper. They each took a seat on either side of Larry's desk, and Larry turned to his computer screen.

"Give me one moment, let me just bring up your file," he said.

Luca looked through the only window in the room at the neighboring concrete office building, a bunch of other worker bees buzzing around their little cubicles, all of them looking just as bored and purposeless. *Rats in a fucking maze,* he thought. He'd have gone back to prison before he ever worked in a place like that. At least on the inside, they weren't under any illusions—they all knew they were in prison.

"Right, Luca Messetti, found you," said Larry, turning back to Luca. "Now, before we get started, I wanted to put something out there. I'm not a cop, I am not trying to *get* you. I like to think of myself as more of a social worker. My job is to make sure your transition back into society is as seamless as possible, and I want to help you as much as I can."

Good start, thought Luca.

"So," Larry went on, "in these meetings, we will usually start by talking about your living situation. Where are you staying right now, by the way?"

He said it so casually, like they were old friends catching up. Luca knew he had to give an address, but he decided to test the boundaries a little, play his hunch. "I'm in a hotel downtown, but that's only temporary. I'm moving in with a friend in a couple days, but I don't have the address with me right now."

Larry stalled for a moment, contemplating his response. Then he nodded to himself, "Sure... that's not a problem. Just make sure to bring it with you to the next meeting."

Bingo, Luca thought.

"When is the next meeting?"

"Good question. So, as you may know, everyone who is released on parole undergoes a risk assessment, and the results of the assessment determine their supervision level. High risks report every week, moderate twice a month, and low once a month. Unfortunately, your case has been labeled as high risk."

"High risk of what?" Luca knew the answer—high risk of him fucking up and getting tossed back in prison—but he wanted to hear how Larry would put it. He didn't disappoint.

"I like to say that *you* are at risk," he said, interlocking his fingers on his desk like a shrink. "You spent many years incarcerated and may find it hard to reinsert yourself into society. But don't worry. With my help, we should get you down to low risk before long. That way, our meetings will become monthly for the duration of your supervision. Sound good to you?"

"Sounds great," said Luca, working him like a mark.

The family photos on Larry's desk showed a wife and two young boys, but he wasn't wearing a ring, just the pale mark where a ring used to be. With his submissive demeanor, he didn't strike Luca as the divorcée type, so Luca figured she was dead. Either way, the pathetic—*we're buddies*—look on his long face spoke volumes. This was a civil servant probably making only slightly more than a McDonald's drive-thru attendant, who still came to this shitty job with a smile on his face. He was the type of guy who would get cut off in traffic and say—*what can you do?*

He was a putz.

He was perfect.

"Great. Where was I? Oh yeah, the meeting structure. So, after housing, we talk about employment; we've got a great workforce center across the street that can help you find jobs. Unfortunately, with a felony on your record, you're going to be looking at basic labor jobs, but it's better than nothing, believe me. After employment, we discuss personal well-being, address any questions or concerns, *et cetera*. Then finally, we test for drug and alcohol use."

Luca nodded. He was never a big user of drugs—a few hits

of hash and an eight-ball of coke from time to time, but that was it.

"I know it can be difficult," said Larry, "especially with all the temptations in this city, but you have to stay strong. Any violations of your parole terms will see you back in prison."

Luca pursed his lips into something that could pass for a smile, and he thought to himself: *America, the good old land of the free.* It didn't matter, though. He found out what he needed to know—that Larry wasn't going to be a problem. And a few missed meetings here or there shouldn't be an issue.

When he left Larry's office, Luca called Brooks from his burner phone for an update. He didn't expect him to have much information yet, he just wanted to stay on his ass. But when Brooks answered the phone, he said, "I got what you need, meet me at the bar in an hour."

"Not the bar," said Luca. "Neutral grounds. Somewhere public."

"Public? Okay, what about MacArthur Park?"

Luca grinned to himself. "I got a better idea. Meet me at the Angelus Rosedale Cemetery."

Brooks sighed. "You shitting me?"

"Park on Washington, head right when you walk through the gates and take a seat on one of the benches."

"Fine. One hour."

"Can hardly wait."

Angelus Rosedale Cemetery looked like something out of a Tim Burton movie; tall, carved statues stood over sinking headstones bearing faded inscriptions, and stringy weeds sprouted just about everywhere. It was the type of place where you'd find senators buried next to mobsters, buried next to movie stars. It also used to be one of Luca's favorite stash spots, so he knew the emergency exit points like the back of his hand.

He watched through his helmet from across the street to make sure Brooks arrived alone, and he did. When Luca walked inside, Brooks was waiting on a bench, hunched over like a question mark, sucking on a cigar. His gold detective badge glimmered on his hip like a jewel in a dust pile.

Luca approached in a slow saunter, his leather boots squeaking under his step, the scent of dry grass clippings taking him back to his childhood. When Brooks noticed Luca, he looked straight ahead, pretending not to know him. Luca slid onto the bench next to him, and they sat in silence, staring blankly ahead like they were watching a ball game.

After a minute or so, Brooks looked around, then pulled a folded newspaper from his jacket and placed it on the bench between them. Inside the newspaper would be an envelope, and inside the envelope would be what Luca wanted. But he didn't take it. Instead, he just glanced at it and said, "That was fast. Shows what you can do with the *right* persuasion."

Brooks shrugged, unamused. "I just asked the *right* people."

"Which people would that be?"

Brooks smiled a *fuck-you* smile and said, "My people."

Luca gestured to the newspaper with his chin. "And our friend? How long's he been back?"

"Three months or so," Brooks said, glancing down at the newspaper as if willing Luca to take it so he could leave. But Luca wasn't done with his questions.

"But why now?"

It had crossed Luca's mind that Jimmy wanted him to know where he was, like he was leaving breadcrumbs, whispers of information given through the right channels. It wouldn't be hard for Jimmy to find out that Luca was getting out, and he must have known he would come for him. Maybe it was a trap —why else would Jimmy show his face now?

But then Brooks gave an answer that put those worries at ease.

"Maybe he just came back home to die. He's sick. The lungs. My source tells me the type of care he's getting means he's only got months, maybe even weeks."

"A few months, huh?" Luca said. "That's plenty of time to make him tell me where his money is, then rip his kneecaps off with a claw hammer."

Brooks sighed an old man's sigh. "The money's gone, Luca."

"What?"

"We saw his financials; he's broke. And he's living in some shitty rental house up on the hill in the valley. Looks like he's got nothing."

"You're lying!" barked Luca, anger filling his hoarse voice.

Brooks nodded at the newspaper. "See for yourself. It's been a long time, he could have spent it all years ago. You know how Jimmy likes to spend."

That son of a bitch, Luca thought.

"He's only got months, huh? Well, we'll shorten that time span up real fast."

Brooks sucked on his cigar, the smoke curling up past his eyes. "Look, just make sure your guy's discreet, okay? I don't want this turning into a mess."

"I ain't using a hitter," said Luca.

"What? Are you stupid?"

Luca turned on the bench to face Brooks, his eyes burning holes in the side of the detective's head. Brooks kept looking forward, and said, "I'm just saying. Who do you think they're gonna finger for the job? You just got out. They'll connect the dots, even if it takes them a while."

Luca spoke through gritted teeth, his body vibrating with rage, "That bastard took everything from me. I spent forty percent of my life behind bars 'cause of that piece of shit. And you want me to trust some other guy with this? Fuck no. If there ain't no money left, then I want his fucking head. *And I'm gonna be the one to rip it off.*"

Brooks tossed his cigar on the floor and stomped it out. "If you screw up, you'll get twenty-five to life to dwell on your mistake."

"Why do you give a shit?"

"About you? I don't. But I can't have it getting back to me."

Luca reached out for the newspaper. "It won't."

But Brooks grabbed it and held on. "You can't take that risk. This isn't the old days. You can't go around shooting people like a fucking cowboy. This..." He noticed an old couple approaching from the patch behind the bench, dry grass crunching under their feet. Both men kept quiet as the couple joined the path and headed toward the front gate. When the couple was out of earshot, Brooks turned back. Luca slid closer to him, their faces a few inches apart.

"You giving me orders now, Brooks?"

"I'm just saying..."

"What?" Luca snapped.

Brooks stiffened and clenched his jaw. "Be smart, Luca. Get a hitter, get an alibi. You don't want Jimmy to be the reason you go *back* behind bars."

Luca withdrew slightly, silently seething. As much as it infuriated him to admit it, Brooks did have a point. Luca recalled Hooper's story about the tree and wondered if there wasn't another meaning hidden within it, one he hadn't considered before. What if, instead of the old man trying to get rid of the tree himself, he got someone else to do it for him?

Luca gave Brooks a look that told him he'd think about it,

and Brooks removed his hand from the newspaper. Luca casually unfolded it and took the envelope from within.

"You were supposed to take the whole newspaper," Brooks said.

"I don't read 'em," said Luca, rising to his feet and placing the envelope into his pocket. "Thanks for the tip. I'll be seeing you soon."

Luca left Brooks on the bench shaking his head, but looking relieved their interaction was over. As he walked to the V-Star, Luca racked his brains on who he could use for a job like this. Running down the very short list of potentials who weren't dead or in jail, he could only think of one worth talking to: Benny "Gums" Nolan.

But there was a problem. The corpse Luca left to be cremated in the smoldering Chevy Tahoe after the heist—the kid, Casey—was Benny Gums's little brother.

16

ANTON

Bar 91 was closed—chairs upturned on tables, the tile floor still glazed from the morning cleaning crew—but Anton had a key. He picked his way through the tables, slipped up the rear stairs, wrapped on the door, and yelled, "Diego?"

Diego lived in a small one-bedroom apartment above the bar, a dingy place with low ceilings that Anton had only set foot in once. Anton knocked again, then placed his ear to the heavy oak door and heard the muffled thud of heavy metal music.

"God damn it."

He fished his phone from his pocket and navigated to his recent calls list. As he thumbed to the top, the door crept open a few inches, and the matte black barrel of a Desert Eagle handgun poked through the gap.

Anton jumped and dropped his phone. "Whoa, what the fuck!"

The door opened the rest of the way, revealing Diego wrapped in a towel. He cursed in Russian, then spoke in his thick accent and broken English, "What the hell you doing, man? I tell you to call when you downstairs."

"You're not answering your phone," barked Anton. "You said it was urgent."

Diego lowered the gun and glanced back into his apartment. "Oh, sorry, my man. I get a little... paranoid, you know? I thought you might be police."

Anton shook his head and let out a long sigh.

"Lucky I see it's you," said Diego, suddenly smiling through his thick beard. "This gun makes a big mess, my man."

Anton laughed through his nerves, and Diego clapped him on the back. "I'll be downstairs in a minute. And don't worry, we have some time."

Ten minutes later, Diego was back in his usual spot behind the bar, slicing some orange pieces to add to the two glasses of Blue Moon (the only beer they had on tap).

"So..." Diego said, a teenager's mischievous grin across his face.

"So, what?" Anton asked.

"Come on, guy. Don't play this game on me. I'm talking about the girl. You took her back to your place, no?"

Anton smirked. "What do you think?"

"So... how was it?"

"Let's just say, she won't be forgetting last night in a hurry."

A toothy smile blew across Diego's face. "Of course not, my guy." He garnished the beers, then slid one across to Anton. "Who is this girl, anyway?"

Anton sipped and shrugged. "Nobody."

"She didn't look like a nobody to me, my man. From where I was standing, it looked like you had history."

"You a psychologist now?"

Diego threw up his hands. "I'm just saying. I saw that ring on her finger, and it didn't slow her down one bit."

"Well, I just told her how it was going to go down."

"Oh yeah?" said Diego, his voice laced with skepticism. "What you say, exactly?"

"I just said, 'Look, I know you've got a man, but I don't care. Tonight you're coming home with me. And that's the way it's going to be.'"

"And that worked? Nice girl like this?"

Anton raised his glass. "You're damn right."

Another smile spread across Diego's face, this one even bigger than the last. "Well, cheers to that, my friend."

As they clinked glasses, Anton's mind drifted to the night before. The thrill of the chase was still alive inside him, and the satisfaction of the prize stirred up old feelings of lust and domination. He knew there was no way he could come back to LA without taking another little piece of her. He was actually a little surprised how easy it was. But he was equally surprised by the way she left: slipping out while he was showering without saying a word. He'd guessed she'd sobered up and felt guilty. But it didn't matter; he had gotten all he wanted out of her.

"So," he said, resting his forearm on the bar, "you going to tell me what this meeting's about?"

Diego sighed. "Wish I knew. She told me to be at her office at one o'clock. And to bring you."

"Why me?"

Diego shrugged and leaned back against the backside of the bar. "She didn't say."

By *she,* Diego meant Karina, the boss of the Los Angeles arm of the organization. Technically, she was only the acting boss until her husband Nicholai finished serving his prison sentence in Moscow, but that wasn't for another 90 years or so.

"It's probably a job," said Diego. "She's had me doing runs with Alex for the past few months. A new group from down south. They're not exactly... how do you say this..." he snapped his fingers a few times, groping for the word, "*trustworthy*. That's it. Maybe she wants an extra body with us this time."

"Wait," said Anton, his face scrunched into a question. "By down south, you don't mean..."

"That's right."

"You gotta be shitting me. What the hell is she thinking?"

Diego took a long sip of his beer, then swallowed hard against the carbonation. "Who knows, my guy. I never understand what she does. I just take orders, you know?"

Anton shook his head firmly and took a long sip of his own. He liked Diego, but when he wasn't carrying out low-level, high-risk tasks—like burying bodies or ferrying money and drugs across the city—the guy worked as a goddamn bartender. The two men simply weren't of the same... caliber. Diego's father was a poor Russian immigrant, whereas Anton's had commanded respect from every person in the organization. Things were always going to be different back in LA without his father around, but there was one thing Anton knew was for sure: he couldn't get stuck doing grunt work for Karina—that was a god damn death sentence.

Karina's office was in a warehouse on Union Pacific Avenue, a street of boxy buildings painted bird-shit gray, with barred windows and graffiti tattoos. Anton and Diego pulled around the back and parked the Mercedes in the lot off East 15th, next to a couple of blacked-out Range Rovers. The cars might have looked a little suspicious in such a neighborhood, if it wasn't for the sign out front: *J.O.A. Metal Artwork and Sculptures*. The business wasn't just a front, either. In fact, if anyone felt so inclined as to pull the financials, they would find a thriving business with auction sales from across the country.

They entered through the back door and slipped through a workshop—a long space with bright florescent lights and strips of twisted steel protruding from heavy machinery. All the equipment was brand-new: workbenches, bandsaws, drill presses, benders.

Beyond the workshop was a short hallway, Karina's office at one end and the gallery at the other. But as they approached door number one, the big guy standing outside—whose face Anton knew but name he couldn't remember—held out his hand, revealing a submachine gun under his jacket, and said, "She's in a meeting; wait in the gallery."

So, they did.

Despite the building's crusty facade, the gallery was immaculate; a bright white space with a dozen or so abstract expressionist sculptures sitting on plinths or hanging suspended from ceiling cables. Each one was lit by rows of LED track lighting or up-lights built into the polished concrete floor. Some of the pieces were spectacular—pure creative vision transferred from the artist's brain to reality.

But the most beautiful thing in the room wasn't a sculpture —*she* was sitting over near the front entry door. The only employee at the only desk in the space. And while Diego went to get his caffeine fix at the Nespresso machine, Anton went over to admire her.

She was wearing a white blouse, her sandy hair tied up in a ponytail, lightly chewing the end of her pen while staring down at her laptop. As she heard Anton's footsteps approaching, she looked up, and her lips curled into a smile around the pen.

"Well, well. We meet again," she said, her voice soft and flirtatious.

"I told you I'd be back," said Anton.

Her name was Becca, or Bella—or some other reasonable facsimile—and their flirting was the only positive takeaway from Anton's last, and first, trip to Karina's office a month or so prior.

"How have you been?" she asked.

"You know, surviving." Anton waved his arm across the gallery. "You been busy trying to make all of these disappear?"

"Yes, sir," she said slowly, in that same frisky tone. "So, how are you enjoying being back in LA?"

He sat side-saddle on the end of her desk, his right leg cocked, his left foot on the floor. "It's changed. So many new places. All the cool spots I used to know are gone."

"Sounds like you need a guide. Maybe I could show you a few things."

"Oh, I bet you could. What do you have in mind?"

She propped her elbow on the desk and looked up at him with playful, hungry eyes. "I have a couple of—"

The clicking of heels on concrete stopped Becca mid-sentence, and Anton could tell by the way her face and body hardened—and the fact she'd forgotten how to speak—that it was Karina who was approaching. He spun on the desk, and Karina stopped fifteen feet from them, holding Anton under her flat gaze.

Karina stood at about five foot three, with straight red hair over pale skin, as flawless as a drop of dew, that made her look fifteen years younger than her actual age of fifty. And with her thin frame, big hazel eyes, and high cheekbones, it would be easy to mistake her as nothing more than a delicate, beautiful woman. In fact, many men had, and they were still finding pieces of them.

Diego dumped his nearly full coffee in the trash and headed over, but Karina ignored him and kept her gaze on Anton.

"Anton," she said in a sarcastically happy voice, her accent even thicker than Diego's. "Please remind me. What is this American saying... 'You don't dip your pen in the ink'?"

Anton carefully slipped off the desk and cleared his throat. "Uh, you mean, 'You don't dip your pen in the company ink'?"

Karina clapped her hands and beamed a smile. "That's it; you don't dip your pen in company ink. I like this one." She looked at Becca, then back at Anton. "I would remember this if I were you, Anton. Because if you don't, I will have your pen cut off and shoved down your fucking throat."

In contrast to the modern design of the gallery, the back office resembled a study from a stately home; dark oak flooring, stacked bookshelves, and rigid, leather armchairs. A fair-haired guy was occupying one of the chairs when Karina led Diego and Anton in. He was sitting in the corner, next to the thick taupe curtains that blocked out the eager California sun, holding a newspaper at eye level. He didn't look up at Anton and Diego, but they could feel him taking them in at the same time as he studied the obituary column. His name was Ruslan. He was Karina's bodyguard and hitman, and a general legend in the organization.

His tailor-fitted black Brioni suit and gray loafers were his way of trying to replicate Karina's persona of a wolf in sheep's clothing. But some telltale signs pointed to his true nature: like the swirls of tattooed ink curling out from under his cuffs and collar, the mound of battered flesh posing as a nose, or—most noticeably—his right eye, which had been carved out with a prison shiv and replaced by a false one at least three shades darker than his real, pale-blue iris. The truth was, you could dress him up in a clergyman's robes, and you still couldn't disguise who, or what, he really was. Being in a room with him was like being in a cage with a sleeping lion.

Karina took a seat at her desk, which was raised on a foot-high platform, and lit a long, thin cigarette. Anton and Diego remained standing, hands at their sides, like soldiers waiting to receive orders.

"There is a job tonight," she said. "A pickup. And Alex is... indisposed, so I want you," she pointed her cigarette at Anton, "to take his place."

Shit, Anton almost said aloud. It was what he'd been afraid of. Although mere involvement with the organization brought a risk of prison or death, he'd never had to do any of the grunt work, the type of work that puts one in situations where the risk is multiplied exponentially. His father always saw to that.

"A pickup?" he said. "I don't usually do that type of thing."

"Excuse me?" said Karina, her tone suggesting she'd heard just fine.

Anton raised his chin and kept his voice firm. "I said I don't usually go on those types of runs."

She took a drag of her cigarette and studied him with that same flat gaze. "You think I care what you usually do? Or what you want?"

"Well, no, but in New York..."

"This isn't New York!" she barked. "You can't just walk around playing gangster here. You're in LA now—my city. And it's time to get your fucking hands dirty."

Anton quickly considered his options; there was no way he was just going to roll over, but he had to choose his arguments carefully. He took a half step forward, and Ruslan lowered the newspaper slightly, his attention shifting to the conversation.

"I understand I need to put in work," said Anton. "I just feel, with my experience, maybe I could be used better in other areas." He wanted to come off confident and sure, like he was making a simple statement of logic. But there was no mistaking the hint of desperation in his voice, the almost childish, forced attempt at an excuse. Karina heard it, she even smiled at him, a hollow, twisted grin.

"You listen to me, stupid fuck," she said. "You are just a body here. You do as I say. If I want you to lick my boot-heel, that's what you'll do. Do you understand me?"

Ruslan let out a soft chuckle, and a burst of rage tore through Anton's tense body. It was one thing Karina pulling rank and sending him on low-level errands, but it was out of line the way she belittled him like he was nothing. He wanted to let the anger out, to scream that she could *go to fucking hell.* But he wasn't stupid, he knew it wasn't the right time for a confrontation. Standing in her office with Ruslan in the corner, arguing with Karina was like challenging someone to a duel with hand grenades—nothing good would come of it. Instead, he had to be patient, bide his time.

He bowed his head slightly and said, "I understand," then retracted the half-step. Ruslan raised his newspaper to its original height.

Karina stubbed out her cigarette in a crystal ashtray, then shifted her gaze to some of the paperwork on her desk, as though she was no longer interested in the conversation; an indication she was wrapping up.

"The meet is at the same time and location as the last pickup. Come back tonight at midnight; Ruslan will have the van and money waiting."

"Of course," said Diego. Then he nodded to Anton, and they both motioned to leave, but Karina stopped them.

"Oh, one more thing." She looked Anton dead in the eyes. "Don't fuck this up."

17

SCARLETT

By the time Scarlett got to Jimmy's house, she felt wilted and small, as though the last twenty-four hours had aged her significantly. And her anger at the old man's request was still very present, still festering like an infected wound.

But when she saw him waiting at the card table, the pieces on the chessboard untouched from the day before, her emotion moved to pity. He was still just sitting there, waiting to restart the game, a forlorn figure with nothing and no one else in his life. And despite all the craziness going on in hers, it somehow made Scarlett feel lucky.

"Good morning," said Jimmy, hopefully.

"Hello," said Scarlett, her voice flat and lifeless.

He wheeled away from the table, and she set down her bag and began the usual routine in silence. When she got through checking his blood pressure, he looked at her and said, "We need to talk about yesterday."

"Please don't," she said, and instantly regretted talking so close to his face. He would have smelled the alcohol on her breath. But there wasn't any judgment in his eyes. How could there be? Who wouldn't want to drink after the conversation they'd had?

"Look," he said, "I thought about it, and... you were right, I am selfish. I'm sorry for asking that of you, and I won't ask again."

Scarlett placed her equipment back into her bag and stood upright. "Really?"

"I promise. But on one condition." He gestured at the chessboard. "We finish our game."

She held up her palm and twisted her lips around a curt response, but before she could speak, he said, "Please? I just want to forget about last time and pretend we're two regular people having a normal conversation over a game. I know talking doesn't sound like much, but it would truly bring this old man a bit of joy in the short time he has left."

The comment stung Scarlett, and any reason she had to push back dissolved. So she smiled weakly, nodded, and slid into the chair opposite Jimmy.

They played for thirty minutes or so in mostly silence. Jimmy tried asking Scarlett conversational questions about other patients, about her wedding plans, but she didn't give much in the way of a response, avoiding any forced elaborations.

Then, somewhat out of nowhere, he said, "So, Scarlett *Laurent*," emphasizing her last name. "Do you speak French?"

Scarlett glanced down at the ID badge clipped to her scrubs, her name printed at the bottom, the font tight and bold and medical blue. In the tiny photo above the words, her eyes were squinted, and her lips slightly parted, the tranquil expression of someone who'd just been kissed. She'd always hated that photo. It reminded her of that naïve girl that just wanted to be happy. And it reminded her that she still was that girl.

"Only a little," she said finally.

"Me too," Jimmy replied. "*Un petit peu.*"

Scarlett raised her eyebrows and gave him a slight nod of approval, and he seemed to like it.

"So, Jimmy *Francis*, I guess that makes you a good old Irishman, huh?"

"My parents were from Ulster," he said, snagging one of her pawns with his queen. "They moved to Boston just before I was born, like every other Irish couple."

"What were they like?"

"My parents?"

She nodded encouragingly, happy to be talking about him rather than herself for once.

"They were good people, good souls."

Scarlett lifted one of her bishops and motioned to take one of Jimmy's knights, but he cleared his throat and gave her a slight shake of the head. She couldn't see the danger he was referring to, but decided to heed his warning, and took one of his pawns instead.

"So, you grew up in Boston?"

"Oh, Scarlett," said Jimmy. "I really appreciate you making an effort here, it means the world to me. But you don't wanna hear my story. It's not a happy one."

"Sure I do. The best stories aren't the happy ones. They're the real ones. Besides, you're the one who wanted to talk."

He let out a deep, heavy sigh. The type of sigh reserved for old men about to recall a suppressed, mournful moment from the past. He tilted his face up to the ceiling, his eyes going small with memory.

"I was *born* in Boston, but we moved to Vegas when I was a kid. My mother inherited a crappy old pawn shop from an estranged uncle or cousin, or someone, I don't remember. My parent's plan was to head over, sell the place, take the cash, and leave. But my dad, the hopeless romantic that he was, fell in love with the place.

"He didn't know the first thing about running a pawn shop, but he worked his ass off, and over the years, it became his pride and joy. I'd head there straight from school and spend hours examining whatever trinkets, antiques, or sports memorabilia he'd picked up that day. I loved it. By the time I was eleven or twelve, I could estimate the value of anything, from an old Charvel guitar, to an antique seventeenth-century sword, to a two-carat canary diamond engagement ring. We had so much fun. It was *almost* perfect."

Jimmy slid his bishop across and took Scarlett's rook. They were down to the final stretch of the game, only a few pieces left on the board. Scarlett pinched her king between her index and middle fingers, but again Jimmy shook his head, so she released it and moved one of her pawns toward his king.

He smiled, then went on, "The problem was, we inherited more than just the business. With the shop came an old agreement with the kind of people that you wouldn't want agreements with. I still remember my father telling me to run along home whenever they came to the store; enormous, gray men in baggy suits and horn-rimmed glasses. They would smile at me and ruffle my hair, their mouths full of gold molars, and their faces leathery from the Vegas sun. Sometimes they'd even give me a few dollars and say, *you be a good kid now, you hear? You're gonna run this store one day.*

"I was a kid, but I knew who they were. The mob had run Vegas since the early fifties, and they had so much money coming in, they were running out of places to launder it. So they'd turn to small cash business owners. I never judged my father, even though he probably took a small cut. Not when saying *no* meant a bullet."

Jimmy paused for a moment as if considering whether to go on, so Scarlett leaned in and said, "What happened?"

He sighed. "Well, that's the sad part. The last time I saw my father talking to men in suits, it was at our house instead of the shop. And those men were thinner, paler, and lacked the charisma of the mob guys. I remember hearing raised voices and sneaking downstairs to find those men in my living room. I don't remember exactly what they were saying, but my mom was crying, and my dad was hugging her, and I remember knowing it was bad. I later realized they were FBI agents, offering my father another deal he couldn't refuse.

"A few days later, I stayed at a friend's house after baseball practice, and when I got dropped home in the morning, I found both my parents murdered in their own bed. There was blood everywhere, splattered up the headboard, across the white curtains. My mother's eyes were still open, like she was searching for the life that'd been pulled from her. I was terrified, of course. I figured whoever did it would have killed me too, if I'd been home. And the last people my parents spoke to were wearing badges, so I didn't know who to trust.

"So I stuffed a backpack full of clothes, collected my life savings from a tin can under my bed, and ran away. I ran and ran until I found myself at a Greyhound bus station four miles from my house. I hopped on the first bus I saw, and it happened to be going to Los Angeles."

The muscles in Jimmy's face tightened, as if a liquid pain had seeped in and solidified.

"I got on that bus to find safety. *Safety*," he repeated, and let out a laugh; a curt, bitter one. "A thirteen-your-old orphan, alone in LA. Words like *naïve, ironic*... just don't quite cut it."

Then his eyes went vacant for a moment, no doubt replaying the countless tortures his child-self had been subject to. It was Scarlett's misfortune to have seen dozens of old men break down, overwhelmed by sadness, either over their impending fate or that of their spouse. But sitting there, watching him as that mask of pain slipped over his face, it broke a piece of her. A piece that, until then, she wasn't sure truly existed. That poor man who'd been through more than she could ever really know and still had more to come.

Scarlett wiped the tears welling in her eyes with the back of her hand, and Jimmy said, "I'm sorry. I told you it was sad."

"It's okay. I'm glad you told me, and I... I'm sorry about your parents."

"Yeah. Me too."

A somber silence fell on the room for a moment, both of them a little exhausted from the story. Then, in what seemed an attempt to lighten the mood, Jimmy nodded at the board and said, "Go ahead. It's your turn."

Scarlett glanced down, and it became instantly clear just how well he'd been guiding her through the game. She slowly slid her queen to corner his king, then she looked up, and he flashed her a joyful, proud, yet pained smile, and said, "Checkmate."

For reasons she didn't fully understand, a hurricane of emotions tore through her and tears flooded her eyes. The sadness, the guilt, the self-loathing, and self-pity, all cascading down upon her. She quickly stood up and took three steps toward the door, not really knowing what she was doing, then stopped and hung her head.

"Scarlett, are you okay?"

She just stood there a moment, a hunched statue. Then she wiped her tears again and muttered something under her breath so softly she wasn't sure she'd even really said it. Something her brain was thinking, but her ears weren't ready to hear.

"What?" said Jimmy. "I couldn't hear you."

Scarlett turned back to him and looked into his eyes. Her usual self, so unsure and indecisive, sank into darkness. For the first time in years, she allowed herself to follow her instincts.

She took a deep breath. "I'll do it."

18

LUCA

The orange sun was dying behind the rooftops as dusk crept over the busy city. Luca dropped the bike in the parking lot, took a shower, then put on the new boots, jeans, and shirt he'd picked up on the way back. With his Beretta tucked into the small of his back, he left the motel on foot and weaved through the back alleys and side streets. Hookers and addicts appeared on corners and in doorways like nocturnal insects coming out to feed. He was heading toward the Vanilla Club—the place he hoped to find Benny Gums.

Benny was the only person who might be able to help take care of Jimmy. But it was a risk going to see him, because Luca had no idea what Benny knew about the heist, or how his little brother Casey had died. Considering Benny hadn't come for Luca in prison, one had to assume he didn't know shit. But he still wouldn't be happy to see Luca; not when he'd talked Casey into coming on the job that got him killed.

The Vanilla Club had been renovated since Luca's last visit, but it still looked like every other strip joint around—pulsing neon lights above blacked-out windows with posters of girls in bikinis; the promise of paradise for sale. Two truck-sized bouncers in black trench coats stood near the entrance, one bald and one in a red wool hat. The guy in the hat was yelling at a homeless man who was scrounging through a mound of cigarette butts near the curb as if he'd misplaced a winning lottery ticket down there.

"I told you to get the fuck out of here," the bouncer in the hat said.

"I got a right to be on the sidewalk," said the homeless guy. "You don't own the sidewalk."

The bouncer stepped over to him, said, "The hell I don't," then kicked him in the ass, sending him face planting into the road. Then the sentry dutifully returned to his post as the homeless guy struggled to his feet, yelled, "Fuck you," then limped off into the night.

As Luca got to the door, the bald bouncer reached out his hand and said, "ID, sir."

"What, are you shitting me?" said Luca.

If the bouncer *was* shitting him, he didn't show it. He just stared back with charged bloodshot eyes. The eyes of a man amped up on cocaine and steroids, ready to show the world just how tough he was.

"I look under twenty-one to you, pal?"

The guy with the hat moved to a back-up position beside his partner. "There a problem here?"

"You better hope not, cupcake," said Luca. "I wanna see the boss. I wanna see Benny."

The bouncers exchanged nervous looks—probably assuming Luca was a cop—then the guy in the hat turned his back and spoke quietly into his radio. A few minutes later, the familiar face of Tony appeared in the entryway behind the bouncers.

Tony was enormous—perhaps the biggest man Luca had

ever known—with deadpan eyes, a low-hanging jaw, and a broad frame that made the two bouncers look like fifth graders.

"Tony," Luca said with a smirk. "How's it hanging, big guy?"

It was a busy night in the Vanilla Club. At least thirty *customers* were sitting under flashing lights, whistling and cheering as a girl with a sleeve tattoo worked the stage. Rap music vibrated through the building, and the smells of liquor and cheap cologne chased each other around the room like flies in a jar.

A busty waitress with a tray of empty beer bottles crossed their path as Tony led Luca through the club, toward a door labeled "*Staff only.*" Tony held the door open, and Luca walked through first to a narrow hallway that looked like a giant's artery—red fluorescent lights shone on crimson walls and the painted concrete floor. The hallway ran from the club to the back rooms, one of which was Benny's office. It was designed to be a tight space to avoid large groups of people—cops—from flooding in at once.

Suddenly, Tony's huge hands were spinning Luca around to face the wall. Luca had expected to be searched, so he went along with it, spreading his legs wide and letting his palms fall flush. As Tony patted him down, Luca craned his head and said, "This how you greet all your old friends?"

A door a few feet down the hallway opened, and a short guy with a polka-dot bowtie appeared in the opening. The squawking of high-pitched voices came from behind Bowtie, and Luca saw through the cloud of hairspray and cigarette smoke that it was the girl's dressing room. A couple girls were touching up their makeup in front of the grubby, scratched mirror, while another straightened out scrunched dollar bills on the countertop. None of them so much as glanced at Luca.

Bowtie let the dressing room door close behind him and

stepped over to join Tony just as he located the Beretta at the small of Luca's back. He handed it to Bowtie without a word, then worked his way down Luca's left leg, then his right. When he was finished, he grabbed Luca's shoulder with his catcher's mitt of a hand and spun him back around. Luca glanced at Bowtie and gave him a *you satisfied?* look, but he didn't react. He looked young, maybe only twenty. Tony's *protégé*.

Tony squatted down slightly, so his eyes were level with Luca's, and Luca puckered his lips. In return, Tony plunged his hand down the front of Luca's pants and began rummaging around.

"Woah, what the fuck, man?" said Luca. "Not with the new guy watching."

Bowtie grinned, but Tony's face remained like stone, his bear-like brown eyes narrowing as he felt around Luca's testicles and penis.

"Look," said Luca, getting agitated, "I appreciate the vote of confidence. But, my package ain't big enough to hide another piece underneath. So why don't you get your fucking hand out of there before we have a problem?"

"I'm not looking for a gun," Tony said as he pulled his hand out. "I'm looking for a wire."

"A wire?"

Tony held his hand in the direction of Bowtie, who produced a tiny bottle of hand sanitizer and squirted some into Tony's palm.

"A wire?" Luca repeated. "What are you trying to say?"

"You still got a chip on your shoulder, huh?" said Tony, rubbing in the clear gel. "I thought all that time away would have changed you."

Luca smiled. "Yeah, well, I ain't ever gonna stop flirting with you, big boy."

If the hallway was an artery, Benny's office was the heart—a big red room, with red leather couches, mirrored-glass coffee tables, and gold accents everywhere. Benny was sitting at his desk when they entered, reading glasses perched on his nose, peering down at a stack of papers only slightly shorter than the tree it was cut from. He was wearing a navy-blue suit jacket with a white, open-collared shirt and no jewelry. Almost the exact opposite of the leopard print silk and six gold chains he used to wear before Luca went away. He looked up from the paperwork with a face devoid of menace, or warmth, or hate, or any emotion at all. And Luca wasn't sure if he was ready to shake his hand and welcome him back, or shoot him.

"They finally let you out, huh?" Benny said.

"Yep," said Luca. "Good behavior."

"That right?"

Bowtie stepped forward and handed the Beretta to Benny, who smiled at it, and tucked it in a drawer under his desk. Then he turned his smile to Luca, a smile of pure gold against his dark skin. Benny got the name *Gums* after he crossed a group of Albanians and they pulled out every tooth in his head with a pair of pliers. Benny walked around for two years with bare gums like a baby while he plotted his revenge. But he finally caught up with them, and when he did, not one of them lived. Benny was just a small-time pimp back then, but the story got around. And when he got the implants, that row of pure gold reminded people of what happened if you fucked with him.

But now, sitting at his desk, reading through papers in his crisp suit, the gold looked childish, even borderline pathetic.

He gestured to the empty chair facing his desk. "Take a seat."

Luca sat, and neither of them spoke for a full twenty seconds, the silence thick with anticipation. Luca thought, *Screw it*, and decided to address the elephant in the room; if

Benny did hold him responsible for his brother's death, then so be it.

"Hey, look, I'm sorry about Casey. He was a good kid."

Something twitched in Benny's eyes, but the emotion was too subtle to place, and when he spoke next, his voice was soft, even curious. "Ya know," he slipped off his reading glasses and placed them on the desk, "he didn't even tell me he was going on that job. You know how I found out?"

Luca shook his head.

"Some cops picked me up and took me in for questioning, thinking I was involved somehow. After like twenty hours of telling them I didn't know shit, this one fucking detective—Grimes, I think his name was—he tosses a photograph of a burned body in front of me, tells me it's Casey. First, I think he's lying, right? Plus he won't let me have my phone call. But then my lawyer comes in, tells me the cop's telling the truth. They found Casey burned to a fucking crisp, said the fire was started with gasoline, and they found a bullet in his gut."

Benny paused, as if waiting for Luca to provide an explanation, but all he said was, "Yeah, it's messed up."

Benny glanced down at the paperwork on his desk, then fixed his gaze back on Luca. "You know what I kept asking myself back then?... *Why*?"

"Why what?"

"Why did he do it? I had money, he didn't need to go on that job, or any job." His eyes shifted to the empty space beside his desk, as if the ghost of his dead brother might be standing there, ready to answer his questions. "Maybe it was my fault. Maybe I was a bad brother." He turned back to Luca with searching eyes. "You think I'm a bad brother, Luca?"

It must have been seventy-five degrees in that room, but it felt like a block of ice had melted on Luca's spine.

"I think the kid was trying to be his own man," he said. "Step out from your shadow, make you proud."

"Think so, huh?"

Benny's face was still unreadable, and with Bowtie and Tony still standing at the back of the room, Luca didn't like his odds of getting out if things went south. But after another tense silence, Benny exhaled slowly and said, "Truth is, you can't dwell on shit like that. You gotta make peace and move on. Nobody can change the past—not even God."

Luca's body relaxed, and only then did he realize he'd been tensed, ready for an attack from behind.

"So, there ain't no bad blood between us?" he said. "You know, because of that night."

Benny flashed a look of genuine confusion, like Luca had just asked what his star sign was. "If there was, you think you'd be sat there right now?"

Luca looked back, and both Bowtie and Tony flashed malicious smiles.

"I guess not."

Benny reached into his desk drawer, producing a bottle of Blue Label and a couple of whiskey glasses. He poured two fingers of the golden liquid into each glass and slid one across to Luca. "It's good to see you out, man."

Luca took the glass, raised it. "To Casey."

"To Casey," Benny repeated, and they both inhaled their drinks.

The shot burned its way down Luca's throat and settled in his stomach like a flare in a barrel. It was the first time he'd tasted alcohol since before his arrest, not counting the toilet brewed prison hooch.

Benny slammed his glass on the desk and said, "Another," and Luca thought about his PO's warning about the drug and alcohol testing.

Fuck that pencil-pushing prick, he thought. No way Larry —*awesome to meet you*—Pratt was going to write him up for some whiskey, at least not before trying to council him first.

After pounding the second shot, Benny wiped his mouth with his sleeve. "They treat you okay up there?"

"Well enough."

"Anderson still the warden?"

"No, it's a guy called Silverman."

Benny grunted, picked up a pen and jotted down the name on a post-it note.

"How's business?" Luca asked.

Benny beamed a smile and spread his arms wide, signifying his empire. "Business is booming. Got myself two more clubs in LA," he pointed at the stack of paper on his desk, "and about to sign the lease on a new one over in Vegas. That one's gonna be a money machine, let me tell you."

"Good to hear."

Benny poured another drink. But this time he sipped from the glass instead of shooting it, and Luca almost thanked him. All those years of forced sobriety, he wasn't sure how many two-finger shots of room temperature whiskey he could take.

"So, you came to ask me about business, or is there something I can help you with?"

"Hopefully, the latter."

"I'm listening."

Luca shifted in his seat. "I need help. With a job."

"A job? You shitting me, right? That last one got my brother killed and you serving a dub, and now you come in here talking about a new one?"

"It ain't like that. It's not that sort of job."

"Then what is it?"

Luca looked back at Bowtie, and Benny said, "He's cool. You ain't gotta worry about him. Spit it out, what do ya need?"

Luca leaned in and spoke in a hushed tone, "It's a hit."

Benny laughed. "Shit, Luca, you got work already? How long you been out, like a week?"

"Two days."

He laughed some more and slapped his desk with his palm. "God damn, man. You always were a crazy son of a bitch."

"So, can you help me?"

"I haven't seen you in all this time, and the first thing you do is ask me to hit someone for you? Come on, man."

"Look, I had to come to you. I've got no one else to go to."

"I can't help you, man."

"You can't, or you won't?"

"A bit of both, I guess." Benny finished off his drink and stared at the empty glass, as if admiring the craftsmanship. "Truth is, times have changed since you went away. The cops cracked down on organized crime in a big way while you were inside. Flipping people left and right. Got niggas I've known my whole life turning state witness."

"That's why pretty boy was searching me for a wire?"

"Can never be too careful nowadays. Shit, they almost got me at least five times. I'm lucky I wasn't up in the pen with you. But it's different now, I'm nearly all the way legitimate. And this Vegas club, it's gonna change the game, baby. I can't let anything jeopardize that. You understand? I've worked too damn hard."

"You're legitimate?" Luca said with a chuckle. "You still sell pussy to tricks whether they're fucking or not."

"I provide a service," said Benny. "Just like a burger joint or a laundromat; people need this."

"They need it?"

"Hell yeah, they do. Shit, we're always so quick to talk about how females are the ones driven by their emotions and hormones. Yet night after night, guys come in here and hand over their hard-earned cash to feel the purely artificial wanting of a woman. They know what this place is. No wool's been pulled over their eyes. But they still come here because it satisfies their needs. It's supply and demand, man, like any other business. And I'm a businessman. I mean, you tell me how else a brother supposed to get ahead in this city."

Benny's self-righteous tone was like that of a man who hadn't sold drugs and rented women and killed people, and Luca wasn't sure if he was trying to convince himself more than anyone else. That's how Luca found a lot of cons were, especially in prison. Always trying to shift responsibility and point fingers or blame circumstances.

But not Luca. He knew what he was, and he embraced it.

Benny poured yet another drink. "Look, you want some advice? Let it go, man. Whatever it is, just let it go. We're too old for that crazy shit."

Luca squeezed his glass so tightly his knuckles turned white, and he thought it might shatter right there in his hand. "I'm sick of people telling me what I'm too old to do."

"Truth hurts, man. We're dinosaurs, you and me. The last remnants of a different time."

Luca sipped the whiskey and let it sit in his mouth, burning the tender flesh on the inside of his cheeks.

He figured there was only one way he could get Benny to help him. One thing he could try, one thing he could say.

19

LUCA

Luca swallowed the mouthful of burning whiskey he'd been savoring, and stared into Benny Gums's eyes, the bright red office turning fuzzy in his peripheral. "The guy I want you to hit. It's Jimmy."

Benny gave a bemused look. "What?"

"The hit, it's on Jimmy."

"Bullshit. He's *been* gone."

"Well, he's back."

"So, what? That doesn't mean shit to me, anyway. I told you all that shit is in the past."

Luca leaned in to the desk and added a hint of drama to his voice. "That night, it was fucked from the get-go. Jimmy planned it all, then he left me in jail and your brother dead."

"What you tryin' to say?

"I didn't see the cop shoot Casey, and when I got to the car, he was already unconscious. I wanted to drop him at the hospital, but Jimmy... he wouldn't do it." Luca paused for effect. "By the time we got to the lot, Casey was already dead."

Benny's eyes narrowed, the image of his brother's murdered body no doubt flashing across his mind.

"Jimmy insisted on burning the body to slow down the cops. Then, after I got arrested, it got me thinking... maybe it was Jimmy who shot Casey."

Benny shook his head slowly. "I knew Jimmy. He was a crook and a thief, but he was no killer."

"He was a rat that put me away for twenty-five years so he could take the money. You think he wouldn't bump off your kid brother for his cut? Hell, even if he didn't shoot Casey, you think he didn't have plans to get him locked up too? The whole job was a fucking set up."

Luca could almost see the cogs turning behind Benny's eyes, a scenario he hadn't even considered before. The slightest hint of revenge fluttered across his face, and then, in an instant, it was gone.

"Look," he said, "even if you're right, I told you I can't do anything that'll jeopardize what I'm building. Not over some shit that *might* have happened twenty-five years ago."

Luca shifted in his seat, and his anger boiled over. "So you're gonna do nothing? What the fuck is wrong with you. That was your brother!"

Tony took a step forward, but Benny raised a hand in his direction and nodded, telling him to be cool.

"Hey, we go back a long time," said Benny, "and I can't even imagine how pissed off I'd be after doing a quarter because of some rat. So I'll forgive you for coming into my office and shooting your mouth off. But this is the only time I'm gonna do that, you hear? Now, I'm going to say it clearly so you understand: I am *not* going to help you—got it? I've told you what I think you should do, take it or leave it. But..." He reached down to his desk drawer, pulled out Luca's Beretta, and slapped it on the desk between them. "You wanna kill that motherfucker so bad, go do it yourself."

Luca slowly reached over for the gun, but Benny picked it up, released the clip, and emptied each bullet one by one. When the gun was empty, he tossed it to Luca who caught it in his left hand.

Benny smiled his golden smile and winked. "As I said, can never be too careful."

Luca took the gun, downed his drink, and stormed out of Benny's office and through the artery hallway, which seemed to tilt and move, courtesy of the whiskey. He'd planned to leave the club and head back to the motel, but as he reached the bar area, he thought, *Screw it, one for the road.*

As the bartender poured his drink, a Dewers on the rocks, Luca took a seat on a barstool and glanced over at the blonde girl working the stage. Her back was against the pole, long tanned legs zigzagging down to a pair of sequined heels, the neon club lights pulsating off her body. A weedy guy in the front row threw down a couple of bills, and the girl dropped to her haunches and began thrusting her hips in front of his face. The guy's eyes were wide with lust, his grin even wider, giving the girl his best—*you want some of this*—look, as if he'd just picked her up at a bar. She smiled and licked her lips, but there was something dead and robotic about her gaze; the vacant eyes of a doll.

It made Luca think of Benny and his blasé responses and lack of action, like the fire in his gut had been put out with a bag of sand. That goddamn pussy. If that were Luca's brother, he'd kill anyone that happened to be on the same block at the time, just in case they had something to do with it.

Or was Benny right, and the times had changed? Is that why men came to the Vanilla Club, because it's one of the few places left where they can openly express their animalistic urge for a visceral connection? He'd seen how people acted now, walking around like they weren't the same species that lived off instincts not long ago. Like they didn't still have those same urges to hunt and fuck and kill.

Luca still had those urges. Now it was time to act on them.

When he was halfway through his drink, Luca noticed Bowtie appear at his side.

"Fuck do you want?" he said over the thumping music.

"Benny wanted me to tell you that there's no hard feelings. He wanted me to bring you a gift. To celebrate you getting out."

"Oh yeah?"

Bowtie waved at someone behind Luca. Luca turned to find a stunning brunette walking toward them. She stopped about six inches from Luca's face and said, "Hi," throwing a few extra I's on the end of the word.

Bowtie looked at the girl. "Natasha, this is an old friend of Benny's. I want you to take care of him."

She smiled. "He's handsome."

She must have been new because her eyes bore no sign of the doll-like inertness that lived in the eyes of the blonde on stage. This girl was bright and sparky, full of life.

Bowtie leaned into Luca's ear. "She can suck the cork out of a wine bottle this one. Have fun."

A finger of excitement touched Luca as he stared into the girl's eyes, the club just a blur behind her. He *was* going to have fun.

Natasha led him to one of the private rooms with white leather couches that stank of crotch and cleaning solution. He placed the Beretta on a side table and took a seat as a new song blasted out of the speakers. It was more angry rap with a slow beat and heavy bass, but Natasha sure seemed to like it. Her hips swayed to the beat as she untied her bikini top and dropped it to the floor. Her perfectly round breasts were held in place by tight young skin, and just above her navel was the subtle hint of abs. It was an athlete's body, the body of a dancer.

She placed her knee between Luca's thighs and rubbed her breasts in his face, her pink nipples grazing his cheekbones. Then she leaned down, her cherry-scented lips brushing Luca's ear and whispered, "I'm gonna take really good care of you." Nimble fingers unhooked his belt, and her breath descended his neck.

At that moment, vulnerable to the touch of a young goddess about to please him in ways he hadn't felt in a lifetime, Benny's words, Brooks's words, Hooper's words all flashed across the drunken haze of his brain. Suddenly, all he could think about was Jimmy.

He could see the smug face Jimmy must have worn after he was arrested. The same smug face he was probably still wearing now. Luca saw himself on death row, two guards walking him down the grainy narrow hallway toward the electric chair, both of them laughing like a couple of hyenas, eyes wide and mouths frothing. And then he enters the chamber and sees the only person in the viewing room, the only one who'd come to see him fry: Jimmy, his mouth twisted, smug face in all its glory.

Natasha lifted her head and looked at Luca, his limp penis in her left hand, her oversized eyelashes fluttering over liquid sapphire eyes. "What's the matter, baby? You don't think I'm sexy?"

A dizzying wave of anger swept through Luca's body like the venom of a viper, and he was suddenly on his feet, sending the girl flying back onto the floor.

"What the hell?" she said, grabbing her bikini top and covering up. "What's your problem?"

Luca re-zipped his pants. "No, you're not sexy. You're a dirty whore."

She clambered to her feet. "It ain't my fault you can't get hard. You're just a pathetic old man."

His stare bored into her, fire in his eyes and hands balled into fists. She clambered to her feet and matched his stare, not backing down, her defiant stance daring him to hurt her. But even in his drunken state, Luca didn't take the bait. Before letting himself turn her beautiful face into a red mush, he grabbed his gun and stormed out of there.

During the walk back to the motel, the streets were deserted, like a 1940s European town after an air raid warning. Luca marched along the sidewalk, past graffiti-covered store shutters and burned-out trash cans. Anger, shame, and hate bubbled inside him like a vat of oil over a blue flame. The streets may have been empty and silent, but the voices in his head were deafening.

Maybe they're right, he thought. *Maybe I don't have what it takes anymore. Maybe I am just an old man. Maybe I'm nothing.*

He turned onto the narrow alleyway that cut across the last three blocks to the motel, glass from a hundred broken beer bottles crunching under his feet. It was dark, the only light coming from the few building security lights which hung low on the walls above the rear of the buildings, creating long spans of blackness. Through the corner of his eye, Luca saw a shadow shift, as if it were alive, like a fluid, black demon. The shadow took the shape of a man dressed in all black, his messy beard and yellow, bloodshot eyes the only thing visible. Luca stopped walking, but he didn't speak, he didn't make a sound.

The mugger lifted his arm and brandished a three-inch switchblade, the thin steel glinting under the security lights. They both stood there in silence for a moment, taking in the situation, sizing each other up, the few seconds of calm before what came next.

Then, in a scratchy tweaker's voice, the man said, "Empty your pockets. I want it all."

"That right?" said Luca.

"I ain't playing with you. Do it now."

The corner of Luca's mouth raised into a smirk. "I don't think so."

He reached to the small of his back and pulled out the empty Beretta, letting it hang by his side. Even in the darkness, he saw the mugger's eyes widen, his pupils flicking from Luca's face to the gun and back.

"Look-a-here," Luca said. "Seems you brought a knife to a gunfight. I always wanted to say that." He chuckled, then let the smirk fade. "Drop it."

The mugger backed up a half step. "Hey, man, look, I'm sorry..."

But Luca cocked the hammer back. "Drop it!"

"Okay, okay."

The mugger bent down and placed the knife on the concrete, then raised back up slowly. His hunched posture and darting eyes told of his intentions of running, probably hoping Luca wouldn't shoot him in the back, or maybe hoping he would miss. Luca looked the guy up and down, and he saw a vulture, lurking in the shadows, trying to pick the meat off people's bones. Maybe he'd been watching, maybe he knew where Luca was staying, maybe he knew everything. He couldn't get away with what he'd done—not a chance.

Luca stepped forward and slapped the guy behind the ear with the butt of the gun, the crack of metal on bone ripping through the alley. The mugger stumbled sideways, the blow providing him with his own personal earthquake, then he spun around wildly with flailing arms. Luca grabbed him and threw him against one of the buildings. They struggled for a moment, all forearms and elbows as the mugger tried to grab the gun. He was a few inches taller than Luca, but his long limbs grew weak and tired under Luca's weight. Luca drove his forehead into the middle of the guy's face, and the guy's nose exploded, blood spurting in every direction. Luca headbutted him again and again and again, the sound of boots slapping against wet mud. When the guy's body went limp in his arms, Luca dropped him to his hands and knees and drove his shin into his ribs. The mugger wheezed and gasped for air, blood dripping from his face onto the concrete.

"You like that?" said Luca. "That feel good?"

He didn't even look around to see if anyone was watching, adrenaline coursing through his veins, making him feel alive—making him feel like a man. He reached into the guy's pants pocket and pulled out a brown leather wallet. He ignored the cards, pocketed the forty-two dollars in cash—the irony of the mugger becoming the mugged not lost on him—then pulled out the guy's driver's license. The guy's name was *Marshal Teal*, and he looked a lot younger and healthier in the photo. Luca pocketed the license, then searched the inside flaps of the wallet where he found a passport-size photo of a young girl, no more than five, with plump rosy cheeks and blonde bangs. *She looks happy*, Luca thought. Maybe too happy to belong to the beaten scum wheezing at his feet. He kicked Marshal in the ribs again, then lowered the photo to where he could see. "Who is this?"

Marshal groaned and looked at the photo but didn't speak. Luca kicked him again and said, "Who is this, you fucking cockroach?"

He choked out a response, his words fast and desperate, "It's my daughter. Please, man. I'm sorry."

"No. Not yet. But you will be."

Luca kicked him again, this time in his stomach, and the guy vomited onto the concrete, some of the yellowish bile splatting onto Luca's shoe.

Luca yelled, "You filthy bastard," wiped his shoe on Marshal's pant leg, then tossed the photograph into the pile of vomit. "Look at her, you stupid fuck. You're never going to see her again."

Marshal started begging through a mouthful of blood, and Luca brought the butt of the gun down on the back of his head, the sound like a coconut cracking under a hammer. His body fell limp to the floor, and Luca stepped back and took a deep breath of the night air.

Luca knew what he'd done was stupid and risky, but he didn't care—not at all. Because those voices, that self-doubt, it had all evaporated. And he was hard as a rock.

20

ANTON

"Where the hell are they?" said Anton.

"Relax, my man," said Diego from the driver's seat. "They'll be here."

"This is bullshit," snapped Anton, checking his phone, "they're almost an hour late. They're not coming."

They were parked up on a hillside, on a dirt road in the dead of night, the only light coming from their dipped headlights and the distant twinkle of the city skyline to their right.

"They're coming," Diego said. "You try smuggling that much shit across the border and see what kind of time *you* make."

A few more minutes went by, and Anton's anxiousness crept toward panic. He was exactly where he didn't want to be: two hours south of the city in the middle of nowhere, in a piece of shit van filled with dirty bills, waiting for some goddamn banditos. He was used to doing business in New York, in offices and warehouses and high-rises, and now he was up on some ridge in the dark like a cowboy, totally exposed.

"We need to get out of here, man," he said, barely masking

his acute sense of desperation. "What if they were caught? There could be cops on their way up this hill right now."

Diego shot him a glance that told him he was considering it. Up on the hillside, away from the chaos of the city, the still night air was heavy with anticipation that only seemed to be accentuated by the constant chirping of the surrounding crickets. Diego looked straight ahead for a moment, then his right hand found the key resting in the ignition, and he opened his mouth to speak, froze for a beat, then said, "They're here."

Anton squinted through the windshield, but all he could see were flurries of dirt floating by the headlights like specs of brown snow over the blackness beyond.

"Where? I don't see shit."

"They're here, trust me."

After a few more seconds, a boxy shape formed on the edge of the darkness, quickly revealing itself as a pickup truck. Then a second shape formed—another truck. The reason they weren't visible sooner was that both vehicles had their lights off, navigating the winding dirt road by memory or GPS or some Mexican psychic voodoo.

The trucks pulled up beside each other and parked. The truck on the left flashed its lights once.

Diego said, "Be careful, Anton. These real slippery guys."

"What do you mean?"

"I mean, these just delivery men. They risk their ass and get paid shit. They may have crazy ideas of taking this van full of money and starting a new life in America, you understand?"

"Oh, shit."

"Relax, my man. Just stay frosty." He grabbed the door handle. "Let's do this."

They climbed out of the van and Anton tried to squint through the darkness, his heart beating overtime. All four doors of the pickup trucks opened and six men climbed out, their shadowy frames barely lit by the van's headlights, the long noses of automatic rifles hanging by their sides.

Diego called out, "You're late," but the men didn't reply, and a long tense silence ensued. Then suddenly, one of the truck's light bar flicked on and Diego and Anton were blinded in a haze of white. Anton quickly raised his hand to face level, but the light seeped through the gaps in his fingers, a full-frontal attack on his eyes.

"What the fuck?" Diego barked.

Three or four, fast, high-pitched voices began talking over each other in Spanish. Then there was the unmistakable sound of one of the rifles being cocked.

"Woah, whoa!" Anton screamed. "Don't shoot, don't shoot."

He looked over to Diego who was shielding his face from the light with one hand, his other hand reaching for the small of his back. "Don't pull your gun," said Anton. "They'll kill us both."

But Diego ignored the warning and kept reaching.

The shrieking rose another few octaves, and another gun was cocked, and Anton figured they were dead. Everything seemed to move in slow motion; his body simultaneously tensed and loosened as air left his lungs.

Then a man called out in a sing-song voice, "Who the fuck is he, man? I don't know this gringo."

Anton looked to Diego who froze, his hand firmly clasped around the handle of his Desert Eagle. "What?"

The voice called back, "You didn't mention any new guys, man. I don't know him."

"You making a joke on me?" yelled Diego. "He is one of our guys."

"How do we know?" the voice yelled.

"Because if he was DEA, there would be cops all over this

hill. Now turn those fucking lights off before you bring more attention on us."

The Spanish chatter began again, but this time the voices were calmer and slower.

Then, after a few seconds, the light cut out, and Anton tried to fight off the cloud of white still occupying his retinas. He heard the shuffle of feet and gained his sight back just in time to see a short Hispanic man with a pompadour haircut extend his hand to Diego. "I'm sorry, man. The guys, they get a little... nervous, eh."

"Yeah, well," Diego said, "The cops are probably sending out a helicopter thanks to your light show."

"It's okay, *pendejo*. The rocks and trees block the light on this side. They can only see the light from the road." The man jerked his thumb at Anton. "Who's the new guy?"

"This is Anton. Anton, this is Elvis. Our man on the other side of the border."

"Elvis?" said Anton, the tremor in his voice betraying him.

"That's right," said Elvis. "You know, like the king, eh."

Elvis was barely five foot four with skin like leather and a diamond encrusted front tooth that looked like it had come from a swap-meet. He held out his hand, and as Anton shook it, shadowy figures appeared behind him, moving from the trucks to the van, each of them carrying a large brown box, their feet shuffling in the dirt. They were kids, with soft-featured young faces, but eyes that seemed borrowed from older, more tortured souls.

Elvis yelled, "*Rapido, rapido,*" at them. Then he looked at Diego. "So, amigo, you got my fucking money, man?"

Anton's heart still raced as they cruised under the yellow street lights along Gopher Canyon Road, heading toward Highway

76, the back of the van filled with seventy kilos of as-close-to-pure black tar heroin as you could buy. But, despite being sent on such a bullshit job, he still basked in the sense of achievement, if only just from walking away with his life.

Even Diego slapped the dash a few times and said, "Holy shit, those Mexicans are cuckoo. I got a little nervous back there."

"Yeah, no shit."

"You should have seen your face, my guy. I thought you were going to faint like a little girl."

"Bullshit. I knew we had it under control."

Diego snickered. "Sure, you did."

"Since when have we been dealing with the cartels, anyway?" Anton asked.

"Since El Chapo was extradited to the US."

Anton flashed him a confused look from the driver seat. He'd insisted on driving; Diego drove too slowly, and Anton was desperate to get off that ridge, to get home.

"Well, as soon as he got sentenced, all hell broke loose in Mexico. The government tried to cripple the drug trade by taking out the head of the most powerful cartel. But they don't get it, man. They don't understand that when you cut the head off a snake, sometimes it doesn't die; three more heads just grow in its place."

"So more cartels popped up?"

"That's right. And as the big players like the Sinaloa and Jalisco cartels fought over the trade routes, little guys like Elvis and the Cabroca cartel expanded."

Anton swung a right onto East Vista Way, a dark two-lane road that led down to the Highway.

"But why didn't we buy off the big cartels before?"

"They already have distributors set up here, guy. And besides, they only sell to other Mexicans. Elvis and the Cabrocas, they don't care who they sell to, as long as the buyer has cash. They're even willing to bring the product all the way up here."

Despite the hatred Anton felt for Karina, he had to give it to her; even with Nicholai locked up in Moscow, she was still running the organization with extreme efficiency, establishing trade routes and making new business connections with groups that were previously considered unreachable.

Diego shifted in his seat, then took the aux cable resting in the cup holder and connected it to his phone. After a few moments, the car was enveloped by the guttural screams of a Russian heavy metal band, the song so raw and angry Anton felt like he was being violated somehow.

He turned the volume way down and said, "What the hell is this shit?"

"What? You don't like music?"

"I know music," said Anton, "and this ain't it."

Diego rolled his eyes. "You're soft, you know that?"

"Fuck you." Anton flicked the audio source to the radio, found 102.7. *Gold On The Ceiling* by Black Keys was in its opening riff. He bobbed his head and smiled. "Now, this is music, my friend."

Diego waved a dismissive hand. "This? You're too American. You forget your roots."

He flicked the source back to the aux, and the snarl of guitar chords and the roaring of voices assaulted Anton's eardrums once again. Diego began roaring along to the song, his palms facing up, with an intense focus in his face like he was trying to raise someone from the dead.

Anton shook his head, flicking it back to the Black Keys, and that's when he noticed them; the blue-and-red lights dancing in the side-view mirror. He'd been too busy fighting Diego on the music to spot them sooner.

"Come on," said Diego, "We need to toughen you up." He reached out for the source button, but Anton quickly switched the stereo off.

"We've got a squad car behind us," he said. "They're lighting us up."

Diego glanced down at the side-view mirror on his side, then sank down in his seat, as if that would somehow make him invisible to them.

"What the fuck should we do?" said Anton. "Do we try and run?"

"In this?"

"Shit!" yelled Anton, gripping the steering wheel until his knuckles turned white.

"Just relax. You probably have a taillight out. No way they can know where we've come from. Just pull over, but be ready."

Anton slowly pulled the van over next to the gravel embankment abutting the road and stopped. The cops stopped about twenty feet behind them and stayed in the car, probably running the license plate number through their computer. Anton suddenly became very aware of just how quiet the road was. There were no other vehicles on the road but theirs and the one behind them—the one occupied by two armed officers itching to get the next big arrest that would land them on the front page of the Los Angeles Times. He tried to look casual as he stared at them through the mirror, but beads of sweat were forming at his hairline and making a break for his face. He made a decision there and then that he would shoot his way out if he had to. But he prayed it wouldn't come to that.

"Is this van clean?" he asked.

"Of course," said Diego, although he sounded far from certain. "But..."

He slipped his Desert Eagle from behind his back and

rested it under his right thigh. Anton followed suit and placed his pistol under his seat.

A few seconds later, both doors of the squad car flung open, and the cops climbed out in perfect synchronicity. It was two men, one big and bulky, the other thin and wiry. As they walked toward the van, the twin beams of an approaching car's headlights rounded the bend fifty feet further down the road.

The cops stopped walking, looking at each other as if they'd forgotten something in the car.

"What are they doing?" said Anton

"What?" Diego adjusted to get a better look through his mirror.

The headlights, and the car it belonged to, cruised past them, and the cops began moving again, their heads low, faces shadowed under flat-brimmed police hats. It wasn't until the thin cop got three feet from the driver's side window that Anton noticed something was very wrong.

It was his face. It looked like he'd dipped his head in a vat of acid, and his skin was starting to melt off, liquid flesh slowly slipping off bone. The *mask* was like none Anton had ever seen; a thin rubber depiction of another person's face, a second skin, the lips and nose not quite matching the symmetry of his real features.

Diego yelled, "Oh shit!" and Anton knew the larger cop was at his window in a similar mask. Then, both the driver's side and passenger side windows shattered, the glass caving in on them like an avalanche of tiny crystals. Diego tried to raise his gun as Anton pulled his from under his seat, but the cops—or whatever they really were—shoved guns in their faces, and one of them screamed, "Drop your weapons, or we'll blow your mother-fucking heads off."

Diego and Anton glanced at each other and dropped their guns into the foot-wells. Then Anton motioned to say something but everything went dark and swimmy and warm, like he'd fallen into a giant bathtub, the left side of his head simultaneously numb and screaming with pain.

He must have blacked out for at least five seconds, because the next thing he knew, his face hit the asphalt. The cop grabbed his wrists and cuffed them behind his back, then dragged him to his feet. He tried to fight him off, but the blow had muddled his brain, and he couldn't focus his energy to the right parts of his body. The cop dragged him around to the back of the van and tossed him into the gravel embankment at the side of the road. Diego was already waiting there, cuffed, with blood streaming from an open wound below his right eye. The bigger cop stood over him.

"Who are you?" said Anton from the ground, his words slurred. "You ain't cops."

The *cops* laughed, and one of them said, "You must be the smart one."

"You know who you're fucking with?" Diego hissed.

But they ignored him, and the thin one turned and rounded the van to the driver's side. Then the door slammed shut, the engine caught, and the van pulled away. Anton looked over to the cop car to see the bigger cop climbing in behind the wheel.

The whole thing took less than a minute, maybe less than half. They were definitely pros, maybe even ex-military. The way they moved with the precision and speed of a formula one pit crew. They were good, no doubt about it. But they did make one mistake.

In their hurry, the big cop didn't notice the snub-nosed .38 Diego had in an ankle holster. And as the squad car snaked toward them, the screech of spinning tires on asphalt, Diego managed to slip his cuffs under his legs and grab the gun. He shifted onto his side, raised his gun with a steady hand, and fired three quick shots at the windshield.

The gunfire cracked through the night like thunder, and the bullets hit the glass and morphed into tight webs the size of baseballs. But the glass didn't break. As the car sped past them, Diego unloaded the rest of his bullets, each shot hitting the target, and each one doing as much damage as a flea hitting a hippo.

Anton couldn't believe it: the car was bulletproof.

As it sped off into the night, Diego slumped onto his back and said, "Well, shit."

Anton couldn't have put it better himself.

21

LUCA

Luca woke up fully clothed and with the worst hangover of his life. The taste in his mouth was so horrific, it was like he'd been exploring the floors of the Vanilla Club's bathrooms with his tongue. And when he sat up in bed, he realized holding down vomit was going to be a big part of his day. But much worse than the hangover was the fact that his hands, face, and clothes were covered in another man's blood.

How stupid could I be? he thought. Before he had been released, he'd planned to be careful, to not take too many risks. But killing a guy only a few blocks from the motel was one hell of a risk. It was amazing the cops hadn't knocked on his door already, canvassing the area for potential witnesses.

He climbed out of bed, made a cup of the motel's instant coffee, took a sip, spat it out, and then got in the shower. It took about four minutes for the water to get hot, but the blanket of cold did a better job of waking him up than the powdered shit the motel was trying to pass for coffee would have. He scrubbed at his hands and arms, the dry blood sticking to his skin like dead bugs on a windshield, the water picking up a pale orange hue by the time it disappeared into the plughole.

Once he got out of the shower, he cleaned it, then turned his attention to the clothes. They were caked in blood and any other DNA samples that sorry prick might have left behind. The new jeans, boots, and shirt all had to go, not to mention the mugger's switchblade he'd picked up as a souvenir. The question was, *how to get rid of them?* Just tossing them in the dumpster in the motel parking lot wasn't an option. Burning was a good way to go, but if someone spotted the black smoke from the rubber-soled boots and put it out—or even worse, called the cops—then he'd be in real deep shit.

Decisions, decisions, he thought. But after deliberating for twenty minutes or so, he came up with a plan. He scrubbed the blood stains on the clothes until the blotchy burgundy took on a pale, pinkish hue, tucked the knife into one of the boots, then tossed everything into the plastic store bag they came in, and headed down to the V-Star.

It wasn't hard to find the perfect spot for his needs. He took a right on East Washington and headed straight for the LA river, the earthy scent of the crushed gravel and sand from the material plants filling his helmet. As he reached the section of East Washington where the road morphed into a bridge over the giant concrete slab the city laughably called a river, he slowed and fixed his gaze on the graffiti-covered columns jutting up to the overhead train tracks, the chain-link fence at the base of the columns, and at the homeless encampment beyond it.

The encampment was made up of seven or eight tents, cardboard sheeting, plastic barrels, and wood crates. The purple, blue, and orange of the tents blended into the colorful graffiti on the gray of the concrete.

Without stopping, Luca pulled the bag from the side pouch

of the V-Star and tossed it over the fence into the middle of the encampment. And within seconds, he saw two men scurry out from their respective *homes* and grab it, like rats after a dropped piece of food. Luca drove on for about two-hundred yards, pulled a U-turn, and headed back.

As he passed by, he saw the guys had unpacked the bag and were inspecting its contents. Even through the helmet, Luca could see their pale-green faces and hooded, red eyes; probably the only two people in the city suffering from a worse hangover than him. One of them was checking the size of the shirt against his torso, while the other held one of the boots up at eye level, studying it like it was alive.

With the clothes taken care of, it was time to focus on Jimmy. But despite how much fun it was taking out that piece of shit in the alley, Luca knew he couldn't play it that loose with his old friend. No more risks. He needed to know the entry and exit points, the security he was running. If he had a dog, or if he had any drop-in visitors. Luca would need to case the joint, sit on it for a couple of days.

And to do that, he needed supplies and equipment.

Luca cruised along 7th street—past the rows of liquor stores, laundromats, and record stores with "going out of business" signs—and stopped outside the first pawn shop he found. It sat on the corner of Westlake Avenue, a big neon "open" sign lit up above the doorway.

A bell jingled above Luca's head as he slipped through the door, announcing his arrival. The only two people inside—a guy in his fifties who Luca presumed was the owner, and the woman he was serving—froze and stared at him as if he'd instructed them to do so.

The owner looked like a cross between a Texan and a

hippie in his baggy denim shirt, black bolo tie, circle-rimmed glasses, and long, gray hair hanging in a loose ponytail. He was at the register counting out twenty-dollar bills in front of the woman, who had bird-nest hair and darting eyes. She was wearing a thin, blue jacket, despite it being ninety degrees outside, and Luca recognized the beige dress poking out at the bottom as a maid's uniform. And by the looks of the diamond necklace she was pawning, he guessed she worked at one of the upscale hotels in Hollywood where rich, flashy types tended to get blackout drunk and misplace things.

Finders keepers, he thought.

Luca said, "Howdy," and gave them a nod.

They looked at each other, then back at Luca, and the owner said, "Hi, be with you in a second," then went back to counting out the bills.

"Take your time," Luca said and began perusing the contents of the store. It was a room of organized randomness. Acoustic and electric guitars hung above worn out suitcases. Bulky white computers and printers sat next to baseball bats and gloves. And all the good stuff—jewelry, ammunition, knives—were wrapped around the cash register.

He crossed through the middle of the space—beat up power tools on his left, home stereo systems on his right—and found what he was looking for in a tall glass case. All kinds of different brands and models stacked side by side. It was amazing how little they'd changed in the last twenty-five years. Sure, they might have a sleeker design, more accessories, and more buttons, but really, they were just the same—black, compact, and extremely dangerous in the wrong hands. As he eyed them, trying to decide which one best suited his needs, the entry bell jingled behind him, and he turned to find the woman gone and the owner approaching.

"See anything you like?" he said.

Luca shrugged. "They all look the same to me."

"Well, what features are you looking for?"

"I need something with good range."

The owner scratched the stubble on his chin, then pointed at the one that looked the newest.

"If you need range," he said, "this baby's your best bet. Lightweight, reliable. You can't go wrong with this one."

"That right?" said Luca.

"You wanna check it out?"

Luca nodded, and the owner fished in his pocket and pulled out a jailer's ring of keys. He somehow found the right key in only a few seconds, slotted it into the stainless-steel ratchet lock, and popped it open. He slid open the case, and Luca reached in and grabbed it, eyeing it under the fluorescents.

"She's a beauty, right?"

"She?" said Luca.

He never understood why people referred to cars and boats and other objects as females. Calling them *she or her* when they're *things,* made of metal and plastic and rubber and wires and computer chips. Maybe he was different, but he preferred his females made of blood and bones, and, well, maybe a little bit of plastic.

Luca twirled it around in his hands.

"You know how to use one of those?" the owner asked.

"Point and shoot, right?"

"I guess," he said. "This is a Panasonic FZ1000. It's one of the best bridge cameras on the market."

"Bridge camera?"

"That's right. It's got most of the capabilities of a DSL without the hefty price tag."

"Well, I do like a bargain," said Luca

"It shoots at twenty megapixels, three-inch LED screen, all

that good stuff. But the best bit's the zoom; you can get up real close without losing focus, and without having to buy one of those big ass lenses. What you're holding is all you need. And a memory card, of course."

Luca nodded. The guy knew his cameras. He reminded him of Jimmy that way. Luca wondered if he could rattle off that kind of information about all the other 299 items in the store, even the 270 that were garbage. He wondered, but didn't care enough to ask.

"Yup," the owner continued. "This one is the best bang for your buck, no doubt about it. It takes great 4K video too. All you gotta do is press this..."

He reached out a finger, and Luca dropped the camera by his side, leaving the owner pointing at nothing.

"I don't care about video. How much do you want for it?"

The owner moved his bony finger up to his temple and scratched at his hairline. "Three-fifty. And I can throw in an SD memory card."

Luca glanced down at the camera. "Two hundred, and I'll take it."

"That's six hundred in the stores or online."

"I look like I give a fuck? Two hundred, or I'm gone."

The owner clapped his hands. "Okay, you got a deal. I'll box it up for you right now."

"Don't need a box, just ring it up."

"Yes, sir."

Luca followed him over to the register, counting out the cash as he walked. When they got there, the owner fetched the SD memory card from a stand beside the register and tossed it onto the glass between them. Luca ran his gaze along the boxes of bullets stacked on the back wall—roundheads, metal jackets, hollow points. Little soldiers of death, neatly packaged, ever ready and eager to fulfill their gruesome destiny. He held out the cash, but when the owner took it, he held on. "One more thing. I assume from your last customer that you, ah… value discretion. Am I right?"

"What customer?" said the owner.

Luca gestured to the door. "The maid with the necklace."

A wry smile formed across the owner's face, "I'm sorry, sir. I'm not sure what you're talking about. I haven't served anybody all day."

Luca mirrored his smile. "In that case, grab me one of those boxes of forty-cal hollow points."

22

SCARLETT

Scarlett woke to the churning of her thoughts, and a dense wave of anxiety told her that after today, after what she had to do for the old man, her life would never be the same again. She slowly rolled over and was shocked to find Josh asleep beside her. But then she had a flashback memory of him climbing into bed in the middle of the night, while she remained in that fuzzy state between asleep and awake.

Josh opened his eyes, stretched his arms above his head, and gave her a smile. "Good morning, beautiful."

Despite the fact she'd truly missed him, her guilt and paranoia wouldn't allow Scarlett to slip into loving fiancé mode. So she just said, "What time did you come in?"

"Somewhere around two," he said, rolling onto his side and slipping his hand around her waist. He blinked hard, trying to rid his eyes of the tired fog that coated them. "Man, I hate red-eye flights."

"I thought you were flying back this morning?"

He pulled her in so she could feel his warm body against hers; he snaked his left leg around her right.

"I couldn't wait until this morning. I wanted to sleep in the same bed as you, and I wanted to see that cute little face of yours when I woke up."

The safety of his embrace began to soothe Scarlett's anxiety, and when he reached for the tip of her nose with his finger, she crinkled it under his touch the way he liked.

"I'm sorry," he said. "For the other night, I mean. I know you were just trying to be adventurous with the handcuffs and the... you know. I shouldn't have..."

"No," Scarlett interrupted, not able to bear an apology after what she'd done. "Please, don't. It's okay."

"No, it's not. I owe you an explanation."

Scarlett opened her mouth to speak, but Josh softly slipped his finger over her lips and said, "Please."

She sighed lightly and nodded, and he tucked a rogue strand of hair behind her ear.

"I appreciate you trying to be spontaneous and creative," he said. "I really do. And it's not that I'm a prude, or that I don't think about doing those types of things. But when I look at you, I see my wife, I see the mother of my children, I see my soulmate."

"Then why don't you feel comfortable enough to do those things with me?"

"Look, I want to be open and adventurous and share in life's experiences with you, but I also respect you too much to degrade you in any way. I know that makes me sound old fashioned or whatever, but it's how I feel. I can't just pretend you're some girl to fool around with and treat like nothing. Not when you're my everything."

Suddenly it all made sense. It wasn't that Josh lacked passion or desire, or that Scarlett couldn't invoke those types of emotions in him; it was the deep love and respect he felt for her. Yvonne was right—she *was* lucky to have Josh, and the prospect of losing him had given her a newfound respect for what she had.

He scooted even closer to her, their faces only a few inches apart. "Having said that," he said, "it doesn't mean we can't have fun. It doesn't mean I don't want you."

He kissed her lips softly, then began sliding down under the covers, dropping kisses on her chest and stomach. Scarlett whispered, "Wait," unsure if she was ready. But he kept moving, and his tongue found the sensitive skin below her navel, and her whole body tensed. His tongue moved even lower then, drawing a line down her body. She tried to enjoy it, to allow the sensation to stir those powerful feelings from within. But blurred images flashed across her brain, that night with Anton, the crazy passion, the betrayal. Her body went rigid, and she grabbed Josh's arms, pulling him up toward her.

He looked up at her from under the covers. "What is it?"

"I just... I need to get to work."

"So be late. You gotta live a little."

"I can't, I..."

"Hey," said Josh, "just close your eyes and relax, okay?"

With his fingertip, he traced the line of kisses down the front of her body, and she shivered.

"Just relax," he said, then slipped back down farther under the covers.

Scarlett used all her concentration to fight off the images of Anton and focus on the physical sensations. And after a while, she did something she could seldom do—she just let go.

Making love with Josh that morning was the best it had ever been. Scarlett completely surrendered herself to his careful movements, and it felt like the first time they'd ever truly made love the way it should be done. Like all the other times were failed attempts at finding the right formula, mere practice for that very moment. As they swam under each other's skin, he drank her in with eyes glazed in the shine of desire and appetite. His strong hands gripped her thighs; her nails sank into the flesh of his back. It wasn't long before her soft groans and sudden gasps built and built until she shuddered, and they shared in a euphoric, blissful release. Then they lay there, damp and spent, their hearts thumping in rhythm as they came back down to Earth one deep breath at a time.

Josh looked at her, the way he used to look at her when they first started dating, that searching stare; a look filled with so much more than just lust, but a knowing look of pure love and acceptance and boundless curiosity.

"I love you, Scar."

And with those words, suddenly, everything felt right in the world. It was like a switch had been flicked, and life had shifted back on course. At that moment, she knew that anything she felt for Anton was purely artificial, and the mistake she'd made would never happen again.

How could I have ever been so selfish as to want more than this? Scarlett thought. *Everything I'll ever need is in this room.*

But before she could fully revel in her newfound appreciation for what she had—for what she'd always had—a question sprung to the forefront of her brain; *What about Mr. Francis? Do I still help him? Do I take that risk?*

Usually, Scarlett was the type of person to curl into a shell of comfort and safety, hiding away from this type of potential danger. But this time, it was different. Something inside her wouldn't let her go back on the promise she'd made. And it wasn't just about the guilt she'd felt for cheating on Josh; it was about doing the right thing and keeping her word. It was about taking action and being a good person.

She'd been complaining for so long about feeling useless in her job, and this was the first opportunity where she could actually really help someone. She wasn't going to let him down.

Jimmy was waiting for Scarlett in his wheelchair when she entered the cramped living room. He closed the Bible in his lap and looked up at her with quiet gratitude. "You came?"

"It wasn't easy," she said, setting down her bag, her brain flooding with all the reasons not to do what she was about to do.

"Big decisions rarely are."

Scarlett pointed to the Bible. "I've heard that's a good one," she said nervously.

Jimmy managed a chuckle. "Sure is." He looked down at the book, considering it, then held it out to Scarlett. "I want you to take this."

"Oh, I couldn't."

"Please, I want you to have it. Hopefully, it will help you find what you've been looking for."

"Thank you. Truly."

Scarlett took the book with a sweat drenched hand and placed it in her bag. Then they waited there in silence for a while, taking each other and the situation in as a blanket of warm, yellow light crept across the thick carpet toward them. It was going to be another beautiful Saturday, of course. And it was strange for Scarlett to think that, out there, trips to the beach and water fights and barbecues were being planned, while in here, a poor old man was preparing himself to leave this crazy, scary, incredible, and ultimately beautiful world behind.

"I take it you managed to get what you needed?" Jimmy asked.

The plan was simple—with his lungs in such a severely weakened state, by removing his oxygen supply tubes and giving him a dose of a drug that would cause respiratory depression, his lungs would fail, and he would die. Choosing and finding the drug was the tricky part; it's not like they had Pancuronium Bromide or potassium chloride lying around the medical center. And even if they did, if those substances showed up on a toxicology report after Jimmy's death—unlikely as it was they would run one—questions would be raised. But luckily, one thing they *did* have access to was Morphine.

Scarlett fished the two disposable syringes from her bag and held them out. Jimmy's eyes locked on to them, the agents of his death but a foot away.

"Are you sure about this?" she asked. "You know we don't have to go through with it."

"I've never been more sure of anything in my life." But she couldn't tell if he really believed that or not, so she pressed him.

"Once I do this, there will be nothing I can do to stop it. You understand that, right?"

He smiled. "Scarlett, I'm already dead. I know what I'm asking you to do seems scary. But please, believe me, I'm ready. Just... give me one minute."

He lowered his head and closed his eyes, and she followed suit.

"Dear Heavenly Father. I ask that you forgive me for my sins. I repent for all the bad I have done, and I pray that you accept me into heaven. Have mercy on my soul. Amen."

Scarlett said, "Amen," and it surprised her how good it felt to say it. Like maybe, if there was a god, he would be looking down on them with support and approval. A small part of her even hoped that was the case, because one thing was for certain: once this was done, it could never be undone.

Jimmy gave her a look that told her he was ready. She nodded and tore both syringes from their white wrappers, her mind focused on not trembling. He looked up at her then with those gray eyes that seemed to be filled with both boundless wisdom and endless questions.

"Will it hurt?"

Scarlett spoke through the lump in her throat, "Well, you won't feel pain as such, but you're not going to be able to breathe, so you're going to feel anxious."

"I've not been able to breathe for years. That, I can handle."

She stacked the syringes together and hovered them over his thigh. But she couldn't go any further, like there was an invisible force stopping her. Jimmy placed his hand on hers, smiled, and said, "It's okay. You take your time."

Scarlett took a few long, deep breaths and slipped the needles in, then pumped the clear liquid from the plastic tubes and into Jimmy's bloodstream.

He nodded in sullen acknowledgment, and something prompted Scarlett to lean down and hug him tightly. Jimmy hugged back, seeming to relish in the final embrace. As Scarlett pulled away, she reached up to his face and pulled the breathing tube from his nose, letting it hang at his chest as a single tear welled in his left eye and spilled down his cheek.

It didn't take long for life to slip from him, and instead of the calm, serene look Scarlett hoped to see on his face, there was something else, something she tried to convince herself wasn't regret. He opened his mouth to say something, but no words came out.

"What is it? What are you trying to say?" Scarlett asked, her hands on his shoulders.

He swallowed hard and tried again, forcing the words out with what little air he had left in his lungs.

"I'm... sorry..."

Then, he died.

23

LUCA

One look at Jimmy's *house*, and Luca knew there was no money left. The place looked like a construction trailer that'd been abandoned on a decrepit job site. Jimmy was the type of guy who'd buy three-thousand-dollar suits and only stay in hotels that had elevator attendants. There was no way he was staying in that house unless he was flat broke. Especially if he was alone and dying. Maybe someone ripped him off, or maybe he got cute with the wrong guy and they beat the piss out of him and took his money. *One can only hope*, Luca thought.

He'd parked the V-star fifty yards down the street and cut through to the steep hillside at the rear of the property. It was covered in tall grass and prickly bushes the color of dust. It looked like a giant tinderbox, daring the scorching sun to provide it with a spark.

Luca followed a ridgeline until he got a good view of Jimmy's place and had no problem picking the right lookout spot—a flat patch with some shade and a direct line of sight into Jimmy's living room.

Even though he had good intel that Jimmy was in the

house, when Luca got horizontal and peered through the camera lens, what he felt could only be described as pure shock. Luca had waited so long, and there Jimmy was: a physical manifestation of years of hate and anger, just sitting there in a wheelchair, a ghost of the man he once knew, meek and lifeless, waiting for death.

For two hours, he watched carefully as nothing happened—nothing at all. Jimmy just sat there reading from a book in his lap, not even moving to take a piss.

Even in the shade, the heat was beating Luca up, sweat pouring out of him like a water tank with a shotgun wound. And the hangover that had subsided earlier was back with a vengeance. Only two hours, and he was already considering ditching the stakeout plan and just taking Jimmy out.

But then something *did* happen—nothing related to Jimmy, but some excitement nonetheless. A scratching sound came from a big, brown rock about a foot away from his right ear. Luca turned his head to get eyes on whatever had made the sound, and some of the soil fell away from below the rock. A scorpion emerged, stinger raised, pointing at Luca's face. It was a big son of a bitch too; at least five-inches long, with a dark-brown body and gold legs, stinger, and pinchers. Luca remembered hearing once that you can gauge how poisonous a scorpion is by the size of its body, but couldn't remember if it was the bigger ones that were more poisonous or the little ones. Either way, he wasn't taking any chances.

He slowly reached behind his back, grabbed the nose end of his pistol, and pulled it from his waistband. As he brought it around his body, the scorpion twitched, then scurried toward his face. Luca brought the butt of the gun down hard, crushing its alien-like body. Instinctively, its tail thrust against the gun handle, ticking against the metal like a tiny pickaxe. Luca brought the gun down on it again, just to make sure it was dead, then flicked it several feet away.

As he began to wonder just how many potentially deadly insects might be surrounding him, something stole his attention. A car pulled into Jimmy's gravel driveway, spitting up a trail of dust. Luca peered at it through the camera and found it was a silver Honda with a pretty woman behind the wheel. He snapped photos of the license plate and got some shots of her as she climbed out. He realized then that she was a nurse, and he was wrong—she wasn't pretty, she was goddamn gorgeous.

But this girl gave him a lot more than something nice to look at. Because once she got to the front door, she picked up a fake rock, pulled out a key to Jimmy's house, and let herself in.

Bingo, that's it, Luca thought. Forget the heat and fucking scorpions. The truth was, he knew it the second he saw that son of a bitch that he wasn't going to be able to wait to kill him. And now he had a key. He could slip in and out, and no one would even know. Hell, he could even make it look like an accident if he was feeling creative—and he was a creative guy.

Once the nurse was inside, she moved out of shot, so Luca refocused on the living room and waited. A few seconds later, she reappeared in his lens and stood in front of Jimmy. They talked for a bit, then they just stood there, neither of them speaking, just staring at each other like a weird prearranged game of statues. What followed was one of the strangest, most unexpected things Luca had ever seen—and he'd seen some stuff.

The nurse pulled something from her bag that looked like two, white candy bars. But when she removed the wrappers and held them over Jimmy's thigh, Luca knew they were syringes. At first, Luca didn't know what he was seeing, but he could feel it in his bones that it was something big. So he quickly pulled his face from the viewfinder and stared at all the buttons and switches on his camera, desperately trying to figure out how to record. He eventually found the right button and put the viewfinder back to his eye in time to see Jimmy's hand on the girl's, trying to stop her. But the weak fuck couldn't prevent her from driving the syringes in. Then she leaned in to him, and Luca thought she was giving Jimmy a hug, but when she pulled away, she'd removed his breathing tubes. Then she just stood there and watched as Jimmy's body went limp in the chair, and—Luca couldn't fucking believe it—he was gone.

When the ambulance came and took the body away, the EMT crew may as well have been UPS drivers picking up a package—like they knew this place would be on their route. And when they spoke to the nurse, she looked calm and collected, like she was ordering takeout.

But after the ambulance drove away, its lights and siren off, Luca watched the nurse get into her car and sob into her hands. She stayed like that for a while, a whimpering mess, then she left, and Luca sat there on that hillside completely fucking baffled.

He had no idea what the hell had just happened. But he did know one thing: he was going to find out.

24

DETECTIVE BROOKS

"Jesus Christ," said Brooks. "I'm at risk of losing my lunch."

The body was facedown, the pool of blood around his head merging with a pile of yellow vomit. And either just before, or just after death, the victim had voided his bowels, and the stench was making Brooks nauseous. But what was most unsettling was that in the middle of the vomit was a photo of a little girl.

The alleyway was taped off and guarded by a half dozen squad cars at each end. A crime scene investigation unit made sketches and scoured the alley for potential pieces of evidence among the broken glass and loose pieces of trash.

"Do we know the cause of death?" asked Detective Chen. She was on her haunches near Brooks's feet, her head cocked to one side as she studied the victim's face.

A forensic officer by the name of Patterson was on his knees next to the body in a full-body suit with a hood, gloves, and booties. He looked up from fishing through his suitcase and said, "Blunt force trauma to the head. Maybe from a hammer, but I won't be able to tell for sure until we get him back to the lab."

Brooks looked up and down the alley. It was in a shitty part of the city known for drugs and prostitution and all manner of indecencies. "Probably drug deal or robbery gone wrong," he ventured.

"I don't think so," said Chen. "I mean, why put the photo in the vomit? It seems a little personal to me." She looked at Patterson. "Any ID on the body?"

Patterson pointed to a yellow evidence marker near Brooks's foot with the number one printed on it. "We found his wallet there, no ID in it, but the good news is we did find this." Patterson pulled a clear evidence bag from his briefcase, and inside the bag was an expired credit card bearing the name *Marshal Teal*.

"What's the bad news?" asked Brooks cynically.

"The wallet is coarse, grainy leather. Means getting fingerprints will be nearly impossible. And the only other physical piece of evidence we have is the photograph, and that's been sitting in the vomit all night, so..." He shrugged.

"Shit," said Chen. She raised to her full height. "I'm going to use one of the squad cars to run a search on Marshal Teal."

"Knock yourself out," said Brooks.

Chen turned and headed toward the nearest end of the alley, and Patterson said, "You see the Dodgers game last night? They really put a hurting on the Phillies."

"Yeah, I saw Freese got two," said Brooks.

"That's right. I took my boy to the game. He almost caught a foul ball, but some asshole in a tank top snatched it before he could get it. Can you believe that shit? What kind of prick steals that opportunity away from a kid?"

Brooks shrugged. "There's always assholes around. What can you do?"

Patterson looked as though he was wrestling with that thought as he pulled a pair of extra-long tweezers from his briefcase. Then he shrugged as well and said, "Yeah, I guess so." He reached over to the vomit with the tweezers and clasped the end of the photo. Then he lifted it out of the sludge and shook off some of the residues.

He was about to slip it into an evidence bag, when Brooks said, "Hold up a sec."

Patterson froze, and Brooks pulled out his camera phone and snapped a few photos of the little girl's face. It would be awhile until the photo was tested in the lab, so having a copy on his phone might come in useful.

The kid looked happy, Brooks thought. Her pink cheeks plumped around a wide smile. She looked on the verge of candid laughter, as if whoever was taking the photo was pulling a funny face at her.

A few minutes later, Chen reappeared with an enthusiastic look on her face. "Only one Marshal Teal in LA," she said, "and the photo looks like a match. He's got a long list of arrests, mostly for possession."

Brooks reexamined the dead guy in light of this new info, and even through the bruising and dried blood, he could still tell the guy was an addict. The thinning hair, sunken cheeks, and brown teeth—all telltale signs of his vices.

He looked back to Chen. "Anything else?"

"Yeah, I've got a last known address. 832 El Vista."

Brooks grinned. "So let's go."

832 El Vista was a duplex, and the landlord was a short woman by the name of Donna. She had scraggly gray hair, hunched shoulders, and pink hands and forearms. It looked like she'd been scrubbing the floors with a hand brush, Brooks thought.

"Yeah, he rented the unit above me for five years or so," Donna said. "He was a pretty good tenant until he started smoking that shit. Then he started trying to pay his rent with excuses, so I had to kick his ass out about six months ago."

She was standing on the other side of a closed screen door as at least one mastiff-sized dog barked vigorously from a back room.

"You know where he went?" asked Chen. She was the lead investigator on the case, and Brooks was more than happy to let her do the talking while he hung back and occasionally glanced around the neighborhood. Some kids rummaged through a heap of discarded furniture. An old man smoked a joint on his porch.

"No idea," said Donna. "But if you find him, tell him he still owes me money for the damage he did to the bathroom."

"Actually," said Chen, "I'm sorry to tell you this, but Mr. Teal is dead."

Donna barely reacted, her gaze never wavering, a tiny smirk twisting her lips. "Yeah, I figured as much."

Chen shot Brooks a glance, then said, "Why do you say that?"

"He was a junkie. Ain't that what junkies do?"

Brooks almost laughed at that. It was one of the soundest pieces of logic he'd heard in a long time.

He felt his face curling into a smile, so he quickly said, "Did he leave any stuff here?"

"Yeah, but I tossed it all a few months after he left."

The barking grew louder, and Donna looked back into the apartment and yelled, "Shut up in there," but the dogs kept at it.

"What about friends," asked Chen. "You know if he had any?"

"Never brought anybody around here."

Chen shifted in place, her frustration becoming evident. "What about a daughter?

"Yeah, he had a little girl."

Brooks pulled out his cell phone, stepped forward, and held up the photo of the girl. "This her?"

Donna lifted the reading glasses that were dangling around her neck, perched them on her nose, and squinted. "Yup, that was her."

"Why do you say *was*?" asked Chen, concern riding her voice.

"The mother took her. Up and moved to Florida about three years back. And before you ask, I don't know where."

Chen sighed audibly, and the dogs grew louder still; their guttural barks booming through the small apartment.

"Anyway," said Donna, turning away, "if you'll excuse me, my animals are hungry."

Chen opened her mouth to speak, but Donna was already back inside, closing the door behind her.

Brooks chuckled. "Nice lady. I might have to ask her out."

As they walked back to the Cadillac, Chen was rigid, her jaw and fists clenched, her fury smoldering underneath her stony expression. Brooks didn't need to ask what was wrong; he understood her frustration, even if he didn't feel it. It was less than two hours after the investigation had begun, and they were at a dead end. The case would remain open, and the daughter and her mother would be found and questioned in Florida, but with no witnesses or leads, the chances of finding the killer were slim to none.

"Doesn't it piss you off?" said Chen out of nowhere.

Brooks chewed his ketchup soaked fries, swallowed, and said, "Doesn't what piss me off?"

They were sitting in a corner booth in a greasy diner on Western Avenue. Brooks was devouring his double cheeseburger, fries, and Coke, while Chen ignored her Caesar salad with light dressing.

"That someone can get beaten to death in the middle of one of the most developed cities in the world, and we don't have shit."

"I hear you. It's a tough break, that's all."

"It's more than that," said Chen, exasperated. "I mean, how many total cases have you worked?"

Brooks shrugged, said, "In my whole career? Fuck if I know," and took a big bite of his burger, sending cheese and sauce spilling onto his plate.

"Exactly. And how many did you clear?"

Brooks chuckled and spoke around his food, "What is this, my review?"

"I'm serious, how many?"

It was the last conversation Brooks wanted to have, but he knew she wasn't going to let him eat in peace. He set his burger down, sat back in his seat, and said, "I don't know. Less than half, I guess."

Chen spread her arms, like a little validatory dance. "Exactly. Doesn't that piss you off?"

"Wait until you've got a few more years on the job, you'll get used to it."

"Come on, don't patronize me, Brooks."

"I'm not, I mean it. And you're not wrong."

"Then, what am I?"

"I don't know, is there a nicer word for naïve?"

Chen scoffed and rolled her eyes, and Brooks tried to recover. "Look, you remember the first dead body you ever saw?"

"Of course," said Chen earnestly.

"Me too. She was a hooker, about twenty-five or so. I was a rookie back then, the first one on the scene. I found her in a motel room, naked, her tangled blonde hair spilling off the end of the bed. She was lying there so peacefully that at first, I wasn't sure if she was just sleeping. It was like..." He searched his brain for the right analogy. "Have you ever seen a flower, and you don't know if it's real or fake? But when you touch it and feel the synthetic petals, it immediately becomes so obviously fake that there's no way you could ever see it as real again. You notice all the little details, like the rounded end of the stem, and the tiny wisps of fabric at the edge of the petals. Then you don't know how you even saw it as real in the first place."

Chen nodded. "Yeah, I guess."

"That's exactly how I felt when I reached out and felt her cold skin, you know? I noticed that her eyes were open, then the marks around her neck. She went from being a naked, passed-out girl to a decomposing corpse the second my fingers touched her. It was like she died twice."

Brooks looked down, and an image of the girl flashed across his brain, and for a moment, he felt a flicker of something akin to sadness in his gut. He took a beat to shake the memory, then looked up at Chen. "I'm not ashamed to say that moment changed me. I was torn up over it for days. I didn't want to eat, I couldn't sleep. And the bottle of Johnny Walker I kept on my nightstand only made matters worse."

Chen's eyes glazed over for a moment, and Brooks knew she was reliving her own similar memory.

"But," said Brooks, snapping Chen out of her trance. "Since then, I've seen more bodies in this city than I could or would ever *want* to count. I've seen it all. Groups of young men no older than twenty ripped apart by AK47s. Rotten corpses left for weeks until the neighbors call in about the putrid stench seeping through the walls. An infant handcuffed to their bedpost by their parent who never returned from scoring crack. Just about every fucked-up thing you could imagine, really. And once you've seen all that, you not only become immune to the horrors of death, but you learn one important lesson."

"Yeah, and what's that?"

"That evil isn't something you can fight, or even find. It's the world. It's mankind. And nothing will ever change that. You take away all this stuff, you strip us down to our bare-naked selves, and you are left with two things: love and murder."

Chen didn't seem to like that. She shook her head and said, "You always been this much of a cynic?"

Brooks laughed. "A perk of the job, I guess."

25

ANTON

The skinny guy screamed in horror as he dangled off the roof of the five-story apartment building. His face was turning plum, and he was flailing his arms around like he thought he could ward off gravity.

"Please, pull me up! Don't do this."

Anton and Diego each had one of the guy's ankles hooked under their arm, their bodies tense under the strain of holding the man's weight. Three kids toting skateboards watched from the concrete below. None of them seemed too concerned, as though this was common practice in this part of town.

"Please, man. I'll tell you whatever you want!" yelled the skinny guy.

He'd said his name was Leo.

Since Anton and Diego had been held up and relieved of the van filled with heroin, the whole organization had been scouring the city, trying to find the men responsible. They'd been talking to connections, pulling people off the street, kicking in doors. But so far, they'd found nothing. No one knew anything about the robbery, let alone the guys who'd disguised themselves as cops—either that, or they weren't talking. But the latter was unlikely, considering how hard the questions were being asked.

As they had been nearing the end of the list of potential people to interrogate, Anton remembered a guy he used to know who was involved in the heroin trade. So they had headed down to the Strip to find him.

"Where's Randel?" yelled Anton.

"I'll tell you! I'll tell you! Just pull me up, man. Please!"

Anton looked to Diego, who nodded, and they pulled Leo up so he was sitting on the ledge of the parapet wall. Leo sucked in quick short breaths as the excess blood drained from his face.

"Well," said Diego.

"He's at the docks."

"Which docks," said Anton.

"San Pedro. The wharf at Fish Harbor. He's meeting his contact down there."

Diego grabbed Leo around the neck and said, "If you make us come back here..." He pushed Leo back a few inches.

"I swear, man! He's at the docks."

Anton and Diego pulled up in Anton's Mercedes and parked in a corner spot, then ambled down the wide pathway toward the action, their heads on swivels, the only two people for miles wearing suits.

Warm afternoon sunlight kissed the wharf and danced on the calm water as dockhands and fishermen ferried crates and buckets to the creaking boats. Flocks of gulls circled and cried overhead, and the whole place was blanketed in the thick stench of fish guts, salt, and diesel.

"What does this guy look like?" asked Diego.

"He's black, average height, muscular."

Diego sighed and said, "This is a waste of time. The men who hit us were pros. They would not be stupid enough to talk to anyone about their plan."

Anton agreed but didn't say so. After all, what choice did they have? Any lead was worth following up on to avoid going back to Karina empty-handed. To say she'd gone *ballistic* when she found out about the hold-up would be an understatement, and now she was demanding blood.

"This place fucking stinks," said Anton as he glanced at an ice chest filled with kelp bass. He'd only gone fishing once in his life, a deep-sea day trip out of San Diego. The tide had been unexpectedly rough, and Anton spent the whole day with his head in a fish bucket. He vowed never to go again.

When they got fifty feet into the crowd, Diego said, "That him?"

He was pointing at a black man standing next to a brand-new trawler. He had his back turned and was talking to an old salty dog of a guy in a green slicker.

"I don't know," said Anton, squinting through the sun.

At first glance, the man looked too fat to be Randel, but as he turned his face in Anton's direction, there was no doubt it was him, just a softer, rounder version, like an athlete post-retirement.

Before Anton had a chance to say anything, Randel noticed them, did a quick double-take, then froze—a deer in the headlights.

"That's him."

"He's going to run," said Diego.

Randel hesitated, then bolted in the opposite direction, leaving the guy in the green slicker with a dumbfounded look on his face.

"Shit!" said Anton.

"Give me your keys," Diego snapped.

"What, why?"

"Just give!"

Anton fished out his keys, and Diego snatched them and began running back toward the Mercedes.

Anton shook his head, "Goddamn it," and gave chase after Randel.

Although Randel had a head start, he was slow, running in a step-step-limp motion, as though he was recovering from a hip injury. But Anton was quick. He soon found himself gaining on the other man as he dodged and weaved around dockhands and piles of coiled rope.

Randel reached the end of the loading area and darted through an open doorway into a warehouse. When Anton reached the doorway, a group of three workers in orange overalls tried to exit through the same space, and Anton had to push his way past them, sending one man falling onto his back.

"Hey, watch it, asshole!" the guy called from the floor.

The warehouse was a corrugated iron shell filled with rows of blue plastic boxes which formed long blue corridors. Anton sprinted down the main corridor after Randel, still gaining on him.

A sharp beeping sound rang through the space as a forklift truck backed into the corridor, and Anton had to sidestep like a running back, but managed to keep his footing and keep moving.

Further down the walkway, Randel glanced back with the frightened look of a man who knew he was going to be caught. Then he quickly reached out and yanked over a stack of the boxes, and Anton ran straight into them, knees first. He stumbled and hit the ground hard, his wrists and elbows taking the brunt of the impact.

"Motherfucker!" he yelled through the pain.

From the floor, he could see Randel charging toward a door at the back of the warehouse. Anton clambered to his feet, and pain shot through his knee and down through his shin. It wasn't a break, but it hurt like hell, and sprinting was out of the question. But his rage pushed him on in the form of a slow jog.

Beyond the rear warehouse door was an alley leading on to a secondary parking lot. Randel was nearing the end when Anton stepped onto it, both men limping along like wounded soldiers trying to make it to an evacuation point.

Randel pulled out a set of keys from his pocket and looked back at Anton with a defiant smile. But as he reached the end of the alley, a flash of purple lurched into view from the right, and suddenly Randel was on the ground, yelping in pain.

The flash of purple was Anton's Mercedes.

Diego hopped out and marched over to Randel, who was whining from the cement and yelling, "What the fuck?!"

Diego seized him, pulled him to his feet, and pushed him up against the alley wall.

"You shouldn't have run, chief," he said.

As Anton approached, his brain was swirling with blinding fury. He was pissed at Randel for giving him the runaround, his hurt knee, and the goddamn dents in the Mercedes. He was so mad that he pulled out his pistol, jammed it in Randel's throat, and snarled, "You fucking asshole!"

"Relax," said Diego. "Not here."

"Who the hell are you guys?" said Randel, his eyes narrowed in confusion.

Anton finally lowered the gun and let it hang by his side. "Don't you fucking play dumb, Randel. You ran from us."

"I thought you were the feds, man."

Diego chuckled. "You're not that lucky."

Randel's eyes darted back and forth from Anton and

Diego's faces. Then he settled on Anton for a moment and said, "Wait, I know you," and, "Oh shit."

Diego slapped Randel's chest with the back of his hand and beamed a smile. "Good. Now we are all acquainted. Tell us what you know about the hit last night."

Randel hesitated, and Anton tilted his gun, so it was aimed at his crotch. "Start talking."

"Whoa, whoa, look, all I know is that someone got hit, and it was a big score. That's all I know."

"That's all you know, huh?" Diego said mockingly before landing a vicious right hook into Randel's gut.

The punch caught him unaware, and he dropped to one knee, all the wind rushing out of him at once. Then he began coughing violently, like he'd just been resuscitated after drowning. Diego lowered his head and spoke into his ear, "Maybe we put you in the trunk and take you to the *basement*, huh?"

"Fat fuck wouldn't fit in my trunk," said Anton.

"Well, we don't have to take all of him."

"Fuck, man," said Randel, slowly getting back to his feet. "Look, I just heard a name. That's it."

Anton perked up. "What name?"

Randel looked around like he was scared he might be under surveillance and said, "Eric."

"Eric who?" demanded Anton.

"I don't know his last name, alright. I just heard it was him."

"Bullshit!"

"I swear, man."

Anton glanced at Diego. "You heard of him."

"Eric? Of course not. He's lying. He piece of shit like the others."

"I'm not lying. It's the truth."

Two security guards came through the warehouse door and began marching down the alley. The guard on the left was speaking into her radio. They must have been responding to a call about the chase.

Anton and Diego noticed at the same time, and Anton said, "We'd better get out of here."

Diego nodded then flicked Randel on the forehead. "This isn't over, Mr. Randel."

26

SCARLETT

"You know I was serious when I said I would come with you, right?" said Josh through the Honda's hands-free system. He was already at the office, but he still sounded genuine. Like if Scarlett asked him, he would drop what he was doing and rush right over.

"No, it'll be fine," said Scarlett, as she crawled along the narrow road, searching the acres of dry grass for where she needed to be.

"Are you sure, baby? You haven't been to a patient's funeral for a long time. This guy must have been special."

"Yeah, he was. But really, I'll be fine." Suddenly craving Josh's embrace, she added, "What time do you think you'll be home tonight?"

He went quiet for a moment, and she heard voices with urgent tones in the background. After a few seconds, he said, "Sorry, what did you say?"

"Nothing, it's fine." And it was. That usual sting of annoyance she often felt at playing second fiddle to his work wasn't there. She was just grateful he took a few minutes to call to see if she was okay, the simple gesture carrying new weight. "I love you," she said.

"I love you too, baby."

When she hung up, Scarlett spotted the priest standing patiently down a small hill to her right. So she pulled over as far as the tight road would allow and parked. But it took a few moments for her to gather her strength and actually get out of the car.

Scarlett used to go to a lot of funerals when she first started her job. It became a routine part of her life, like going to the grocery store or filling up at the gas station; just something that had to be done. Most were the same, with grief-stricken faces, hushed sobs, and whispered prayers. Husbands with bowed heads, silent and mournful, cradling their weeping wives. Scarlett arriving alone, unknown to most, often feeling more uncomfortable than anything else.

After going to so many, she inevitably began thinking about her own—who would be there, the types of flowers, the words on her tombstone. Eventually, it became all she could think about for the entire service. It got to the point where she would see herself in the coffin and be forced to face her own mortality.

After a while, it just became too much, and she had to start making excuses to the patient's families—*Sorry, I'm heading out of town that weekend, but thank you for inviting me.*

With Mr. Francis, though, it was different. She'd been an emotional wreck ever since that day at his house, her days filled with sudden trips to the bathroom to hide her sobbing while she fought off blurred flashbacks—the clear liquid leaving the syringe, his face as he slipped away.

But she knew she had to go to the funeral. In some ways, she was even a little eager. Desperately hoping, after it was over, she would be able to close this chapter and move on.

She eventually started down the hill, picking her way

through the gravestones. The priest was standing alone at the mouth of the open grave—a funeral party of one, about to be two. When she reached him, he gave her a tight half-smile. The type of mournful smile you gave to a stranger at such somber events. He was a small man, with pale, sunken cheeks and lips so thin and crooked they looked to have been drawn on by a shaky pencil.

Scarlett took her place on the opposite side of the grave, and the priest began with readings from the Bible. Scarlett's tears came early and flowed throughout, but it felt almost liberating, like a release of sadness and guilt. It was a short service, and it wasn't long before two of the cemetery staff appeared from under the shade of a nearby tree, shovels in hand, ready to fill the hole they'd dug.

After the priest finished reciting his final prayer, he turned to Scarlett, his blue eyes squinting against the sun. "Would you like to say a few words?"

Totally unprepared for a question Scarlett should have guessed would come, she said, "Yes, thank you." She bowed her head, closed her eyes, and desperately tried to remember the poem her mother would say to her at night before bed. She only remembered it because she'd looked it up to read at *her* funeral. Scarlett started tentatively, but once she passed the first line, it came as easily as the alphabet:

"*Day is done, gone the sun, from the hills, from the sky.*
All is well, safely rest, safely rest, all is well.
Fading light dims the sight, and a star gems the sky,
gleaming bright from afar, drawing nigh, falls the night.
Rest, dear one, rest."

Scarlett made her way back up the hill to the sound of dirt scattering over wood. When she reached the Honda, she climbed in and sat there for a while, her eyes still blurred by real tears she'd cried for someone she barely knew. But no matter how little she really knew about him, she would always share a connection with that man, and would never forget him, not for as long as she lived.

When Scarlett placed the key in the ignition, her cell rang from her purse in the passenger footwell. Fishing it out, she found it was a number she didn't recognize, but something prompted her to answer anyway. She put the receiver to her ear, fully expecting it to be a telemarketer offering a free stay at a Marriott of her choice if she only complete a brief survey. "Scarlett speaking."

"Hi, Ms. Laurent, this is Tina Lewis, Mr. Francis's attorney. I sent you the funeral invitation."

"Yes, of course," said Scarlett. "I'm actually there right now."

"Right," said Mrs. Lewis, seemingly uninterested. "I was hoping you were free to stop by my office today."

"Uh, why?" Scarlett asked, immediately regretting how flustered she sounded.

"Nothing serious. Mr. Francis gave me something to hold for safekeeping. He asked me to give it to you after the funeral. I thought you might want to stop by and pick it up."

"What is it?"

"Not sure, really; it's sealed. But I think it's a letter."

"A letter?" she repeated, her throat suddenly dry.

It was one thing staring down at a casket, imagining what Jimmy would say if he had one last opportunity to talk to her, but reading a letter was far too real. When she read his words, it would be his voice she heard in her head, talking to her from the other side. She wasn't sure if she was ready for that.

But if there's one thing that can overpower nervousness, it's curiosity.

. . .

Mrs. Lewis's office was downtown, a part of the city Scarlett tended to avoid whenever possible. Some people loved the bustle of city life, the impressive buildings, the vibrant energy. But for her, it all felt too man-made and claustrophobic, its magnitude and immensity a constant reminder of our insignificance.

At least there was a parking lot half a block from her building, one that, due to it being close to lunch, had plenty of open spots, all for the fair price of ten dollars per thirty minutes.

When Scarlett stepped into the elevator from the lobby, a stocky man got on with her, and the whole ride up, she got the sense that he was taking her in, but not in a sexual way. She couldn't say he was watching her, but she couldn't swear he was looking away, either. Regardless, Scarlett felt slight relief when the elevator deposited her on the eleventh floor, and the man stayed on, heading up higher into the building.

Mrs. Lewis's receptionist—a plump, attractive woman around Scarlett's age—guided Scarlett to a small waiting area made up of four low armchairs and a circular coffee table littered with magazines. Scarlett perched herself on one of the chairs and gazed out of the window, down onto the city below, to the honking cars and trickling flow of pedestrians, all moving with purpose, like worker ants ferrying food back to the nest.

A set of wide double doors opened across from her, and Mrs. Lewis came through the opening, her hands clasped together, a friendly smile atop a pressed navy pantsuit.

"Scarlett. Glad you could make it."

Mrs. Lewis thrust a bony hand in Scarlett's direction, and Scarlett shook it as she stood. She was around fifty, with chin-length brown hair and a sparrow's hard eyes and sharp nose.

"Please, follow me," she said, before glancing over to her receptionist, saying, "Hold my calls please, Amy."

Scarlett had only ever set foot in one lawyer's office before, who had tried and failed to get her off a speeding ticket. He was one of those billboard guys with a cheesy smile and an even cheesier slogan. She remembered his office was small and dark, every flat surface covered by files and paperwork. He even had to move a stack of Manila folders out of a chair before offering it to her.

Mrs. Lewis's office was the opposite of that. The wall to the left was floor-to-ceiling glass, while the wall to the right was lined with plaques and diplomas, with a few pieces of stick-thin furniture in between them. And there wasn't a single sheet of paper out-of-place anywhere.

They took their respective places on either side of the tinted glass desk, and Mrs. Lewis laced her fingertips together, creating a web with her hands. "Thank you for coming in on such short notice."

"Of course," said Scarlett. "No problem."

"How was the funeral?"

"It was... nice. I actually thought you might be there."

Mrs. Lewis gave a look of genuine bemusement. "Really, why?"

"I don't know, I guess. Did you know him for a long time?"

"No, he was a relatively new client. I've had many clients come to me when they are nearing the end. It's important to get your affairs in order, especially if you have no family to survive you."

"Right," said Scarlett.

"Well, anyway," said Mrs. Lewis, all business. "As I mentioned on the phone, I have something..." She reached down to the draw below her desk and pulled out a white card envelope with Scarlett's name written on the front. She held it out and said, "This is for you."

"Thank you," said Scarlett, taking it. "Did he tell you why he left it here?"

Mrs. Lewis narrowed her eyes, seeming surprised by the question. "I don't ask those sorts of questions of my clients. I'm sure you understand."

Scarlett smiled and nodded, thinking, *I don't understand any of this. Not at all.*

Scarlett slipped back across the busy road to the parking lot and into the Honda. Then she stared at the envelope for a full three minutes before building up the courage to open it. Just looking at her name scrawled on the front in Jimmy's shaky handwriting made the hairs on her arms stand up. There was also something small and hard at the bottom of the envelope, and she was more than a little nervous about finding out what it was.

But when she finally opened it and slipped out the first few inches of the piece of paper inside, it wasn't handwriting she saw, it was a cherry-red logo and letterhead that read, *Bank of LA.*

Scarlett read the document once, twice, then a third time before accepting what she'd read to be correct. It was a letter to Mr. Francis, notifying him that one Scarlett Laurent, was successfully made a co-owner of a safe deposit box (*number 211*) at their Hill Street branch.

Setting the letter on the passenger seat, Scarlett tipped the envelope upside down, and a small key fell into her palm. It was gold and only an inch or so long, like a key for a gym locker or a briefcase. At the base was a tiny three-digit number in black lettering—211.

What the hell is going on? What's in that box? And why didn't he tell me about it when he was alive? Why give this to the attorney?

A car horn blared from the street in front of her, and she quickly looked up to find a pickup truck nearly kissing the rear fender of a Prius that was parked curbside with its hazard lights on. The guy in the truck yelled something out of his window, then sped around the Prius while flipping off its driver, an older Middle Eastern man who either hadn't noticed any of this taking place, or pretended not to.

With the excitement over, Scarlett went to look back at the letter when something caught her eye, and a light flicked on in her head: an ignored detail that shouldn't have been overlooked. She checked the address on the letter once more, then looked back up at the tall building beyond the Prius. It was an impressive looking building, its towering beige brick facade signifying its institutional permanence. There was a carved gargoyle statue on the corner above a red sign spanning four-stories. Running down the sign, in bold, black lettering, were the words—*Bank of LA*.

Scarlett flicked her gaze to the street sign at the intersection —Hill Street.

Whatever was going on, the old man had planned it.

The bank's Assistant Manager was tall, at least six-four, and looked like a surfer. He had wavy blond hair, smooth, golden skin, and an easy smile that, from afar, made him look in his late twenties. But when Scarlett got close and started talking, she realized he must have been close to double that.

After thoroughly checking Scarlett's ID and confirming she had possession of the key, the Assistant Manager led Scarlett through a set of steel doors and into a long, thin room lined with hundreds of brass faceplates, each with its own three-digit number.

"There's a viewing room through that door," he said, pointing to a windowless door to the right. "You can take your box in there if you want some privacy from the, ah..." he pointed upward with his index finger and twirled it around, "... you know, cameras. And please, if you need any assistance, don't hesitate to ask."

"Thanks," said Scarlett, and he turned and headed back out.

Box 211 was on the bottom row, about ten feet past the viewing room door. The faceplates on the bottom row were bigger than the others—roughly ten inches by ten inches. She leaned down to 211, slotted the key in, and opened the faceplate revealing the charcoal-steel box within it.

When she slid it out, it hit the floor hard, even with only an inch drop. It was two feet long, and when Scarlett tried to lift it up, she had to strain against its weight. The thing must have weighed thirty pounds, maybe more. Scarlett managed to lug it into the viewing room, which was bathed in pale fluorescent light and completely bare, save for the stainless-steel table in the center. It looked more like an interrogation room than the type of place you'd expect to find in a bank.

She set the box on the table, her curiosity at a level she'd never felt, and lifted it up the lid. A buzz of electricity rushed through her, and it felt like the gravity in the room had been turned way up. She had to clutch the table not only to keep herself standing, but to convince herself through the cool metal under her fingers that she wasn't dreaming.

Staring back at her was a wall of cash. Stacks of hundred-dollar bills wrapped in paper bands, piled up to the brim like clothes packed into a suitcase. Scarlett had never seen this much cash—not even close. It looked like something out of a movie. Each stack was about half-an-inch thick, with $10,000 printed on the face of the paper band—and the box was full of them.

She began pulling them out and placing them on the table in piles of ten, with no intention of counting them all. But once she started, she couldn't stop, it was like she was possessed. When she was done, she stepped back, and a second wave of shock coursed through her blood, the magnitude of the moment settling in stages. She couldn't believe it—she was no longer staring at a *shit load* of cash, she was staring at three million, six hundred and forty thousand dollars.

She stared dumbfounded at the piles on the table, stunned that much money could fit in that small box—but it had. Her hand found her mouth while the same four words repeated in her head over and over and over: *Three-point-six million.*

Three-point-six million.

Three-point-six million.

27

LUCA

The nurse carried the scent of sweet coconut. Luca could picture her getting out of the shower that morning, spreading lotion across her tanned, naked skin. She was even more beautiful up close with her soft features and freckled nose. She was so enticing that he even had thoughts of taking her right then and there in that elevator. She must have felt his lingering eyes on her because she made a sly, subtle attempt to glance over at him. But he saw it. The elevator stopped at the eleventh floor, and she got off, and Luca stayed on. But he'd found what he needed, the brass sign in the lobby reading *Lewis and Bishop, Attorneys*.

Why is she going to see an attorney straight from Jimmy's funeral? He thought.

After that fateful day at Jimmy's house, Luca had Brooks run the girl's plates and managed to find out her address and the medical center she worked out of, although she didn't spend much time there. Luca had been following her ever since, only leaving her at night when he went back to the motel. He'd managed to keep his distance, to avoid being noticed, staying clear of her small residential street on the loud bike. He knew it was a risk getting into that elevator with her, but that itch for information was growing ever stronger, and he had to know what was going on.

He didn't have to wait long in the coffee shop across from the parking lot before she came back down to her car, carrying what looked like a letter. He watched her as she sat it her car for a few minutes, then she got back out and crossed the street to—he couldn't fucking believe it—the Bank of LA. And not just any branch; the Hill Street branch.

Suddenly, everything made sense, and Luca couldn't believe he hadn't thought of it before. No wonder Brooks couldn't find anything on Jimmy's financials; his money wasn't in an account, it was in the same place Jimmy had been storing his money since the 90s. Luca used to give Jimmy shit about it all the time; the only bank robber to keep physical cash in a bank. And Jimmy would say—it's the one place nobody can look as long as you're alive.

But Luca had to be sure. Even in his mind, it felt a little thin—a little too perfect. There are a million things she could be doing in a bank, even though she took that letter in with her. So Luca waited for a while, then headed up the worn granite steps and through the heavy glass doors into the bank. He knew there was a chance she could recognize him from the elevator and suspect he was following her, putting her on alert, but he had to take that chance. If he walked in and she was at one of the ATM's or talking to a teller about a fixed-rate loan, then so be it, he would just have to be more careful from then on. But she wasn't doing either of those things; she wasn't anywhere to be seen.

Luca played his hunch and approached one of the free tellers and asked if he could grab something from his own safe deposit box. The kid looked like he was still learning things about puberty, let alone the various facets of his job, so Luca wasn't concerned when he called over the branch Assistant Manager—a tall, goofy fuck with a terrible haircut.

"Can I help you, sir?" the Assistant Manager asked.

"I need to get something out of my safe deposit box.".

The Assistant Manager flashed an uneasy grin, then glanced over to a large set of steel doors to the left of the tellers. "I'm sorry, sir, but one of our other customers is using the viewing room right now. But if you don't mind waiting, I promise to get you in there as soon as she's out."

She, Luca thought. *Bingo.*

28

ANTON

Karina picked up her gold samovar teapot and poured the steaming liquid into her cup. She set the teapot down, stirred in sugar with a small gold spoon, and said, "So, I hear your efforts have been fruitless, yes?"

"So far," said Anton.

Anton was back in her office for the third time in three days. Ruslan was in his usual spot in the corner, his face buried in the morning's newspaper. But this time, Anton was without Diego, who must have still been out looking. They'd had no luck figuring out who Eric was, and Randel had up and disappeared.

Karina blew on her tea, sipped it, then sat back in her chair. "You have found *nothing*?"

"No, but I think we're getting close."

"Of course you are," she said mockingly.

Anton hadn't slept in thirty-three hours, and his eyes felt like they'd been dipped in salt, but he knew he needed to show how invested he was, how much getting the money back meant to him. He straightened and swallowed hard. "Look, I know I —" but Karina interrupted immediately.

"No, you look. I send you on simple fucking job, and you lose our product. And now, when I ask you to find those responsible, you chase your tail for few days and find nothing." She squinted her eyes and cocked her head to one side, measuring Anton. "Please, remind me what exactly you bring to this organization?"

Before he could answer, she said, "Don't answer that, it will only infuriate me. I will answer for you—nothing. You bring nothing. You walk around like a fucking American playboy gangster. But I see what you really are. You are a pretender. And you would have nothing if you weren't Viktor's son."

"But I *am* Viktor's son," Anton said defiantly.

She held his gaze for a moment, her expression hard, yet inquisitive. Then she stood from her desk and said, "Come. I have something to show you."

Acid churned in Anton's stomach and crept up his throat as they stepped down the narrow staircase into the dark basement, the acrid stench of old blood and sweat thrusting its way up his nostrils. It felt like they were descending into a dungeon at a gulag prison camp or one of the gas chambers in Auschwitz—the air drenched in death and decay, with walls that clung to the final screams of a thousand desperate souls. He'd heard rumors of this place, even from New York, and he couldn't stop the questions from flooding his mind—*Why is she taking me down here? Would she kill me over a few bricks of heroin and a snide remark?*

The answer to that, of course, was a resounding *yes*.

Anton was in front, with Karina at the back and Ruslan in the middle. Anton was half bracing himself for a heavy blow across the head. Or perhaps, as he turned into the basement, he would see a muzzle flash explode in the darkness and a bullet rip through his chest. He wanted to reach for his gun—his fight-or-flight mechanisms twitching like a phantom limb—but he managed to refrain and keep his head. And as he reached the last step, he wasn't met with gunfire. Instead, he turned the corner to find two men in only their underwear, under hanging spotlights in the center of the space. Anton sagged with relief.

One of the poor bastards under the light was covered by a black hood, and the other had a face Anton didn't recognize. The hooded guy was hanging by his arms from a thick chain, his feet curled back, knees almost touching the floor. He had blood running down his chest from wounds that might have been on his face. By the way his body was slumped, Anton guessed he was already dead.

The other, bigger man was definitely alive though, tied to a chair, blood streaming from his nose and lips, a small puddle of sweat at his feet. Two of Anton's suit-wearing comrades were standing beyond them, just outside of the light, their faces masked by the half-darkness.

The torture method for the hooded guy was simple. He was tied up, probably beaten with a wrench or a steel pipe. But for the guy in the chair, Karina—or whoever she'd appointed for the task—had gotten creative. There was an old sports motorcycle suspended from a small crane lift, its back tire only inches from the man's left leg, ready to rip it apart. Seeing that set up made Anton wince, his imagination filling in the blanks of what came next.

As Anton and the others stepped into the light, the guy looked up at them with eyes so pregnant with fear, they looked as though they may burst. Karina pointed at him but looked at Anton. "You recognize this man?"

Anton took a good look at his face, then shook his head. "No."

"His name is Mr. Daniels. He is one of the men who robbed you few nights ago."

The big cop, Anton thought.

The man—Daniels—cleared his throat, spluttered blood onto his chin, and spoke in a desperate voice, "Please, you got the wrong guy."

Karina placed her finger over his bloody lips. "Shush now, do not insult me by lying. That would not be wise." She turned back to Anton. "Do you know how we found him?"

Again, he shook his head *no* and added a shrug. Ruslan stepped to the guy hanging from the chain, pulled off the hood, and a hot buzz ripped through Anton's gut. The guy *was* dead, his face a beaten mess. But that wasn't the shocking part—the shocking part was that it was Diego.

Anton tried to speak, but the words wouldn't form. "Wha... what? I... I don't understand."

"I knew the leak had to have come from within," said Karina. "How else did they know exactly where you would be? And why else would they hit you after you made the trade; why not take the money?" She directed her next questions to Daniels. "I take it you already had a buyer lined up, no? Worth a lot more once you've cut it, am I right, Mr. Daniels?"

Daniels didn't so much as blink, and Karina came back to Anton. "So, I had you both followed. And although *you* just pranced around falling over boxes, Diego was of some value. He led us to this man's warehouse, where there was a special type of vehicle. Would you like to guess what kind of vehicle it was?"

Anton spoke with a flat tone trying to sound neither insolent nor stupid. "A cop car?"

"Bingo! An armor-plated police cruiser with bulletproof windows." She said it slowly, as if each word was its own sentence, its own condemning fact. "It was a very fine coincidence that Diego only chose to shoot at that car and not the van, no?"

"I thought he was trying to avoid hitting the product," Anton snapped, then realized the question was rhetorical. And he suddenly felt so much anger toward Diego. He'd betrayed him *and* made him look like a fool. *Why?* He must have known he would get caught. Maybe he'd gotten sick of working for that crazy bitch and thought this was his way out.

Karina moved closer to Daniels, lifted his chin with her index finger, and said softly, "I know you have a partner. The other cop. Where is he? I want what you stole from us."

Daniels tried to clear his throat again, this time swallowing the blood. "I told you, I don't know what you're talking about."

Karina smiled, knowing she was about to inflict pain. Daniels opened his mouth to speak but decided against it.

"I know you are not alone in this. That's why you are still alive. But you must give me the location of your partner. You do this for me, and I promise you will die quickly. But if you don't," she patted the seat of the motorcycle and smiled again. "This could take weeks."

Daniels shook his head rapidly. "I don't know."

She slowly lent down to his eye level and spoke in a long, flirty tone, "Come on, you can tell me."

Daniels stuttered, "I... I... I swear."

"Well, that *is* a shame." She stroked his cheek, then stood upright and nodded to Ruslan, who stepped over to the bike and twisted the key in the ignition. The lights of the bike flicked on, and it made an electric whirring sound.

"No, wait, please!"

Ruslan pressed the ignition button, and the bike came alive, purring like a gas-powered panther. He pulled the clutch, flicked the bike into first gear, then released the clutch and pinned the throttle back. The sound was deafening, the deep purr growing to the screaming roar of fire and metal. The thick tire spun with the speed of a disk saw mere inches from the guy's leg, and through the smoke pouring out of the exhaust, Anton saw his face turn the color of spoiled meat.

Despite the chaos, Anton couldn't help but admire the bike idea, whether Karina had thought of it or not. It was genius, albeit a little elaborate. Most people would just beat a guy if they want to get information out of them, but if you go too far, they might die before they get a chance to talk. Which is likely what happened to Diego. But even the sound of that bike echoing around this small space would scare most men into talking. That high-pitched metallic grind of machine parts, giving a stark reminder of just how soft organic tissue really is.

Karina nodded to Ruslan, and he released the throttle slightly, lowering the revs.

"Give me a name!" yelled Karina over the roar of the bike.

Daniels screamed out through tears, "I don't know! I swear! I swear!" and Anton, for one, believed him. But it didn't matter what he believed, or anyone else in that room for that matter. Nothing could help Daniels now.

Karina nodded once more to Ruslan, who pinned the throttle back again, the roar somehow even louder, the reverberation occupying and dominating every millimeter of the space. Then Ruslan grabbed the seat of the bike and swung it into the guy's thigh, the black rubber tearing his flesh like sandpaper on a peach. Blood sprayed, and Anton wanted to look away, but he couldn't show any signs of weakness—not in front of Karina. Instead, he stared at Daniels's bloodied face, a face locked in a scream, his voice lost in the roar.

Anton's stomach began darting around his gut like a spider stuck in a glass jar, and he had to swallow hard to stop from heaving. It wasn't as if he was totally new to death; he'd been the last face two different men had seen before they'd gone down for the long sleep. But a bullet from ten feet away wasn't the same as torture; it wasn't this. Suddenly Daniels's eyes rolled back, and his head fell limp onto his right shoulder, passed out from the pain.

Ruslan moved the bike away and kicked it into neutral, and the roar was replaced by laughter from the suits in the darkness. With his ears ringing and nostrils filled with the smell of burning flesh, Anton looked over to Karina and found eyes brimming with sadistic pleasure.

When she snapped out of it, she caught Anton looking, then stepped toward him and leaned in as if to tell him a secret. He gave her his ear, and she said, "Whether he talks or not, we've lost big, you understand? We've lost money, product, respect. And you let it happen. Now is the time for you to be useful. The time for you to be a man of action," She paused and moved even closer, her lips brushing his ear. "Come back to me with something soon, or do not come back at all."

29

DETECTIVE BROOKS

It was still early evening when Brooks got to the new crime scene. The sun was slipping down the sky to the West, leaving a beautiful orange glow over the city. But luckily, there were no eager onlookers with their iPhones out trying to be the next Kelly Lange. Just a few uniformed cops sitting in their cruiser at the end of the street, with a handful more holding the tape line across the opening of the small rear loading bay.

Brooks parked the Deville behind the medical examiner's van, and when he pulled himself out of the car, his back shot a bolt of pain up to his brain. Just a friendly reminder that even the simplest of movements were off-limits—especially after a long day. He did manage to keep hold of his Dunkin' Donuts coffee, though. Lord knows that if he'd dropped it, whoever was in the loading bay would have to wait an extra hour or so for Brooks to start working their case. They probably wouldn't care, though, given their current situation.

It'd been a few days since Luca told Brooks he saw Jimmy's nurse murder him. A story Brooks would have laughed at if it didn't come with video evidence. And they'd gotten no closer to finding out why she did it. Luca was following her around the clock, while Brooks looked into her, but they had nothing. Brooks even went back to speak to Eric, but he was gone—the warehouse cleaned out and abandoned. It was unlikely he would have any information on her, anyway. The nurse was clean—no record, no secrets. Brooks was even starting to wonder just what he saw in the video—a murder, or something else.

Either way, he was starting to lose interest. He was almost back to life as usual, free of Luca and his bullshit. And for Brooks, that meant a call from dispatch—another good old homicide.

As he pulled the lid off to take his first sip of the coffee, Brooks noticed Chen walking toward him, sporting a fretful expression. As she got close, he asked, "What have we got?"

"We've got a mess," she said, her eyes wide and eyebrows raised. "Garbage guys route brings them by here twice a week. But when they opened the dumpster today... Well, you'll see."

"Yippee," said Brooks. "I love surprises." He blew on his coffee, sipped it. "Any witnesses?"

"Not yet. All we've got are the garbage guys, and they're on their way to the station to give statements. We also interviewed two employees of the bakery who stayed late to prep for the morning bread run. They didn't hear or see anything, but the bread ovens are on the far side of the building, so..." She shrugged.

"What else?"

"I've got some uniforms going door to door to check the cameras of the surrounding businesses. Hopefully, one of them caught the license plate as the perps were leaving."

"Perps?" said Brooks. "Plural?"

"Oh, I think so," said Chen, with a quick nod of her head.

Brooks took another sip of coffee, then said, "Well, time to clock back in, I guess."

Chen fell in beside him, and as they moved toward the tape line, Brooks said, "You hear anything back from Florida PD on the mother and daughter of Marshal Teal?"

"They're still trying to track them down."

"Any other leads?"

"Nope," Chen said dejectedly.

"Too bad," said Brooks, and for a moment, he thought he might actually have meant it.

Brooks badged one of the young cops who held up the tape for them to duck under. And when he straightened back up on the other side, his back gave him another nudge of pain, reminding him of what they'd talked about when he'd gotten out of the car.

The loading bay was not much wider than a truck, and shorter than the distance from a pitcher's mound to the plate. A narrow gray strip lined with graffiti tags and cardboard, with two dumpsters at the end. It was designed to bring food deliveries in and trash out through the bakery's shutter doors. The whole thing was cast in heavy shadows and filled with the scent of baking bread, that sweet and almost sour aroma that somehow smelled warm.

Two forensic officers were flashing photos while Patterson adjusted one of the standing LED lights that poured white light down into the open dumpster on the right. He noticed Brooks and said, "You've come to see the freak show, huh?"

Brooks shot Chen an inquisitive look. "Is it that bad?"

She grimaced. "I have to be honest, I've never seen anything like it."

Brooks let out a long, tired groan. He didn't take Chen or Patterson for the dramatic types, so he braced himself for something awful; a maimed kid, perhaps. But when he got to the open dumpster and leaned in to look inside, his blood froze and a dense buzzing invaded his skull.

Buried among the trash bags and newspapers and sticky grime, was the mutilated body of Daniels. He had burns everywhere except his face—thick black streaks, like he'd been scolded by a thin layer of boiling tar. But that wasn't the worst part. He was cradling something in his arms like a mother would cradle a newborn baby. It was the severed head of a bearded man Brooks didn't recognize.

Brooks had to put his hand to his mouth and fight back the urge to gag. After taking a moment, he pointed to the burns and said, "What the hell is this?"

Before Chen could answer, Patterson said, "It looks like rubber—probably from tire burns."

"Tire burns?" said Brooks. "My god."

"Yep," said Chen. "Could have kept him alive a long time like that. But what's bothering me is why the hell would they leave them out here like this for anyone to find? Wouldn't they want to get rid of the bodies?"

Brooks cleared his throat and tried to look away, but he couldn't. "Maybe they were trying to send a message."

"One hell of a message," said Patterson. "Those poor bastards must have pissed off the wrong people."

Brooks's shock and revulsion suddenly morphed into terror as he thought about the people responsible for this mess coming after him. Considering he didn't recognize the face of the severed head, it was likely Daniels was murdered for something unrelated to Brooks. Maybe something to do with that cop car. But he couldn't be sure. And even if Brooks hadn't been involved, Daniels may have given his name up just to make the pain stop. Lord knows Brooks would have told them anything if it was him.

A loud voice boomed in his head, years of frustration

forming into words: *I'm done with this shit. I want out of this place.*

At that moment, his phone rang in his pocket, and in his panic, he answered without checking the caller ID and said, "Brooks, homicide."

It was Luca's croaky voice on the other line, slow and deliberate, probably more than a few beers deep. "We need to meet."

Brooks carefully turned his back to Chen and stepped out of earshot. "I can't, I'm busy."

"Trust me, we need to talk. You're going to like this."

"I doubt that very much."

"Trust me," he repeated. "I figured it out. I know why she did it."

Luca didn't sound like his usual self. Yes, he was probably drunk, but that wasn't it. His tone was light, almost enthusiastic. And the threatening, malevolent undertone that typically lived in his voice was gone.

Brooks craned his head and saw Chen watching with eager eyes, probably hoping he was receiving some new information about an open case. He cupped the phone tight to his ear and said, "Where?"

"Murphy's," said Luca. "One hour." Then he hung up.

"What's up?" Chen asked when Brooks turned back.

"Oh nothing, just personal stuff. A, uh... medical thing," he lied.

"Everything okay?"

"Sure. Well, kind of." Brooks gestured to his car. "I've got to make a few calls. Why don't you work with the uniforms to set up a blockade? If the TV people get wind of this, they're going to be all over us."

Chen looked a little unsure for a moment, then caught herself and nodded. "Ten-four."

When Brooks got to his Cadillac, he dialed both the

numbers he had for Eric, knowing he wouldn't answer—and he didn't. Dead or alive, Eric was gone, and Brooks was never going to see him again. He just hoped whoever killed Daniels hadn't been watching the warehouse when he had gone to visit.

Fuck, he thought. *I need to leave this city and never come back.*

30

LUCA

Murphy's pub was a tacky Irish bar with sports memorabilia pinned to every square inch of the wall and ceiling space. Luca usually hated drinking in any place that offered more than just a beer and stool, but it was the only place he could find that was empty, save for the bartender, who was on glass washing duty. Or at least it *was* empty until some schmuck in a Hawaiian Shirt came in and sat down two seats over from Luca at the bar. He was about Luca's age, the small bit of hair he had left was the color of a ripe peach, and his skin glowed pink from too many hours spent under the California sun—a tourist, Luca decided. Probably had his family drop him off at the nearest bar before they headed off to see the Hollywood Walk of Fame.

Hawaiian Shirt ordered a beer, and they both sipped in silence while the bartender moved on to wiping down tables. Then, out of nowhere, Hawaiian Shirt threw out his hands as if he was about to catch a football from a looping pass and said, "Can you believe this shit?"

Luca followed his eyes up and found a pretty news anchor on the almost-muted TV above the bar, delivering some breaking news. Apparently, a schizophrenic manic depressive named Clarence Rudolf thought it'd be smart to shoot up a mall in North Carolina. Seventeen dead, another twenty-eight wounded.

"It's just crazy," Hawaiian Shirt said. "I mean, how many of these shootings need to happen before Washington does something?"

Luca gave the guy a sideways glance and said, "Do what?"

"Well, they could ban assault rifles and high capacity magazines. Background checks and increased gun safety laws. They could fix the goddamn mental health system and bring back mental hospitals. I mean, they need to try something." He turned on his stool to face Luca. "You know, I looked it up, and there have been more mass shootings this year already than the whole of last year. There's more than one a day. Can you believe that? You can't even go to the goddamn mall anymore without worrying about getting shot."

Luca figured he would have a bit of fun with the guy, so he sipped his beer and said casually, "You want to know what I think? I think it's lazy."

"The reporting?" Hawaiian Shirt said excitedly. "I've been saying the same thing." His voice was high and animated, as though he'd been searching for someone to discuss this topic with all day. "They're too scared to say it how it is, to hit the real points of the arguments. It's just—"

"No, I'm not talking about the journalists," Luca said. He pointed to the mugshot of Clarence on the TV. "I'm talking about him. He wants to kill a bunch of people, so he buys a gun and shoots at them until the cops show up and take him out, or he takes himself out. That's just lazy and uncreative. Hell, it's downright sloppy. You want to take out a bunch of people, get a big body count, you have to put the time in, you need to do the planning, you need patience and perseverance."

The guy's mouth was gaping, and Luca could tell he wanted to haul ass out of the bar. But his body wouldn't move, his muscles all performing a synchronized mutiny.

"I mean, shit, just off the top of my head—you get a job at a toothpaste factory, work there for six or seven months until you earn the trust of your coworkers. Then, when no one is looking, you slip an industrial-sized bottle of cyanide into the mixing vat. You'll take out at least a few hundred before they figure out the source of the problem and issue a recall, right? And by then, you'll be long gone."

Hawaiian Shirt smiled awkwardly, the twisted face of a frightened child in a new, uncomfortable situation they don't quite understand. He said, "Uh-huh. Right." Then he reached into his pocket, tossed down a few dollars next to his nearly full beer, and started to stand.

But Luca reached over and grabbed his arm, pulling him back down. "Hey, what about this? This is even better. You buy a brick of heroin, right. But not black tar—you get the low-quality stuff, the shittier the better. Then, when you cut it, you lace it with Botulinum and sell it for thirty percent cheaper than anyone else on the street. The bums will eat that shit up. They won't even care when they hear the stories of people dying off some product in circulation. They'll shoot up, anyway. And you can roll by alleyways and underpasses and watch as their nervous systems fail, and they die slowly. You'd be a hero." He let go of the man and spread his hands through the air. "The guy who wiped out the scum of LA."

With his arm free, Hawaiian Shirt backed away toward the door, said, "You've got problems, man," and hauled ass out of the bar. And as Luca turned on his stool to follow him, he found Brooks at a table in the corner, shaking his head.

Luca hadn't noticed him come in, but he must have been there a while, because after Luca swiped Hawaiian Shirt's beer and joined Brooks at the table, Brooks said, "You're a twisted fuck. You know that, right? Like pure evil."

"I'm not evil," Luca said, placing the beers down and taking a seat. "Shit, there's no such thing as good people and bad people, Brooks. You should know that."

"There's not?" Brooks asked, his head cocked to one side.

"No, there's not. We're all just living in each other's worlds."

Brooks let out a nervous chuckle, then pointed at Luca's glass. "How many of those have you had?"

"I'm serious. I learned that from watching movies on the inside."

"Movies?"

"What is this, twenty fucking questions? Yeah, movies. See, movies are different from real life because their worlds are always the same—whether it's *Pulp Fiction* or Casper the friendly fucking ghost. It doesn't matter. Their world is either rated R, or PG, or G whatever, but it stays the same the whole movie. But in real life, it's different. All those worlds cross over and get mixed into one. See that fucking guy who just walked out of here? He lives in a PG-13 world. He probably had a good childhood, felt love, some sadness, maybe some drama, but never any real danger. Sure, he's heard and read about bad things, but never saw them firsthand, never lived them. But for me, I come from a world that's not even rated. The type of movies where the blood and violence is real. No, it's not that I'm bad and he's good. He's just not supposed to be in my world. And I'm sure as shit not supposed to be in his."

"Okay," said Brooks after a considerable pause, as if it was the only word in the English language that he knew. "So, are you going to tell me what the hell is going on, or what?"

Luca looked around the empty bar, made sure the bartender wasn't in earshot, then told Brooks all about the girl and the bank on Hill Street. When he was done, Brooks flicked his head back, smirked, and said, "Bullshit."

"No—real shit. I even waited to see her come out of the vault. The bitch looked like she'd seen Jimmy's ghost in there."

Brooks took a long pull of Hawaiian Shirt's beer, looking like he wanted to rip holes in Luca's theory—but he couldn't. Instead, he just said, "Shit."

"Yeah. That's what I thought."

"But none of this makes sense. Why was he living in that house if he had money? And how did the girl get the key to the safe deposit box? I mean, did he tell her about his stash? Is that why she killed him?"

"All good questions," Luca said. "But what do those questions all have in common? They don't matter. Not one bit. Not anymore."

"Okay, so let's say you're right. What's your plan?"

"What do you think? I'm going to make her hand over the money."

"That easy, huh?" said Brooks.

"I got the tape of her killing Jimmy, don't I?"

Brooks shrugged. "Sounds like you got it all figured out, then. So why did you call me? I told you I want out of this shit."

Luca scratched the stubble around his chin as the thought in his head took the shape of words. "Well, here's how I see it. She doesn't know who Jimmy really was, right? She just thought he was some old guy that nobody would take any notice of. So, when a homicide detective turns up asking questions about ex-cons and stolen money, making implications that something fishy might have gone on but without actually accusing her... well, a girl like that, it's going to put her on edge. So when I roll up with the only piece of evidence that can tie her to a murder, she's going to be throwing the money at me to avoid doing time. You can bet your ass on that."

Brooks screwed up his face, his eyes narrowed, and Luca could almost see his brain running through all the different scenarios, trying to make an educated guess on how they would all pan out. He straightened his shirt cuff and twisted the gold LAPD ring around his finger. "I want a cut."

Luca chuckled. "Oh, you do now, do you?"

"That's right. And you can start throwing threats my way if you want to, but it isn't going to change anything. I can't do this shit anymore. I need a payday."

Brooks's tone was firm, but he was wearing a look of desperation Luca had never seen on him before. He had seen it on others, though. In fact, he knew it well. It meant, *I'm fucked, and I need a way out.* It was a vulnerability that was perfect for exploiting.

"Well, damn, look who finally grew some balls," said Luca. "Okay, Mr. Payday, I'll give you ten percent of whatever we get from the girl."

"Twenty."

Luca wagged a finger at Brooks, a smirk forming on his face. "Don't get greedy, now. I put this together, I made the tape."

"Yeah, and I found Jimmy. We don't even know how much we're talking about here. But you give me twenty percent, and I'll go see the nurse, make sure she doesn't think about going to the cops. Plus, I can keep an ear out at the station and get you a clean vehicle to leave town when this is all over."

Luca squinted at the proposition, pretending to mull it over before flashing a wide alligator grin. "Okay, you got a deal."

But the truth was, it didn't matter what Brooks asked for; that old fuck wasn't getting a goddamn penny.

31

SCARLETT

"Okay, here's another. A female member of staff is at her desk, trying to complete an assignment. A male supervisor approaches to discuss the assignment, and without warning, begins massaging her back."

A sea of red cards went up around the room. They were mid-way through one of the bi-weekly group meetings in one of the cramped rooms at Scarlett's medical center. Rows of bored faces slumped in plastic, stackable chairs like giant school children. This week was sexual harassment training, and Scarlett's manager, Jackie, was reading out hypothetical scenarios, and it was the staff's job to judge if they constituted sexual harassment or not. They had to raise a red card if they thought it did, yellow if they weren't sure, and green if it was okay. Scarlett was just throwing up whatever card anyone else was throwing up, her mind far too distant to concentrate on the questions.

"A male member of staff often sends emails to his female coworkers containing lewd jokes with sexual references. Is this sexual harassment or just a bit of light-hearted office fun?"

Another sea of red went up. Everyone except for an older

guy called Jerry, who flashed everyone a deer-in-the-headlights look before looking up and pretending to be shocked to see a yellow card in his hand.

Scarlett had often heard people say the meetings were the worst part of the job, and that's coming from people who watch others die for a living. They were pretty terrible, though. If it wasn't training, it was hours of managers bombarding the staff with information on new compliance regulations and their ever-diminishing benefits package.

But today, none of that mattered. They could be showing a slide show of graphic car wrecks, and Scarlett would still only see images of that box and that money. She hadn't told anyone, of course—not even Josh. She was too scared of the questions, and she couldn't risk raising any suspicions about Jimmy's death. Besides, why wasn't that money in a bank account where it should be? And why was he living in a crappy house with cheap hospice care when he could afford the best?

But even with those questions, for the first time in a long time, Scarlett felt buoyant and optimistic. She'd taken a huge risk helping Jimmy—another one of her naïve, half-baked schemes to bring her happiness. But by doing it, she'd indirectly unlocked something that could once and for all quash any concerns about her future.

She was rich.

As she pondered the ludicrous situation she was in, detached from Jackie's new scenario about eye contact in the workplace, Scarlett glanced to her right and saw the small face of Lily, the intern, peering through the strip of glass on the exit door. When Lily saw she had Scarlett's attention, she quickly waved for her to come outside and mouthed the words, "*It's urgent.*"

Scarlett tried and failed to get up without making a sound. Heads turned—who's that? Shame her!—and Jackie managed to give Scarlett a death glare without stopping her story as Scarlett hurried over to the door and slipped out.

"There's a man here to see you," said Lily, sounding a little rattled. "He said he's a detective."

"A detective?" said Scarlett. "Like, the police?"

Lily looked at her deadpan as if she'd been asked a trick question. "Uh... yeah, the police. I told him you were in a meeting, but he just said he'd wait, so I took him to your office. I hope that's okay."

A detective? To see me? Scarlett's brain lingered on that for a moment, and she had to swallow hard to control her panic. Then she noticed the mild concern on Lily's face, so she forced a smile and tried to sound relaxed. "Uh, sure, yeah. Thanks. I'll head over there right now."

Scarlett's "office" was a supply closet turned joint workspace that she shared with two other nurses. The space was barely larger than a phone booth and had no windows, but Scarlett spent so little time there it didn't matter.

When she opened the door, she found the detective alone, sitting in her chair, studying a framed photograph of the day Josh proposed. He was older than Scarlett had expected, maybe late sixties, with a gut and thinning gray hair. And when he noticed her, instead of being embarrassed at getting caught with the photo, he simply gazed at her with the look of a man who'd given up caring what other people thought.

He slowly placed the photo on the desk, then his wide mouth creased into a wry smile before he spoke with a loud, confident voice that matched his aura. "You're Ms. Laurent, I presume?"

Scarlett closed the door behind her and said, "Yes. Please, call me Scarlett." Trying to come off as friendly as possible.

"Scarlett," he said, almost as a question to himself. "What a beautiful name."

"Thank you."

She waited for him to speak again, but instead, he just stared at her, his blue eyes neither warm nor hostile. After what felt like a full minute, Scarlett said, "So, how can I help you?"

His eyes narrowed, and he seemed disappointed by her getting to the point. Like breaking an uncomfortable silence had become a social faux pas, and everyone had neglected to mention it to her. He pulled his wallet from his jacket pocket and flashed his detective's badge. "My name's Detective Henry Brooks. I'm with the LAPD." He gestured to one of the other seats. "Please, sit down."

She did so, then crossed her legs, feeling vulnerable under his heavy stare. "What can I do for you, detective?"

"I'm here to talk about a former patient of yours. Mr. Nealson."

"Who?"

Detective Brooks gave his forehead an exaggerated slap like someone out of a Charlie Chaplin movie. "Silly me. I meant Mr. Francis. James Francis."

Scarlett's heart began working double time, and she did her best not to show it. "Of course. What did you want to talk about?"

He pulled a notepad from his jacket pocket, unclipped a pen, and hovered it over the pad. "How well did you know Jimmy, Ms. Laurent?"

Scarlett shrugged. "Not very well. He was a patient of mine before he passed."

"What exactly did you know about him?"

"Just that he was a nice man, no family. He liked to talk and play chess. That's about it."

Detective Brooks looked over the pad at Scarlett, his level gaze telling her she hadn't answered his question satisfactorily. "That's all you know? Nothing else?"

"That's all," said Scarlett. "He wasn't my patient for very long."

Brooks leaned back in his chair and crossed his legs, his small, twisted lower half looking cartoonish sprouting from his broad torso. And when he spoke again, he spoke as if he was addressing the room, even though it was just the two of them in there. "I knew Jimmy many years ago. Back in the late eighties and nineties. Back when he went by the name James Nealson, and he was revered as one of the best thieves in the city."

"Thief?" said Scarlett with a soft laugh. "I think you might mean someone else. This guy was..."

"Jimmy was a convicted felon, Ms. Laurent. He and his crew planned and executed armed robberies all over California, and probably other states too. They robbed banks, drug dealers —anything with a big score. They were meticulous and well organized. And several people lost their lives directly because of the jobs Jimmy planned."

A flash of heat flushed over Scarlett's face, and her hand found her throat. "My god, that's... I had no idea."

"You wouldn't. After his last job back in '94, Jimmy disappeared. And when he finally returned, it was under the name James Francis. Hell, we only just discovered it ourselves."

All Scarlett could say was, "I'm sorry, this is coming as quite a shock."

Detective Brooks didn't respond. Instead, he just looked around the tiny office, casually scanning the shelves as if he was in a boutique clothing store. When he brought his gaze back to Scarlett, he said, "How did Jimmy die, Ms. Laurent?"

"Respiratory failure. He had advanced-stage COPD. His lungs were weak, and they failed."

"Right," he said, jotting something down in his notepad. "Nice way to go."

"Excuse me?"

"Well, all things considered, having your lungs stop working and drifting off into the long night ain't such a bad way to go. Not after the life he led. I know most of his associates didn't get off that lightly."

Scarlett could sense he was trying to elicit a reaction out of her, but she didn't give one. There was something not quite right about this guy. He seemed to be relishing in her reaction as he fed her more information, bit by bit.

Detective Brooks tilted his chin up and asked, "Did he leave you anything after his death?"

"Uh, yes," Scarlett said, a little flustered. "An old Bible."

"A Bible?" A frown creased the detective's droopy face. "Are you a religious woman, Scarlett?"

He kept saying her name—Scarlett this and *Ms.* Laurent that. She knew he was trying to work some psychological angle, but to what end?

"No," she said. "Not really."

"Me neither. I believe justice is best served out there on the streets. This city is my church, you know what I mean?"

Scarlett opened her mouth to speak, but whatever response her brain had conjured up died in her throat. The fact was, she had no idea what he meant or what he wanted.

"Nope," he went on. "I've never had much use for a Bible. Did he leave you anything else, anything at all? I mean, a big-time crook like Jimmy, who knows what he had lying around."

He gave her a look a parent gives a child, a look that said—if you confess now, I'll go easy on you. But there was no way she was going to give up that easy. If they had reason to believe she'd done something wrong, they would arrest her, or at least bring her in for interrogation, wouldn't they? She held his gaze and said, "No, nothing."

He nodded slowly, but his eyes told her that he knew she

was lying. And Scarlett was suddenly struck with an urge to get him out of there.

"With all due respect, detective," she said. "Why did you come here?" There was an element of challenge in her tone, and Brooks seemed to pick up on it as he sat straighter.

"Well, I just thought I'd stop by and tell you who Jimmy really was. And... to warn you, I guess."

"Warn me of what?"

"Jimmy left behind a lot of enemies, Ms. Laurent."

"What does that mean?" said Scarlett, a defensive snap in her voice.

"Well, in his last job alone, he left one of his crew dead and had the other sent to prison. Not to mention all the money he's relieved people of over the years. If such people were to find out that James Francis was Jimmy Nealson, as we have, they might come looking for answers. Just something to be aware of."

Scarlett suddenly felt like she was sinking into her chair, all this new information overwhelming her.

Detective Brooks slowly got to his feet and said, "Well, I have to go. You know how it is; murderers to catch." He winked, then fished a business card from his pocket and placed it on her desk. "You want to talk to me about anything, you call me."

Who was this cop? And why was he acting like he knew something Scarlett didn't? She hadn't met many cops before, no detectives she could recall. But she'd seen enough TV to know this guy was playing a game. One she didn't want to be a part of.

When she spoke again, her voice was dry and small and sounded like it belonged to someone triple her age. "Nice to meet you, detective."

She stood and held out her hand to shake, but Detective

Brooks raised it to his mouth and presented it with a kiss. "The pleasure is all mine."

As he slipped passed her toward the door, a question formed in Scarlett's brain, and although she knew it wasn't smart, she couldn't stop herself from asking: "How did you know that James Francis was Jimmy Nealson?"

Detective Brooks turned back. "Excuse me?"

"You said that James Nealson disappeared, and you've just now discovered that he came back as James Francis. How did you find that out?"

He gave her a wide fervent grin and said, "I'm a detective, Scarlett. I'm good at figuring stuff out." Then he was out of the office, the door closing behind him.

Questions began swirling around Scarlett's head like cars caught in a twister. And she needed answers. With no one else to turn to, she quickly pulled out her cell and dialed the attorney.

Her assistant, Amy, answered on the sixth ring. "Hello, Lewis and Bishop, how may I help you?"

"Can I speak to Mrs. Lewis? It's Scarlett Laurent."

"I'm sorry, she's unavailable. Can I take a message?"

"When will she be free to talk?"

Amy sighed, sounding put out. "Let me check her schedule. One moment, please."

Scarlett chewed a hangnail as she waited, her conversation with the detective replaying in her head. "So it looks like she has back-to-back meetings until lunch, then she's out for the afternoon. I can't really say when she'll be free."

Scarlett hung up without a word and pulled her car keys from her purse.

. . .

Amy was at her desk, filing her nails, the bored look of a teenager slapped across her face. She shifted in her seat when she noticed Scarlett and tucked the nail file into her lap.

"Ms. Laurent, I thought I..."

She trailed off as Scarlett marched straight passed her and headed for the doors to Mrs. Lewis's office. She didn't know what had come over her, she wasn't even thinking about what she was doing, she just had to know if those stories were true.

Amy yelled, "Wait, you can't go in there!" but Scarlett was already shoving the doors open. Mrs. Lewis was at her desk with her landline phone receiver up to her ear, a bemused look spreading across her face. She gave Scarlett a strange, forced smile, then said, "I'll call you back," into the receiver and slowly hung up. "Ms. Laurent, is everything okay?"

"Look, I'm sorry, but did you know about Mr. Francis?" said Scarlet, her voice shaky.

Amy appeared beside her. "I tried to stop her, but she just ignored me."

"It's quite alright," said Mrs. Lewis. "Thank you, Amy."

Amy sighed, then stormed out and slammed the door shut behind her. Mrs. Lewis leaned back in her chair and interlocked her fingers, adopting the calm demeanor of a psychiatrist. "I take it you also received a visit from the good detective?" she said. "Quite the unpleasant character, isn't he?"

"You've met him?"

"He came by first thing this morning." She waved her hand over her immaculately tidy desk. "Disrupted my whole schedule."

"What did he ask you?"

Mrs. Lewis looked annoyed by the question but answered, anyway. "He was curious about Mr. Francis's movements over the past few years. And I told him that Mr. Francis was a new client who I'd only spoken to a few times. The last time being when he asked me to hold on to that package for you."

Scarlett must have lost her ability to hide her reactions because Mrs. Lewis leaned forward, suddenly all business. "Look, to my knowledge, Mr. Francis was never involved in any unlawful activity. And besides, even if the tales of daring heists, multiple identities, and double-cross are true, he is deceased now, so it's somewhat irrelevant. But if you ask me, it felt like I was talking to a police officer on the verge of retirement looking to close up some loose ends."

Maybe she's right, Scarlett thought. *Maybe the detective just hated Mr. Francis because he never caught him. Maybe he doesn't suspect me of anything. How could he?*

"I'm sorry," Scarlett said. "I shouldn't have burst in like this. I just..."

"It's okay," said Mrs. Lewis, sounding disingenuous. "This is an... emotional time for you."

Scarlett nodded. "Thank you. I'd better go. I'm sorry —again."

"Of course."

Mrs. Lewis picked up her phone to go back to her call, and Scarlett turned, her tail tucked, and headed through the doors and past Amy to the elevator. She could feel the pure abhorrence emanating from Amy's eyes, and she wanted to apologize but was too embarrassed. Embarrassed and completely rattled. What had she expected to gain from the visit? Even if Mrs. Lewis had confirmed that Jimmy was a felon—then what? Would she turn the money over to the authorities and have them check it for clues? As far as she was concerned, that money belonged to Mr. Francis, and he left it to her—that's it.

It was hers now.

32

LUCA

"She didn't know a thing," said Brooks. "She had no idea."

Luca was lying on the motel bed on the phone, smiling up at the ceiling like a high school kid talking to his crush. "Was she scared?"

"She was scared, all right. I waited outside after we talked, and she came out only a few minutes after me and ran to her car."

"You tail her?"

"Of course," said Brooks. "And get this, she drove straight to the attorney."

"Oh, goody gumdrops. She's going to be perfect."

"Just one thing, though—be careful of the fiancé. He's a young guy around her age. We want to keep him out of the picture."

"I'm always careful, detective," said Luca. "Now... what's her address again?"

"Wait. You're not thinking about going there today, are you?"

"No time like the present. I gotta strike while the iron's hot."

Brooks sighed down the phone, and his voice gained a cautionary tone. "I just went to see her. That's one hell of a coincidence if you show up on the same day. She's going to suspect something. You need to leave it a day or two, at least."

Luca said, "Fine, I can do that," then hung up, grabbed the keys for the V-Star, and headed to the nurse's house.

The nurse's house was bigger than it looked from the outside. The open-plan space was thoughtfully decorated, with modern furniture and a huge wall-mounted TV. The security, on the other hand—not so great.

Luca sat at the dining table in the dark for over an hour in silence until he heard the scrape of a key in the lock. He tucked half his body behind a corner of a window nook that abutted the table and watched.

The nurse came through the door, hung her keys on a hook, and, without looking in Luca's direction, turned on the lights above the island countertop and wandered into the kitchen. She flicked on the electric kettle, then grabbed a mug from the cabinet and set it down. Then she just stood there for a moment, her brain seemingly lost in a nightmarish thought. She looked fried, like she'd just worked two doubles back to back. But there was a beauty in her pained face, no doubt about it. A tortured beauty. One that can only be obtained through the rigors of life and loss. She looked like a little baby bird fallen from its nest, alone and afraid.

Luca felt a strange excitement at her vulnerability. This beautiful woman standing across the room from him, with no idea he was there and no idea what was going to happen next. He would be lying if he said it didn't turn him on.

The rumble of the kettle grew louder as the water bubbled inside. And as it clicked off, Luca leaned forward in his chair, out of the shadows, and said, "What are you making?"

The nurse jumped and spun to look in his direction, then scrambled for the light switch and flicked it on, illuminating the whole ground floor of the house. When she saw it was not her fiancé, but a stranger sat at her dining table, she let out a half scream then quickly covered her mouth.

"Who the hell are you? What are you doing in my house?"

"Me?" said Luca. "I'm the ghost of Christmas past."

She glanced at the door, her mind no doubt on running, but Luca pulled out his piece and rested it on the table. "That wouldn't be so smart."

She looked at the gun, wide-eyed and terrified, tears starting to well up.

"Take whatever you want, okay? Just please don't hurt me."

"Are you going to answer my question?" he said. "I asked what you were making. It's rude to ignore people."

Her mouth opened, but no words came out, just that look of blind panic.

"Well... is it coffee? Tea? Cocoa?"

Her voice was tiny, like a child still acquiring the confidence to address a room. "Tea... I was making tea."

"There we go. What kind of tea? Black? Green? British? Some cool new shit I don't even know about?"

"Look, I..."

Luca lifted the gun off the table, pointed it at her. "Which type?"

"C-Chamomile!"

"Chamomile? What's that for?"

"Helps you sleep," she said hurriedly.

Luca chuckled and placed the gun back on the table. "Well, go ahead. You mind making one for me too?"

She swallowed hard, nodded, "Sure," then slowly reached up and took down a second mug from the cabinet. As she poured the water over the tea bags, she said, "Please, just tell me what you want?"

"All in good time, sweetie pie. All in good time."

She winced, picked up both mugs, and turned to face Luca, her mouth open and bottom lip quivering. Luca gestured to the seat across from him, "Come on, come join me. I won't bite."

Her footsteps were slow and unsure, like she was walking the plank, the mugs dancing in her trembling hands. She stopped a foot short of the table and said, "Please, I just..."

"Sit down!" Luca hissed. "I won't ask again."

She hesitated, then slowly placed the mugs on the table and took the seat across from him.

"Now, you wanna know who I am? I'll tell ya. I'm an old colleague of a patient of yours, Jimmy Francis. Well, I guess I should say ex-patient now."

A slight shudder ran through the nurse's body, and she did a poor job of hiding it.

"Why are you here?"

"I heard he died," said Luca.

"That's right, he did."

Luca slid the tea closer, picked it up, and blew into it. "How did he die?"

Fear found her eyes, and she tried to blink it away. "What?"

"How did he die?" Luca said slowly, like he was scolding a child.

"His lungs failed. He had advanced-stage COPD."

He gave her a broad smile and took a sip of tea. It wasn't half bad. Then he set it back down, and they just sat there, staring at each other until she plucked up the courage to ask again, "What do you want?"

"What does anyone ever want, sweetie pie? The fucking money."

She shifted in her chair, wrinkles of worry creasing her forehead. "What money?"

Luca wagged his finger at her. "Don't play dumb with me, okay?"

"I'm not, I don't—"

He brought his hand down so hard that both the mugs jumped on the table, and the nurse jumped in her seat.

"Do not lie to me! I'm being very fucking nice to you right now. You have no idea how bad this could get if you start to piss me off. Now, Jimmy left money in that fucking bank, and now you got the keys, correct?"

She hesitated, the moment all too much for her. "Yes."

Luca smiled wide, all teeth. "Good. Now we're getting somewhere. How much is left?"

Again she hesitated—probably trying to come up with a believable figure that was considerably less than was actually there—so Luca leaned in close and yelled, "How much!"

"Three-point-six million."

The words sounded like sex to his ears, a porn star's seductive whisper. He almost couldn't believe it. Despite the fact he knew Jimmy kept money in that bank and he'd left her something with the attorney, it was still a bit of a long shot. But he was right, and that money was going to be his. And even though it wasn't the ten mill or so they'd taken back in the nineties, three-point-six would do just fine. He tried to hide the roar of excitement rushing through his body and act like that was the number he'd expected to hear. "Good. I want it. All of it."

Tears spilled from the corner of the nurse's eyes and rolled down to her jawline. She wiped them away with the back of her hand and left her eyes closed. When she opened them, her despair was replaced by yet another emotion, an emotion that lived in the same neighborhood as determination and courage—the look of a bullied kid finally ready to fight back. She sat up in her chair, glared into Luca's eyes, and said, "No."

Luca laughed. "What did you say?"

"No. That's my money. He left it to me. I'm not giving it to you. I won't."

Luca had to admit he liked her. She had mettle. He'd known guys with body counts who'd put up less of a fight when faced with him and a gun. Even that low-life scum in the alley didn't even think of standing up to him; he just turned into a big rubbery one as soon as he saw the gun.

But what she didn't know was Luca had more than just a pistol, he had video evidence that she was a murderer. But before getting to all that, he decided to fuck with her. He'd take his time and enjoy himself.

"You ever heard of a beluga whale?"

She flashed a confused look, her newfound confidence already fraying.

"A friend of mine told me about 'em. Very fascinating. You see, during the winter, the water freezes, leaving only small openings in the ice. Now, the whales need to stay close to these openings so they can poke their heads up and take a breath. And they can't leave and move onto the next one because these openings are miles apart. So they just wait, trapped under the ice for months, waiting for the ice to melt. They don't even need to hunt and eat, because they can live off their blubber."

Luca picked up his pistol and tucked it into his waistband.

"Now, a passing polar bear picks up their scent, and this is where the fun starts. The bear's hungry, right? He's barely eaten all winter, so he decides to come along and get a piece of the action—and good action it is, too. He stands next to the opening, his big paws in the snow, waiting for the whales to come up for air. And when they do, he strikes, scarring and maiming them until he can pull them out of the water and rip them to fucking pieces right there on the ice."

Luca pulled out his camera from his jacket pocket. Then he placed it on the table between them. The nurse stared at it, genuinely baffled.

"Now, the poor bastards can only hold their breath for twenty minutes or so, so they have to watch their friends get eaten and still keep coming up for air, over and over and over, risking the same fate. Now, if you ask me, there is a strong message there."

Luca turned the screen to face her.

"The message is that, sometimes, you've got no fucking choice."

He pressed the play button, and the video came on right at the moment she jabbed the syringes into Jimmy's leg. Horror danced across her eyes as she stared at the tiny screen, her life unraveling before her. Luca wished he'd got a photograph of her face at that moment, the despair so profound he could smell it.

A smile formed across his face, then the smile became a laugh, and the laugh became a cackle, mocking and contemptuous. It must have filled her with enough rage to forget herself for a second, because she lunged for the camera, both arms outstretched like a football player reaching for the end zone. Luca pulled the camera away with his left hand and grabbed a handful of her hair with his right. She yelped as he stood up and dragged her to her feet. Then he tossed the camera on the table, pulled his gun, and stuck it deep enough down her throat to make her gag. Leaning in close, he said, "Listen here, you stupid bitch. You're going to get me that fucking money, or this video goes to the cops. And if you try anything, I'll kill that chump boyfriend of yours—slowly." She began to sob around the barrel of the Beretta, tears streaming down her cheeks. "Do you understand?"

She slowly nodded her head.

"Good. Now, when the bank opens up tomorrow morning, you're going to get a text with instructions. You follow those instructions, you do everything I tell you, and you might just make it out of this okay."

33

SCARLETT

Scarlett had never known evil like that man, not in her whole life. There was barbaric brutality living in his eyes, like a violent squatter in an abandoned home. One look into them, and she knew he would follow through with every threat he made. It wasn't hard to tell that he'd killed people before, and he'd do it again without hesitation or fear.

When he left, Scarlett's legs crumpled, and she slumped into a pile on the floor. But it didn't feel like it was happening to her—it felt like she was watching someone else's life fold in on itself, and there was nothing she could do to stop it. The worst part was she recognized the guy. He was the guy from the elevator in Mrs. Lewis's building. God knows how long he'd been following her. And it was no coincidence she found him waiting at her house mere hours after the visit from the detective. They must have been in on it together, which was even scarier. She couldn't even go to the police if she wanted to; she wouldn't know who to trust.

She didn't want to get up from the floor, the pure violation of that man's invasion smothering her like a thick film of toxic sweat. But Josh would be home any minute. She was lucky he didn't walk in right as that psychopath was shoving his gun down her throat. If he had, he would have been threatened too—maybe even hurt—and he would know what Scarlett had done. Or maybe Josh would have got out and called the cops—that would have been even worse. At least now Scarlett had some hope of keeping them both alive and her out of prison. But she knew she couldn't do it on her own. She needed help, and there was only one place she could go for that.

She dragged herself upstairs and washed the tears from her face, trying to remove any signs of what she was going through. Then she threw on some workout clothes and a Dodgers hat and headed back downstairs. She planned to head out, then on her way back, pour some water on her shirt and make it look like she'd been running.

But as she fished around in the closet next to the front door for her running sneakers, she heard the unmistakable sound of Josh's Audi pulling into the garage. She found the shoes and quickly threw the first one on, her hands still violently trembling. Before she could move on to the second shoe, Josh came through the door, loosening his tie, his blank expression morphing to a smile as he noticed Scarlett at his feet.

"Hey, baby," he said.

"Hey," said Scarlett, her voice shaky, the voice of someone about to cry. She quickly stood up and gave him a hello hug. "How was your day?"

"It was fine. Same old, same old." He pulled back, looked her up and down. "You going out?"

"Just for a jog. I felt like doing a few laps of the lake."

"Really? Now?" He placed his hand on her hip. "I was kinda hoping we could cuddle on the couch, maybe open a bottle."

"That sounds awesome, but I gotta get my runs in, babe. I want to look good in my wedding dress, remember?"

"Say no more," said Josh, showing his palms in surrender. "I get it. Hey, you want me to come with? I can throw on some shorts. Been a while since I went to the lake."

"No, baby, you relax," said Scarlett, bending down and slipping on her second shoe. "Throw on some comfy clothes. I'll be back in a little bit, and we can cuddle as much as you want."

Josh bent down and placed his hand on Scarlett's lower back, then slid it down onto her butt. She looked up at him, and he grinned. "Can we do a little more than cuddle? I really missed you today."

Scarlet knew that's what he was after the second he touched her hip. Josh, like most men, had a habit of looking for sex at the worst possible time. It's like he sensed when her mental state was coming undone, teetering on meltdown, and that's when he chose to initiate intimacy.

She rose up again and returned his smile. "Of course we can." Then she kissed his lips softly, giving him just enough to think she was into it, but not too much that he'd get excited and try to persuade her to stay. "But now I gotta run before I lose my energy. I'll be back soon, okay?"

Josh stepped aside and said, "Fine," like a disappointed teenager. "Be safe."

"I will," said Scarlett as she reached for the door and headed out.

When she pulled off the driveway, she turned left as if she was heading toward Balboa lake, but when she got to the end of the street, she took a right toward the 101. Toward Hollywood.

34

ANTON

The search for the second cop had come up with nothing, and Anton was seriously thinking about packing a bag and moving back to New York. So, when the doorbell rang, he thought it would be Ruslan or another black suit standing there with a big, shit-eating grin on their face. The last person he expected to see was Scarlett. But there she was, standing on his porch in yoga pants and a Dodger's hat pulled low over her eyes.

"Scarlett? What are you doing here?"

She looked up, and her eyes were glazed with tears. Then her face twisted into a look Anton had never seen on her before, not even during their worst times together.

"Hey, you okay?"

She quickly raised a hand to her face and caught a sob with her palm. Then she threw her body into Anton's, and he caught her in a hug, her whole body shuddering in his arms.

"You have to start talking," said Anton. "You need to tell me what the hell's going on."

She'd been sitting on his couch for almost ten minutes, her hands fidgeting in her lap, eyes studying the coffee table like it was a piece of alien technology they'd just unearthed. Anton's first thought was she was pregnant, which produced a warm, sick feeling in his gut. He made a decision right there that if she was pregnant, she was getting that thing aborted, no ifs, ands, or buts.

He placed his hand on hers and looked into her eyes. "Scar, what is it? What happened? You can talk to me."

When she spoke, her voice was weak and hesitant, teasing out each syllable, like she feared saying the wrong word might trigger a bomb to explode.

"I had a patient and he... he died."

Anton felt a wave of relief—not pregnant.

"Okay," he said. "What about him?"

"Well," Scarlett looked at him for a second, then went back to studying the table, "he was alone, with no family. And well, he... he left me money. A lot of money."

"Well, shit, Scar, isn't that good news? I mean, I'm confused."

"It *was*," she mumbled.

"But..."

"Well, the money's in a bank. In a safe deposit box and, um..."

"And..." Anton said, dragging out the word.

Scarlett stalled for a moment, then began delivering her words measuredly. "A man came to my house today. He said he knew my patient. And that my patient stole from him." She paused, reliving the moment. "He said if I don't give him all the money, he's going to kill me." Scarlett blinked, and two crocodile tears rolled down her cheeks like new rain hitting a windshield. "He stuck a fucking gun down my throat, Anton. I'm terrified."

"Jesus."

"He's crazy. He'll do it, I know he will."

Anton sat back in his chair, wide-eyed, and thought, *Who the fuck is this guy?* Busting into her home in broad daylight and stuffing a gun in her mouth was a ballsy move. Whoever he was, he was definitely serious. *And how did he know about the money?*

"You ever seen this man before?" he asked.

"No. Never. I just got home from work, and he was in my living room, waiting for me."

"Why didn't you go to the cops?"

"He said he'd kill me if I did. And besides..." she reached into the waistband of her yoga pants and pulled out a business card, then held it out to Anton. "This cop came to see me earlier. He was asking all kinds of strange questions about the patient."

Anton took the card and scanned over it.

"Something wasn't right about him, the way he spoke to me. And then I get home, and there's a guy waiting for me with a gun. I mean, something really weird is going on, and I don't know who I can trust."

"So, you came to me?"

"I had no other choice." She began to sob, the balloon sized tears swelling around her eyes, busting, and trickling down her cheeks as her body jerked with sharp, wet breaths. "I'm so scared. I don't know what to do."

If only to stop her crying, Anton wrapped his arm around her and said, "It's okay, I won't let him hurt you."

Scarlett buried her face in his chest and blubbered, "My God, thank you. Thank you."

He held her close, the hairs on the crown of her head brushing against his chin.

"Did he say anything else?"

"Only that he would text me with instructions tomorrow when the bank is open."

"Okay," said Anton, rubbing her arm. "It's going to be okay."

As he held her close, a question that should have been at the forefront of Anton's mind the whole conversation beamed across his brain in neon green. He lifted her head from his chest and looked her in the eyes. "How much money are you talking about, exactly?"

"Three million?" said Karina, and it was the first time Anton had heard surprise in her voice without it being accompanied by annoyance.

"Three-point-six," he corrected.

There was silence on the other line for a moment, then Karina said, "This girl, what is she to you?"

Anton was in the back room, calling Karina from his burner phone. He wandered over into the doorway to make sure Scarlett hadn't left the couch—she hadn't.

"Nothing," he said. "Just a girl."

"Very good," said Karina. "Did she mention anything else?"

Anton debated telling her about the detective but didn't want to sour the good news. Besides, Scarlett was probably just being paranoid.

"No, that's everything."

"Perfect. It's enough to cover the stolen product."

"My thoughts exactly."

"Take Ruslan. This is your primary concern now."

She wants Ruslan with me? Anton couldn't decide if it was a blessing or a curse. Maybe both.

"What do I say to the girl?"

"You must find a way for her to take the money out, then we will step in and take it from whoever has it. Can you do that?"

"Of course," said Anton, unsure how he was going to pull it off.

"Good." Silence fell on the line again, and he thought she'd hung up, then she said, "Anton."

"Yes."

"This is good news. Don't fuck it up." Then she hung up.

After jotting down the number to his burner phone on a Post-it, Anton headed back into the living room where Scarlett was still on the edge of the couch, but this time staring out of the window. As she noticed him come in, she lifted herself a few inches off the couch as if to stand, but then quickly sat back down. With wide, hopeful eyes, she said, "What did they say?"

He took a seat beside her and took her hand. "They are going to help you."

Scarlett's whole body seemed to loosen. "Thank you," she sighed.

"But," Anton said quickly. "They want three-hundred thousand as payment."

He picked the number out of thin air, hoping it sounded reasonable and believable. A flicker of reluctance found Scarlett's eyes, then just as quickly, it vanished. "Okay, that's fine."

"And, you have to do exactly what we tell you. Understand?"

She nodded earnestly. "Tell me what I need to do."

Without knowing precisely what his plan was, he said, "Well, as we don't know who this guy is, we can't go out and get him. So... you're going to have to let him come for you."

"What?"

"You need to go about your life as if we never had this conversation. You won't see us, but we will be following you. Then when he comes tomorrow, we step in."

Scarlett's eyes went small with fear. "So, you're going to use me as bait?"

Anton had to play it carefully. Scarlett was an overthinker; if he didn't make it clear he had a solid plan that involved her keeping the money *and* her life, she would freak out, and he wouldn't be able to control her.

"No. The money is the bait. As soon as he gets the money, that means you're out of harm's way. Then we can pounce on him. If we try and do it any other time, like when you're in the car or near your house, something terrible could happen."

"Is there no other way?" she asked.

"We don't have a choice. This is the way it has to go down. But listen, if you cooperate with him and let him think things are going to *his* plan, then you will be safe—I promise. This guy doesn't want you. He just wants the money."

She motioned to speak but paused, her mouth hanging open.

"You must trust me, Scar. You just need to let him think that he is in control, and we can do the rest. Can you do that?"

She nodded with very little conviction, but he knew she would cooperate. She was too scared not to.

"Good." He handed her the Post-it note. "We'll be watching. But if you need to get a message to me, call this number. You're the only one who has it, so the line will always be open."

Scarlett took the Post-it and stared at it intensely, like she hoped it could explain to her how she'd gotten into this mess, or how this would all play out and if she would be okay.

35

SCARLETT

When morning came, Scarlett got dressed for work, waited for Josh to leave, and called in sick. Then she spent two hours checking her phone while thinking about what she was going to write in the note she planned to leave for Josh. When she finally put pen to paper, the words came slow, but she persisted. She had to, just in case.

She was going to cooperate with that psycho like Anton told her to; she had no other choice. But she had no delusions—even with Anton's help. She knew she could be seriously hurt or even killed. And if that did happen, Josh needed to know everything, not just about the money and the evil bastard that was coming for it. She wrote about what happened with Mr. Francis and even her affair with Anton.

She was at the bottom of the third page when a text came in from a private number. It read: *Corner of Lexington and St Andrews off the 101 in twenty minutes. Bring a suitcase. COME ALONE!*

Scarlett tried to think of how to respond to that kind of message and just settled with, *OK*. Then she quickly dialed

Anton and gave him the address. Anton said he was close and would be right behind her the whole way, but it did little to help Scarlett's nerves. Before leaving, she placed the letter for Josh in the dishwasher, knowing he wouldn't look inside for a couple of days.

Then, for the first time she could remember, she said a prayer.

They pulled into the same parking lot across the street from the bank, passed a vacuous attendant who looked like he was sleep-walking, and found a free space near the back. The son of a bitch had been waiting on the corner with a smug but threatening look on his face when Scarlett had picked him up, and she could tell how excited he was to go rob a bank without so much as a mask.

But when Scarlett placed her hand on the door, he reached across and touched her arm, the gesture telling her to wait. They sat in silence for a moment as Scarlett cautiously scanned the surrounding streets for Anton, but there was no sign of him.

Then the guy spoke in a calm, casual tone, as if he was an old friend bestowing life advice. "You know, I've heard people say that love is the most powerful emotion. It can make you do things, make you act a certain way, it can... control you. But I disagree. It's too messy, too complicated. Love isn't control, it's confusion. Now, fear and pain—they're way more effective." He groped in his pocket and pulled out a blue lighter, then lit it, and stared into the flame. "When I was a kid, my friends and I used to play a game. We would stand in a circle, and each one of us would hold out our lighter, then hover our forearm over the flame and let it bite into our flesh. The last kid to move the arm away was crowned the winner. The most free."

"Sounds like a sick game," said Scarlett.

He smiled, his eyes still fixed on the dancing flame. "Maybe. But most people spend their whole lives not knowing who they really are, pretending to be something they're not. And five seconds into that game, you know who you and everyone else in that circle is."

He let the flame die, then raised his elbow above his head and flashed Scarlett a dozen or so horrific scars on his forearm. He turned to her then, and his smile faded. "Let's find out who you are."

In an instant, he was on her, squeezing her against the car door, trapping her with his weight. She tried to fight back, but he was too strong. He pulled up Scarlett's shirt and pressed the scorching metal top of the lighter just below her ribs. And she screamed as she heard and smelled it searing her flesh. She tried to shift away from the tip, but it only made it slip and find a new piece of virgin skin. After what felt like a lifetime, he finally pulled it away and sat back in his seat as if nothing had happened, his face expressionless. Scarlett put her hand to the wound, then immediately removed it, her whole side tender and on fire. She took deep breaths and gritted her teeth, but it didn't even help a little with the pain.

That sick bastard casually placed the lighter back into his pocket and said, "Please understand: if you try to fuck me on this, I will show you just how little you really know about pain."

36

LUCA

It was the longest wait of Luca's life. Even longer than waiting to be sentenced. He had a horrible feeling that the nurse had called the cops after their little tea party, and they'd set up some kind of sting operation. For all he knew, the FBI was waiting inside for her, and they had operatives in black tactical gear with stubby automatic weapons closing in all around him.

But it wasn't an agent that came out of the bank, gun drawn, yelling instructions. It was the nurse, wheeling the suitcase behind her, struggling against its weight. When she reached the car, Luca just watched as she lugged the case onto the back seat in mournful silence.

She climbed into the driver's seat next, and Luca turned back, opened the suitcase, and rummaged through the beautiful stacks of cash, scouring for tracers and dye-packs. When he was *completely* satisfied, he zipped it back up and said, "Okay, drive."

But the nurse didn't move. She just sat there sneaking glances at the parking lot entrance. Luca followed her gaze but didn't see anything out of the ordinary—no panel vans or Ford Taurus's with tinted windows.

Who the hell is she looking for?

"Let's go! Now!" he ordered. And she hesitantly started the car and found drive. "Hurry up," barked Luca. "Move faster."

As they pulled onto Hill Street, she said, "Where are we going?" with bitterness in her voice.

Luca pointed at East 9th. "Take a right."

She did, and they moved along 9th toward a busy intersection, the nurse checking her rearview every few seconds. The lights turned red up ahead, and she slowed down, but Luca yelled, "Punch the gas, now!" seizing an opportunity to lose any tail they might have picked up.

"I can't, it's red!" she yelled.

But Luca grabbed her knee and shoved her right foot down on the gas, accelerating them through the intersection. The nurse screamed and closed her eyes, so Luca took the wheel and veered the Honda around the four lanes of traffic that were coming at them from the right. Horns blared and tires screeched, but they made it through, leaving any cars that might have been following stuck back at the red light.

The nurse opened her eyes and began to cry, so Luca said, "Now's not the time for tears, sweetie pie. They come later!"

They made it back to the motel without incident, and Luca had the nurse park up near the walkway so he could drag the case straight up to the room.

"You did the smart thing obeying me. Now you can go back to your life, to your fiancé. Just like nothing ever happened," he said, before stepping out of the car.

"This money was never really yours, anyway," he went on. "You remember that. Now, I'm a man of my word; no one will ever see that video of what you did to Jimmy, just as long as the police don't come knocking on my door asking about this money. Do we have an understanding?"

He meant what he said. He had no reason to turn her in, and by keeping the video, it meant he owned her.

The nurse gave two quick, shallow nods—rage bubbling beneath her controlled panic.

"Good. Now do yourself a favor: forget you ever met me, and get the hell out of here, fast."

Luca climbed out of the car, opened the back door, and pulled the suitcase out. As he closed the door, the nurse immediately pulled away and headed for the exit, seemingly anxious to follow the instructions he'd given her.

Dragging the case up the stairs to the walkway, Luca frankly couldn't believe how easily he'd pulled it off. No cops. No issues at the bank. No surprises. Hell, the nurse could've taped a pearl handle .22 to her thigh and popped him in the fucking head right there in the parking lot. Who knows what she was capable of after what went down with Jimmy.

But that didn't happen, and now he was fucking rich.

Back in the room, Luca placed the suitcase on the bed, opened it, and began counting out a separate stack. As he got about halfway through, there was a knock at the door—three slow raps. Luca pulled out his pistol, gingerly approached the door, and found the peephole with his right eye. Then he lowered the gun, opened the door, and said, "You're late."

Brooks was looming in the doorway, a concerned look on his face, the sun bouncing off the detective badge clipped to his belt. He stepped inside, closed the door, and said, "So what happened?"

Luca gestured to the suitcase full of money. "What do you think happened?"

"And the girl?"

"She's a non-issue."

Brooks glanced at him sideways. "You didn't...?"

Luca chuckled. "No, she's fine. But she knows what's good for her."

"Good. But we still better get moving. Just in case she turns stupid and calls the local precinct. There's no telling what people will do in a situation like this." He pointed to the separate stack Luca was laying out. "That my cut?"

"That's right, Mr. Payday. You can finally buy a new fucking suit."

Brooks smirked. "Try a new boat."

"Speaking of vehicles," said Luca. "You bring a car?"

"Yeah. I parked across the street at Denny's."

Luca scrunched his face into a *what the fuck?* look. "Why the hell did you do that?"

"I wanted to make sure I wasn't being tailed, so I slipped through Denny's and left through the back door. Plus, I didn't wanna just leave it outside while we did this shit. Call me paranoid, but I thought I'd play this one safe, considering what happened last time."

"God damn it, give me the keys. I'll bring it up front. You separate the rest of your cut then bring the case down to the car. And stay fucking frosty."

Brooks pulled the keys from his jacket pocket and held them out. Luca took them, then stepped up close to Brooks. "You're in deep now, you hear me? You even think about leaving with a dollar of this money, and you won't live a single day to spend it."

Brooks shrugged and shook his head. "You got the keys. Where the fuck am I going to go with a suitcase full of money?"

He had a point, and Luca knew he wouldn't try to run, even if he could. Plus, if there did happen to be cops on the way to the motel, they would find Brooks in the room when they bust the door down instead of Luca.

Making sure not to crack the door too wide, Luca slipped out, then headed downstairs to the parking lot. The rest of his plan was simple, get the car, pick up Brooks and the money, take him somewhere remote, and get rid of the last loose end.

37

ANTON

Things had started off well for Anton, neither the guy nor even Scarlett had spotted the black SUV. Ruslan was driving with Anton in the back seat, so it looked like he was being chauffeured around, the SUV playing its part as the town car. They were right on Scarlett's ass until she blew that red light, and they were forced to take a quick right. They tried to chase them down the parallel street, but when they rejoined 9th, the Honda was nowhere to be found. They took a gamble and decided to head south for a few blocks, then they tried going west, but it was hopeless. Scarlett and the money were long gone.

They rode around aimlessly for a little while, like a compass-less ship lost in a storm. Then Anton got the call.

"Scarlett?"

"Where the hell are you?" she said, "You said you'd be right behind me at all times. He's already got the money."

"I'm sorry," said Anton, trying to sound genuine. "We couldn't find the right moment, then we lost you when you ran the red light. Where are you now?"

"I just left the parking lot of the Capital Motel on South Central and East 23rd. I saw him going into room twelve."

"Shit, we went West."

Anton gave Ruslan directions, then spoke back into the phone: "Is he still in the room?

"I think so. What should I do?"

"Nothing. Just go find somewhere to lie low. I'll call you when it's done. But Scarlett..."

"What?" she said, her voice soft and shaky.

"Make sure you pick a spot far away from that motel. You don't want to be anywhere near when this goes down."

They made it to the motel in under ten minutes and were lucky not to pass any cops at the speed they were going. The motel was a brick piece of shit that looked like it should've been put out of its misery back in the eighties.

"Should we park across the street and scope out the room?" Anton asked.

"No time," said Ruslan. "We pull up and hit the room right now, and we hit it hard."

They located room twelve on the upper deck, then pulled into the parking lot and backed into the closest empty spot to the left staircase. Anton flicked the safety catch off his Glock while Ruslan cocked a round into the chamber of his twelve gauge Mossberg shotgun and slipped it under his coat. Anton's heart was pounding in his chest; that heavy rush of adrenaline drowning all his senses. But Ruslan, he looked like he was in line at the drive-through, calm and collected, his face like wood.

They hopped out and rounded the car, scoping the parking lot for any potential witnesses, then hit the staircase two steps at a time. When they hit the walkway, they slipped on their ski masks and hurried over to door twelve. Ruslan faced the door, took a big step back, and threw out a kick so hard it almost took the whole motel down. The door flew open with a thunderous crack and wood splinters scattered to the floor.

Anton went in first, his gun leading the way. He only had a few seconds to case the room, but that was more than enough time to know that something wasn't right. He locked eyes with a big gray man who looked nothing like the guy from Scarlett's car. Anton's eyes fell to the money on the bed, then he reached inside his jacket, and an explosive went off somewhere to his right. Buckshot from Ruslan's Mossberg turned the gray man's chest into a plate of tomato spaghetti.

The man let out a guttural wheezing gasp, then fell back onto the bed beside the money. The shock of the situation overwhelmed Anton's brain, and he froze for a moment, his arm still outstretched, his gun pointing at where the gray guy used to be.

Then he thought of Ruslan reporting back to Karina after this was over, how he would describe how Anton reacted. He sucked in a few quick breaths, then stepped over to the guy who looked up at him with eyes pregnant with the same fear he saw in Daniels's eyes, the fear of a man who knows he's about to die. Anton leveled his Glock on the guy's face and pulled the trigger twice, hitting him in the jaw and cheek. His head fell back and his body went limp, and that's when Anton saw it, the thing that had pinged his subconscious the moment he entered the room—the gold LAPD detective badge on the guy's hip.

After stacking the loose money back into the suitcase, Ruslan and Anton burst out of the room, jogged down the hallway, and hit the staircase as fast as the suitcase would allow. When they reached the bottom, they hopped into the SUV and spun out of the parking lot, barely avoiding playing bumper cars with a UPS truck as they whipped left onto 23rd.

Once they were at a safe distance, Anton ripped off his ski mask and banged on the dashboard with a clenched fist and yelled, "Fuck, fuck, fuck!"

The car fell silent for a moment, filled only by the roar of the engine as they weaved through traffic. Then Ruslan spoke, calm and monotone: "The girl."

Anton looked into his cold, unblinking eyes, and without saying a word, Ruslan made it very clear that Scarlett was going to pay for this mistake.

"You fucking fool," yelled Karina. "Do you know the heat you've brought down on us?" Fire burned in her eyes as she shattered a glass paperweight against the wall, the thick shards scattering across the floor like chips of ice.

Anton pointed to the suitcase he'd placed at Karina's feet. "But we got the money," he said. "All of it."

They'd parked in the rear lot of the gallery and brought the suitcase through to Karina's office, but she hadn't even glanced at it.

"You killed a cop. A detective, no less. It's going to cost me that much to get rid of this problem." She banged on the desk with her left hand and rubbed her temples with her right. "Get the nurse bitch on the phone. I want answers."

Anton hesitated as he thought of the cop's business card and Scarlett's warning. This was bad. If Karina found out he'd withheld info about a cop potentially being involved, there was no telling what she would do. And if she was to question Scarlett, it would certainly come up.

"What are you waiting for?" Karina barked. "Call her. Now."

With no other choice, Anton slowly fetched his phone from his pocket and found the number. Scarlett answered on the first ring. "Hello? Anton? What happened?"

Anton groped for words, but before he found any, Karina held out her hand, "Give me the phone."

He held it out at arm's length, and Karina took it, placed it to her ear, and said, "We have your money. If you want to see any of it again, or if you value your life, come to my office —now."

She recited the address, told Scarlett to come to the back door, then hung up.

Anton tried to think, to formulate a plan to get out of this mess, but his brain was barely capable of conjuring a coherent thought, as though his mind was quilted by a fog of panic and anger. It was all Karina's fault. If she hadn't made him go on the drug buy, none of this would have happened. Maybe she knew all along. Maybe she'd planned it, just to have an excuse to get rid of him. Either way, he'd had enough of her shit and wasn't going to let her get away with what she'd done.

The wrath must have been visible on his face because Karina gave him a questioning look. But their stare-off was interrupted by a loud buzzing sound that came from a small black device on Karina's desk. Karina's expression moved to panic, and her eyes shot to Ruslan, who picked up his shotgun and cocked it.

"What's going on?" asked Anton.

Then there were more noises, this time from further away, and Anton, Ruslan, and Karina all fixed their gaze on the office door. There was no mistaking what those noises were—they all knew the sound of gunshots.

38

LUCA

When Luca pulled into the motel parking lot in the piece of shit Acura Brooks had left him at the Denny's, a black SUV went squealing out of the side entrance and onto East 23rd. And he didn't have to look up to see the door to room number twelve wide open to know something very bad had happened.

He quickly hopped out of the Acura and ran upstairs and along the walkway to the room. Brooks's blood was all over the walls, his corpse on the bed, and there was no fucking suitcase. A visceral scream built in Luca's gut, and he wanted to pull out his gun and shoot Brooks a few more times for being stupid enough to let this happen.

But he buried the scream down deep and hauled ass back downstairs, hopped in the car, and peeled off in the direction the SUV had gone.

It took about six blocks for him to find them, switching lanes, but unable to speed through the thick LA traffic. As Luca got close, he had visions of running them off the road or hitting them at a red light. Those goddamn sons of bitches that let him do all the hard work and planning just to swoop in and fuck him over. But the roads were too busy—he couldn't risk getting blocked in. So he followed them, staying five cars or so behind, gripping the wheel hard, his whole body one giant knot of anger.

As they worked their way east, the traffic thinned out, but Luca still kept his distance, waiting for the right moment to strike. There were only two heads in the vehicle, and Luca's plan was to speed up, clip their back end, send them spinning, then unload a clip through the windshield. Messy, sure, but effective.

When the SUV turned onto an industrial road, Luca figured he wasn't going to get a better opportunity. So he racked the slide on his Beretta and prepared to stomp on the gas pedal. But as he did, the SUV's brake lights flared up ahead, and they turned right into the rear gated parking lot of a warehouse building.

Luca slowed right down, ducked in his seat, and rolled by to get a good look at the guys as they hopped out of their vehicle. They were both in suits, and one of them was carrying a shotgun. They didn't look like mob guys but were definitely pros. Luca also clocked one armed guard in uniform at the rear entry door.

He kept going and circled around the block to the front of the building, which had a sign that read: *J.O.A. Metal Artwork and Sculptures*—a front, Luca presumed. There were no windows on the building, not even on the front door, so there was no way of knowing what he was walking into, no way of creating any plan or strategy. But he was sick of making plans, anyway; they kept backfiring on him. This time, it was going to be all gut and instincts, all bullets and fury. And he wasn't leaving without that fucking suitcase.

He parked as close as he could get to the entrance, hopped out, and casually walked up to the front door and slipped inside. It was a bright, open space littered with weird sculptures that looked like giant shell casings melting under a heat lamp. The only person in there was a girl sitting at a desk against the wall. As she looked up and saw him, her automatic receptionist smile quickly faded. "Can I help you, sir?"

Luca didn't speak until he got right up to the desk. "Where are they?"

"Where are who?"

He pulled out his Beretta, let it hang by his side. "The fucks that took my money."

The girl quickly slipped her hand under the desk, so Luca raised his gun and aimed it at her face. "Don't you fucking move."

But she didn't listen, her hand slipping further. Luca reached across and yanked her out of the seat by her hair and pressed his gun to her cheek. She yelled in pain, and he said, "What the hell you reaching for, huh?"

Gripping her close, he rounded the desk and bent down, expecting to see a gun strapped to the underside of the desk, but instead found a small red button.

A silent alarm? What the hell is this place?

Before he could ask, a door at the far end of the space opened, and a big guy with long hair and a submachine gun stepped out. He raised the gun to aim, but Luca spun and shot three times in his direction. The first two shots missed, but the third popped a hole just below the guy's left eye, sending him face-first into the concrete floor, his corpse propping the door open. Beyond him, Luca saw the torso of the rear door guard weaving through heavy machinery in what looked like a workshop.

Luca pulled the dazed girl in front of him, using her body as a shield, the muzzle of his pistol pressed against her temple.

As the guard reached the doorway, he screamed something in a foreign language, and Luca yelled back, "Drop it, or she dies."

The girl screamed and pleaded for her life, but the guard kept his gun trained on Luca as he glanced down at the long-haired man with the hole in the back of his skull. Without a word, the guard began firing, bullets ripping through the girl's flesh, blood spraying Luca's face.

Luca fired back, squeezing the trigger as fast as he could, and managed to hit the guard near the hip and shoulder. He fell back, hurt, but not dead, so Luca let the girl's limp body fall to the floor, took aim, and popped him twice more in the chest.

In less than a minute, three of them were dead, and Luca remained unharmed, none of the bullets having passed through the girl's body into his. He'd been lucky not to get hit, but now wasn't the time for slowing down. He needed to keep surprise and speed as his ally if he wanted to succeed in his mission. He rushed over to the doorway, tucked his pistol behind his back, and yanked the submachine gun—an Uzi 9mm—from the dead guy's hands.

When Luca poked his head around the corner to get a look at the hallway beyond it, a cannon went off, and a basketball-sized cluster of buckshot took a hole out of the wall beside his head. He leaned back, stuck the Uzi into the hallway, and let off a barrage of bullets. The booming rattle echoed around the tight space, shell casings bouncing off the walls and spilling onto the floor.

Another cannon blast went off, and this time, the buckshot tore through the wall and bit into Luca's side, the lead burning through his flesh. Before he could get caught by another shot, he gritted his teeth, stepped out into the hallway, and sprayed the shotgun-wielding son of a bitch with a hail of bullets. The guy's body jerked, and he fell onto his back, but not before getting off one last shot that clipped Luca's left shoulder and ripped into the ceiling behind him.

Luca's left arm roared and went dead at the same time, and he dropped to one knee, the pain dizzyingly strong. A woman yelled something from the room at the end of the hall. It sounded like a man's name—*Russell*, maybe? But Luca's ears were ringing, the pure chaos making him feel like a flash-bang grenade had been released inside his skull.

But no matter how disoriented he was, he knew he had to keep moving, to stay on the attack, his siege on this place in its final push. Summoning all his strength, he pulled himself back to his feet and trudged his way down the hallway, the buckshot in his side making it hard to walk, the Uzi wavering as he trained it on the open door at the end of the hall.

As he neared the doorway, the woman yelled something else, something frantic in the same foreign tongue as the guard. Then a single gunshot went off, one whose path Luca couldn't track. He pressed his body against the wall and took a breath, preparing himself for the last showdown. For all he knew, there was an army of armed men beyond the door, but blood was pouring from his wounds, and he was feeling light, his adrenaline fighting a losing battle. This was it, all or nothing, kill them all and take the money, or die with his gun in his hand. A final *fuck you* to this world.

A bullet tore through the wall beside him, then another, and another—searching for his torso like a real-life game of battleship. Luca gripped the handle of the Uzi with his good arm, then dove knee-level across the doorway and squeezed the trigger tight.

He found a guy in a suit standing, pointing his pistol at the doorway with both hands like a cartoon detective. Luca's bullets drew a line from the guy's left knee to his right shoulder, and he dropped to the floor like a duffle bag full of dumbbells.

Pain shot through Luca's side and down his hip and leg, and all he could do was lay there for a moment, target practice for anyone left alive. But the shot didn't come.

He barely managed to get to his feet, his clothes soaked in blood now, his whole body going numb and cold. Staggering into what looked like an office, his gun barely raised, Luca found a woman slumped in an office chair with a bullet hole in her neck. It didn't make any sense; that bullet must have come from the guy in the suit. *But why would he shoot one of his own?*

Luca didn't dwell on it, though, because beyond the woman, he saw something else—a suitcase, *his* suitcase.

He placed the Uzi on the desk and took three shaky steps towards the money. But as he reached out for it, he felt as though he was sinking into a giant chasm, like Earth was opening up and Hell was swallowing him.

Then, everything went black.

39

SCARLETT

Scarlett clamped her hand across her mouth, desperately holding down vomit. The first bodies belonged to two men who were lying almost on top of each other like they'd been dumped in a pit, and beyond them was a young woman lying on her side in a pool of her own blood.

The back door of the building had been wide open when Scarlett arrived, so she let herself in, blissfully oblivious to the horrors that waited for her. Her mind buzzed with an overwhelming cry of alarm, and every fiber of her being screamed for her to turn and run. But somehow, she kept moving forward, one small step after the other, as if she was being pulled by an invisible rope wrapped around her waist.

When she reached the office at the end of the bullet-riddled hallway, passing another dead man with a thick scar across his eye, she was greeted by the heavy stench of blood and sulfur.

It was a massacre, bodies strewn around the dark room. Then she noticed Anton, his eyes still open, but soulless, that same silver pistol from his bedroom clutched in his hand. A man she'd shared so many intimate moments with, gone forever.

Her panicked gaze shifted to the dead woman seated at the desk, a bullet hole in her throat, then finally settled on the man slumped in a heap, a slack body in the shadowy corner.

She couldn't believe her eyes. It was him, the bastard that took the money. He was slumped against an armchair, leaning over to one side, blood oozing from wounds on his torso and pooling on the dark hardwood floor. Scarlett followed the trail of blood, and that's when she saw it, just to the right of the guy, tucked under the desk—the suitcase.

She gathered her courage and took a step toward it, but the man's head moved slightly, and his eyes fluttered open. He glared at her, a ghost back to life, and she froze.

"You..." he croaked. "You bitch. It was all you."

He began reaching behind his back, and Scarlett knew he was going for a gun. But his wound kept him in slow motion, his face scrunched up in pain. She quickly bent down and grabbed Anton's pistol from his hand and aimed it at the guy's chest.

"Don't do it!" she screamed, squinting through fresh tears.

But he just laughed, an old drunk's laugh, wild and unhinged.

His hand cleared his back, holding a pistol, and Scarlett flinched, her finger tight on her own trigger. But when the guy tried to jerk his arm up, his punctured muscles wouldn't allow it. He yelped in agony, then laughed again, even harder than before.

"Drop it," Scarlett pleaded, the gun feeling twice as heavy now as it shook in her trembling hand.

The man gritted his teeth and began to raise his gun again.

Scarlett braced herself and squeezed hard on the trigger.

The gun boomed and bucked in her hand, and a bullet

struck the man in the center of his chest, jerking his body back. And for the briefest of moments, all that psychotic hate that lived in his eyes gave way to fear.

Then he was gone. She'd killed him.

For several seconds, Scarlett tried to move but couldn't, her hysterical brain firing signals to her unresponsive legs. But then the faint howl of police sirens trickled into the room, and it granted her a spurt of energy. She quickly rolled her sleeve over her shaking hands and frantically wiped her fingerprints from the gun, then tossed it next to Anton's body. Then she grabbed the suitcase and dragged it out of the room and through the bloody hallway, yanking it around the corpses.

She made it out of the back door and over to the Honda, but the sirens were growing louder, closer. As she stuffed the case into the trunk, two cop cars whipped past the side street where she was parked. They skidded to a stop out front of the building.

Scarlett was inside her car as fast as she could, peeling away without looking back. When she got three blocks away, another cop car pulled onto the street ahead of her, its lights flashing and sirens blazing. She slowed her speed, one hand on the wheel, trying to look casual while ducking her head slightly.

Her heart stopped beating as the cop car whipped past her, but it didn't slow down, just kept moving toward the warehouse.

She made it about a mile before she pulled over next to an undeveloped lot, climbed out, and threw up. Snapshots of blood and gore and Anton's lifeless face flashed in front of her eyes as she heaved and coughed and sobbed. She could still feel the gun in her hand.

Good god, I'm a murderer.

When the ground stopped moving under her feet, she wiped her mouth and hurried back to the car. She needed to get back home to hide the money and get the letter she'd left Josh, just in case he came home and found it. After everything she'd been through, the letter could still undo her.

Scarlett pulled up just past her driveway, then backed the Honda up so the trunk was only an inch from the garage door, the parking sensor pinging frantically. Once in the house, she spun into the kitchen and rushed over to the dishwasher, yanked it open, and enjoyed a brief but real moment of relief as the unopened envelope stared back at her. Even faced with the horrors of what she'd seen and done, losing Josh was still at the forefront of her mind. After finally realizing what she had with him, she couldn't face losing it.

She tore the letter to shreds, but as she did, a thudding sound from upstairs made her freeze above the trashcan. Her nerves were still very much on edge, so she instinctively grabbed a carving knife from the chopping block and spun on her heels—but she found only an empty living room.

Had she really heard something or was her ravaged mind playing tricks? She gingerly crossed the house to the bottom of the staircase and aimed her ear up to the second floor, but heard nothing. She didn't want to go upstairs, but she was desperate to be certain of her safety. So she began to head up, taking each step slowly, one by one, her body tense as she gripped the knife. As she took the last few steps and reached the bedroom door, she heard another thud, this time unmistakably the sound of a dresser drawer slamming shut.

Holy shit. Someone's going through my stuff. They've been sent here.

Scarlett turned to flee, nowhere near ready for another violent confrontation, when she heard another sound, this time not a thud, but the light buzzing sound of water running through the pipes—the shower.

Why the hell would they run the shower?

Then it hit her—it was Josh. He must have come home early and parked in the garage, maybe preparing to head off on another business trip. Scarlett composed herself, let the knife hang at her side, and opened the bedroom door.

A massive wave of relief washed over her—it *was* Josh. He was hunched at his underwear drawer, naked, save for a white bath towel wrapped around his waist, the slapping sound of water hitting porcelain echoing around the closed en suite behind him. Josh raised to full height and stared at her, his wide eyes flicking from Scarlett's face to the carving knife in her hand. "What are you doing here, Scar?"

Scarlett set the knife down on the dresser and rushed over to him and wrapped him in a hug.

"I heard noises, I was scared. I didn't know you would be home." Scarlett laughed and cried in one motion as she held him close. "I'm so glad you're here."

But Josh remained emotionless. He didn't even hug back, his arms limp at his side. "I tried to call," he said. "I thought you were with patients."

Then, almost in slow motion, the door to the en suite crept open, and Scarlett turned as Yvonne stepped out wearing a black lace bra and matching crotchless panties. "Hey, I thought I..."

Yvonne stopped mid-sentence and stared at Josh and Scarlett, locked in their one-sided hug. Scarlett slowly stepped back from Josh, and both he and Yvonne opened their mouths, but neither spoke.

Scarlett's mind was already numb from the trauma of the day. It took a few moments for her to fully register exactly what was happening. When she did, she was at the closet, tearing clothes off hangers and stuffing them into a small overnight bag as Yvonne sobbed and pleaded like a child, begging for forgiveness, begging for Scarlett not to tell Danny.

"Please, Scarlett. I didn't mean for this to happen!"

Scarlett wanted to lash out, to scratch and slap and punch Yvonne. She wanted to reach for the knife, to hurt her the way she'd been hurt. But she was too exhausted, too weary from her week from hell. The last thing she needed was more blood on her hands.

Instead, she turned to Yvonne with wild eyes and spoke in a low, deathly tone, "You don't fucking talk to me, you understand?"

Yvonne backed up and sat on the edge of the bed, her hands finding her lap, her head hanging in shame.

Then it was Josh's turn. "It's not what you think, Scar. It was just a mistake." He reached out to touch Scarlett's arms, but she smacked his hand away.

"Don't you fucking touch me!"

Scarlett spun back to the closet and yanked out a few more items. She headed for the stairs, charging down them, clothes spilling from the overnight bag. As she crossed the living space, Josh hurried down the stairs after her, and when she burst out of the front door, he followed, still half-naked.

"Please, Scar, wait!"

Scarlett flung open the driver's door of the Honda and tossed the bag on the passenger seat, more of the clothes spilling down into the footwell.

"Can we talk about this?" He put his hand on her shoulder and stopped her getting into the car. "Please, baby, you know I love you. I made a mistake, but you're my whole world. Please, can we just talk?"

She turned to him, his eyes teary and desperate. But she didn't want to talk. She was sick of men feeding her stories, always trying to manipulate and control her.

She looked down at his left hand on her shoulder and his right hand holding the towel just below his navel. Before she even felt her hand curl to a fist, she punched him, her knuckles cracking against the bridge of his nose.

He stumbled back, cupping his face and dropping the towel. "What the fuck!"

Scarlett ripped off her engagement ring and threw it on the ground at his feet.

Then she climbed into the Honda, started the engine, and drove out of their life, and into *hers*.

When Scarlett first set off, she'd had no idea where she was going. She just drove. But as soon as she' reached the freeway, she knew there was only one place she wanted to be.

Her mind raced the whole drive, the horrors she'd seen flashing across her windshield like movie clips from a projector. She couldn't stop thinking about what Mr. Francis had said—how we are all nothing more than fragile creatures. She thought she'd understood what he meant when he said it—after the dozens of patients she'd seen fade into nothingness, and the way her own mother had been switched off like a lightbulb. But really, she hadn't comprehended what he meant at all, not even close. It wasn't until she was standing in that room, surrounded by corpses, watching that sick bastard die from a bullet she had fired, that she truly understood.

Those were powerful, dangerous people who plotted and schemed and murdered, and with a few little pieces of metal, they were reduced to nothing more than mounds of flesh and blood. After experiencing that, she knew her world would never be the same again. She'd been altered somehow—tainted—pieces of her identity stripped away like siding from a house in a hurricane.

She pulled off the 101 North at San Luis Obispo and merged onto Highway 1 over to Morro Bay, the little seaside town she used to go to as a kid. The drive took over three hours, and it was dark when she got there, but she could still hear the crashing waves and taste the salt in the air as she pulled up across from the small pier.

Scarlett sat there for a long while, listening to the creaking wood and winding rope of the fishing boats bobbing in the water thirty feet away. Those noises always sounded like freedom to her, like adventure, and for a moment, she felt like Jimmy, wanting only to escape it all.

Something made her reach across to the glove box and take out Jimmy's Bible. She looked at it for a while, tracing the faded gold letters while she thought about what Jimmy had said—*I hope this helps you find what you're looking for*. Then she leafed through the heavy book—its musty smell and thick paper a testament to its age—and a thinner, newer sheet fell from the folds and into her lap. It was folded in half, but she could still make out blue ink in the shape of looping handwriting.

Scarlett set the Bible down next to her, picked up the note, unfolded it, and found that it was actually two pages. She read the first line of the first page, and her heart shattered in her chest. It read: *To Scarlett, my beautiful daughter.*

40

JIMMY

To Scarlett,

my beautiful daughter,

The first thing I want to say is sorry. I'm sorry for the lies, for not being there, and for everything I put you through. But I didn't write this letter to ask you to forgive me, I wrote this because you're owed an explanation. I guess the first thing I should tell you is that I wasn't a good man. I was a thief, a criminal. But I never hurt anybody. At least I can say that.

Back in 1994, I pulled off the biggest job of my life, and after it was over, I went to your mother's place. She lived in a tiny studio apartment in Culver City back then. It was the middle of the night when I knocked, and she answered in that faded orange robe she loved, her eyes thick with sleep. Even then, she looked so beautiful, her soft features and smooth skin glowing under the yellow light of the streetlamps.

She was angry because I'd gone dark on her for the few weeks leading up to the job. I knew it was unfair, but I had to, just until it was over—to protect her. Our relationship had blossomed so fast, from a drink at a bar to full-on, heart-pounding love in only a few months. And I'd felt so safe and loved around her that I even told her about my work. But that job was the big one, and I couldn't risk anyone finding out about her, not when we were so close to starting a new life and leaving it all behind.

We sat in her tiny kitchen and smoked cigarettes as I tried to explain myself and begged her to pack a bag and come with me. But she just sat there with a look on her face that I'd never seen before. A look that was worse than fear or anger.

When she finally spoke, she told me that she couldn't come with me, and that I had to go alone. She wouldn't tell me why, so I pressed her and pressed her until she broke down in tears and told me she was pregnant with you. I was happy, I truly was. I hadn't even thought about being a father, but when I heard those words, I was filled with excitement.

But your mother, she was so scared. Scared of police, scared of the people I'd stolen from coming after me or using my family to get to me. I tried to tell her everything would be fine, and we would be safe. But she made me promise to stay away, to never put you in danger. When I said no, she threatened to go to the police and tell them what I'd done. So I agreed, hoping that time would ease her fears and change her mind. But it never did.

The only time she let me see you was at a vacation home up the coast a few times when you were really small. We walked on the beach together, the water kissing our toes. I even tried to teach you chess. Those were the best weekends of my life.

But please don't hold any anger toward your mother. She did what she did to protect you. She wouldn't even take money from me. She was a strong woman, and she loved you more than you'll ever know.

When she died, I'd already been diagnosed with COPD, *and I knew I had to see you and be with you for what time I had left. But I couldn't break my promise. That's why I didn't tell you who I really was. But before my time came, I found out that my past was finally catching up to me, and as long as I was alive, you would be in danger. I knew I had to die for you to be safe, but I didn't want to die alone; I wanted you to be with me. That's why I asked for your help.*

I know that's selfish, and I only hope it doesn't haunt you, but please know it meant the world to me. I made a lot of mistakes in my life, and my biggest regret is not being there to enjoy all the special moments with you, big or small. But the best gift of my life was seeing how you blossomed into the beautiful, strong woman you've become. I want you to know that you are capable of achieving anything you put your mind to. And I will always be watching over you.

All my love,

Your father, James Francis.

P.S. I hope the money brings you peace and happiness. But be careful with it, because it can just as easily bring loneliness and pain.

EPILOGUE

DETECTIVE CHEN

In the hours after the shooting, the Capitol Motel had become a frenzy of activity. Bug-eyed tweakers and chirping reporters stood shoulder to shoulder behind police caution tape, all trying to get a look at the dead cop. Rookie detectives and uniformed officers took statements from motel guests and other potential witnesses, all of them claiming to have seen nothing.

Inside room twelve, forensics officers and blood spatter experts snapped photographs and placed evidence markers next to spent shell casings as Detective Chen stood frozen over the bullet-riddled corpse that used to be Brooks. They were never that close, and she knew what they said about him—the rumors and allegations—but he was always nice to her and hadn't deserved to be put down like this.

Chen's cell buzzed, and when she answered, Sergeant Grimes's heavy voice bellowed down the line.

"What-a-ya got?" He was calling from the blood bath across town at an Art Gallery. A crime scene she'd heard was a bigger, far more gruesome cousin of the one she was in.

Chen took in the red mess that once served as Brooks's

chest cavity and said, "Looks like a hit, Serg. A sloppy hit, but still a hit."

"Shit," said Grimes. "The press is going to be all over my ass on this. What the hell was he doing over there? They find anything?"

She glanced around the shithole of a room, knowing Grimes meant drugs or money. "Nothing yet, but whatever he was doing, it wasn't good."

"Ah, Christ. You get anybody to talk?"

"No, but we're working on it."

Grimes let out a long, deep sigh, and Chen said, "What have you got over there?"

"Here? We got bodies. A lot of them."

"Any familiar faces?"

"You could say that. You heard of Karina Turgenev?"

Chen wracked her brain for a beat, running down the endless list of names tossed around the station these days. "Sounds familiar."

"It should. She runs—or should I say *ran*—the Russian mob in these parts. Took control when her husband Nicholai got extradited back to Russia."

"Russians?" Chen said and looked at Brooks as if she expected him to explain himself. "What the hell happened today?"

"I don't know," sighed Grimes. "I got a tech working on getting me footage from the cameras, but they only have them in the gallery, none in the back office. All I do know is Karina Turgenev was a very serious player. Whatever went down, it was big."

The line fell silent then, both of them taking this in. Then Grimes said, "Look, we got someone from the task force on the way over here to identify the rest of her crew, then I'm coming to you. In the meantime, find me a witness."

"Ten-four," said Chen.

She hung up and was tucking her cell into her pocket when a woman's voice called from the far side of the room, "Hey, detective, I think I've got something."

Chen turned and found a forensic officer by the name of Reed kneeling in the corner of the room, shining her flashlight into a ventilation duct. Chen walked over to join Reed.

"Take a look, about a foot or so back," Reed said.

She took the flashlight, got to her knees, and found a small brown bag tucked into the duct.

"What do you think it is?" Chen asked.

"Could be nothing," said Reed. "But it definitely looks planted there."

"Well, let's get it open."

Ten minutes later, after one of the Techs fetched a screwdriver from his truck, Reed unscrewed the four screws supporting the vent casing and popped it off. Chen reached into the duct with a rubber-gloved hand and pulled out the brown bag. It was so light that, at first, she thought it might be empty. But when she opened it up and peered inside, she saw a driver's license and a small piece of blue plastic.

Chen laid the objects out onto the carpet so everyone in the room could see: a driver's license belonging to none other than Marshal Teal, and a blue SD memory card.

ACKNOWLEDGMENTS

Many people helped in the writing of this book, and I couldn't have done it without you all. Many thanks to my fantastic editor Liz Cartwright who steered me through this whole process. As well as the rest of the editing team, Melanie Kirk, Cass Vanvalk, and Meaghan Summers.

Huge thanks to Jenna Harris, Rachel and Matt Pruchniewski for the help with marketing. Also, to Flor Figueroa for the awesome cover.

Thanks to Jonette Balagtas, Joanna Bazmipour, and Ross Young for answering all my questions about the interesting worlds of nursing and banking.

I'm extremely grateful to my mum and Jude for all of your help and support, this wouldn't have been possible without you. And to the rest of the Owen clan for all the encouragement throughout all my endeavors.

Last but certainly not least, thank you to Jamie Panizales for all the love and advice, and for answering my thousands of questions about everything from how women tick, to how to spell tricky words! You are my rock and my human dictionary.

ABOUT THE AUTHOR

Gareth R.T. Owen is an award-winning author, screenwriter, and filmmaker from Wales, United Kingdom. Gareth's love for stories developed at a very young age and soon blossomed into an obsession. He studied creative writing and screenwriting before moving to Los Angeles, CA, where his work on screen has earned him festival awards including best film and best screenplay. Whether it be enjoying the work of others, or creating himself, Gareth is drawn to gripping psychological thrillers with a gritty tone.

www.GarethRTOwen.com

facebook.com/gareth.rt.owen

instagram.com/gareth.rt.owen

Printed in Great Britain
by Amazon

63371103R00182